Praise for the "outstanding"* anthology
Living Large
featuring stories by Donna Hill, Brenda Jackson, Francis Ray, and Rochelle Alers

"Four touching stories about curvaceous African-American women at pivotal points in their lives. . . . Full of humorous encounters, sweetly charming heroines, and the message that living large and loving one's self are good things, this gem of a book is sure to leave readers happy."
—*Booklist*

"A real winner. . . . Readers of all shapes and sizes, especially those tired of waiflike heroines, will find this anthology the perfect diversion." —*Library Journal*

"This anthology could easily have doubled in size, as each tale screams out for its own book. . . . Four outstanding stories from four outstanding authors."
—*Romantic Times* (Top Pick)

"All four tales in this delightful collection star strong protagonists who make for an entertaining anthology. Fans of contemporary romances . . . will enjoy each contribution in which the road to love is filled with detours."
—Under the Covers

"A nice treat. . . . It was a pleasure to read about strong, likable, plus-sized heroines who have much more to focus on than their waist measurements." —The Best Reviews

"A fantastic book about love and the healthier-sized sisters that it ensnares in its trap. I loved each story. . . . [They] have proven that true love is blind to size, but seeks only what's in the hearts of the people in the relationship to be happy." —The Romance Reader's Connection

Big Girls Don't Cry

Donna Hill

Brenda Jackson

Monica Jackson

Francis Ray

A SIGNET ECLIPSE BOOK

SIGNET ECLIPSE
Published by New American Library, a division of
Penguin Group (USA) Inc., 375 Hudson Street,
New York, New York 10014, USA
Penguin Group (Canada), 10 Alcorn Avenue, Toronto,
Ontario M4V 3B2, Canada (a division of Pearson Penguin Canada Inc.)
Penguin Books Ltd., 80 Strand, London WC2R 0RL, England
Penguin Ireland, 25 St. Stephen's Green, Dublin 2,
Ireland (a division of Penguin Books Ltd.)
Penguin Group (Australia), 250 Camberwell Road, Camberwell, Victoria 3124,
Australia (a division of Pearson Australia Group Pty. Ltd.)
Penguin Books India Pvt. Ltd., 11 Community Centre, Panchsheel Park,
New Delhi - 110 017, India
Penguin Group (NZ), cnr Airborne and Rosedale Roads, Albany,
Auckland 1310, New Zealand (a division of Pearson New Zealand Ltd.)
Penguin Books (South Africa) (Pty.) Ltd., 24 Sturdee Avenue,
Rosebank, Johannesburg 2196, South Africa

Penguin Books Ltd., Registered Offices:
80 Strand, London WC2R 0RL, England

First published by Signet Eclipse, an imprint of New American Library,
a division of Penguin Group (USA) Inc.

First Printing, January 2005
10 9 8 7 6 5 4 3 2 1

Contents

Dr. Love

Donna Hill

Acknowledgments

Many thanks go out to all the incredible readers who have made this series so successful. We deeply appreciate your support.

If you can believe it, you can achieve it.
                                    —Donna

Chapter 1

The blare of the radio alarm clock could no longer be ignored. Tricia Spencer groaned and with reluctance opened her eyes, then squinted against the morning sun that had made its way through the slats in her Levolor blinds. She turned on her side drawing the sheet up over her face only to hear the creak of the bed beneath her. She wasn't sure if it was the springs that needed replacing or if it was the extra pounds she'd piled on in the past month.

Less than a minute ago she was a solid size eighteen and in a blink she'd totally bypassed twenty and was sprinting toward a size twenty-four, and the finish line was no where in sight. Fortunately, she made enough money to replenish her wardrobe when necessity dictated. As President and CEO of ImageNouveau Advertising, she had to look good at all times. She *was* her company's slogan: *image is everything*. One would think that with all the running around she did, the sleepless nights, marathon meetings and days of brainstorming sessions that she would be skinny as a stick.

In Tricia's case the opposite seemed true. The more she worked the more she ate, the more success she attained the more pounds she gained.

Wincing at the sound of the bed straining against her weight, Tricia's cinnamon-toned eyes drifted to the nightstand and the four cartons of Chinese food that she'd wolfed down while mapping out a campaign strategy for her newest client.

Remnants of lo mein, a fried chicken wing and something that was no longer recognizable sat like jurors waiting to cast their verdict about her lousy eating habits.

Tricia forced herself to sit up. With difficulty she swung her legs over the side of the bed and her foot kicked the half gallon carton of vanilla ice cream that she'd used to wash down her Chinese dinner. The melted mess made a neat white trail across the floor, stopped only by the threshold of her bedroom door.

"Today is starting out with a bang," she grumbled and stood. Every muscle in her body seemed to ache and if she didn't know better she'd swear the bathroom was at least a mile away. She pressed her hand to the small of her back and rubbed. Yes, she was definitely going to have to get a new mattress.

Less than an hour later, Tricia looked like the executive that she was. She always looked good in navy blue she mused, turning from side to side to check for runs in her stockings. Leaning closer to the mirror she added the final touches to her makeup, and added just a hint more mascara to bring out her eyes. Everyone always said, "You have such a beautiful face . . . and those eyes." But what they really wanted to say was, "You sure are pretty to be so big." She saw it in the way people put on "special" smiles when they met her for the first time to hide the surprise in their eyes. Tricia was used to it by now. She'd been a big girl for as long as she could remember. But there were some days that it still stung—just a little.

Satisfied that she'd make a dynamite impression, she grabbed her trench coat and briefcase then headed outside.

Not bad for May, she thought, as she walked the long concrete street to her car. The air was warm and the forecasters promised a partly cloudy day with only a chance of showers. She waved at some of her neighbors as she hurried along, mindful that she still had traffic to beat if she intended to get to the office before everyone else. It was one reason why she'd chosen to move to Harlem. On a good day she was no more than a half hour away from the office. The other reason was much more practical with long-term rewards.

When she'd moved onto 115th Street in Harlem ten years earlier, friends and family alike had warned her that the neighborhood and its inhabitants were tough. One block after another was littered with abandoned buildings or buildings that would be better off abandoned. But if there was one secret gift that Tricia always prided herself on, it was her gift of seeing things that no one else could. She knew the value of the fabled brownstones and she watched as the fabric of the surrounding neighborhood began to change and she made her move.

She'd bought her three-story brownstone for a song and a dance. It needed extensive work, but she didn't care. She tackled it one floor at a time until it was restored to its former glory. Now, the shell of a building she'd purchased for a mere seventy-five thousand dollars was worth a half-million and climbing. Contractors couldn't rehab the houses fast enough to satisfy the influx of eager buyers who saw into the future as she did.

Reaching her Volvo, Tricia disengaged the alarm and opened the door. When she got inside, she fastened her seat belt and realized she was breathing harder than usual. A thin line of perspiration ran down her spine. She frowned and took an extra moment to collect herself before putting her car in gear.

Maybe it was time for the checkup she'd been putting off for the past six months. But the truth was, she didn't have the time. Her every waking hour was filled with keeping her company on the top, checking on her ailing mother and her trifling sister. By the time her average day ended, it was usually after one a.m., and the only energy she had left was enough to get out of her clothes and collapse into bed.

"When are you going to take time for yourself?" her best friend Phyllis would ask at least once per week.

"I don't have time to take time for myself," Tricia would routinely answer.

"It's all going to catch up with you one day," Phyllis would warn. "And then I'll be forced to say 'I told you so.'"

Tricia smiled in spite of herself as she wound her

way around the Manhattan traffic. Tricia and Phyllis had been unlikely friends since college. Phyllis was the kind of woman that men pinned up pictures of in their lockers, while Tricia was the one who sat in the corner at dances and was pretty much ignored by the young men on campus. But Phyllis was so much more than beautiful. She was smart, funny and the best friend anyone could ask for.

It was Phyllis who'd shown her the ropes at Howard University, sat with her in the hospital when Tricia's mother had her first stroke, taught her about style and makeup and threw a champagne party for her when Tricia landed her first client.

There were many days that Tricia didn't know what she would have done if Phyllis hadn't been around. But her friend was married now and had been for five years. They were still close, but of course the dynamics of their friendship had changed. They still made time to see each other, but between Tricia's thriving business and Phyllis's family and job obligations, those times were few. So Tricia filled her hours with work and food, which was fine with her—sort of.

Tricia entered her refurbished storefront office in the West Village. She was the first one there. Just the way she liked it. She'd pretty much built the empty space from scratch. Right after graduation, she went to work for Bell, Hanley and Stowe, one of the bigger ad agencies in the city. During her ten years at the company, she worked on some of the most lucrative campaigns: everything from Calvin Klein jeans, billboard ads and commercials for luxury cars to the Super Bowl.

But no matter how innovative her concepts, how fantastic her presentations, she was never given the opportunity to deal one-on-one with the clients. She was fine behind the scenes and in staff meetings, but that's as far as she got.

Of course she couldn't prove it, but she knew it had to do with her weight. She didn't fit the image that Bell, Hanley and Stowe presented to the world—ultra sleek and fashionable.

So one night after five glasses of wine and several buckets of tears, she decided to take her half-drunk friend Phyllis's advice and strike out on her own. That was four years ago and she had never looked back.

Tricia entered her spacious and orderly office, complete with a projection screen, the latest computer technology and a wall of video tapes of every presentation and ad that her company had completed.

She hung up her trench coat and immediately went to the coffeemaker that sat on a table by the window and prepared her daily dose of java.

By the time her staff of eight began filtering in, Tricia had downed three cups of coffee and completed the first draft of her presentation.

" 'Morning, boss."

Tricia looked up from her notes and smiled at her VP, Reginald Porter.

Reginald was also a former employee of Bell, Hanley and Stowe. The day Tricia handed in her resignation Reginald had stopped her in the hallway.

"So you're really leaving," he'd said.

"Yep."

"I don't blame you," he'd confided. "You have so

10

much talent and it's pretty much ignored around here."

She leaned on her right leg and planted a hand on her hip. "That's right and so are yours. That's why I think we would make a great team," she said, surprising him with her proclamation.

Reginald frowned. "Team? What are you talking about?"

Tricia hooked her arm through his. "Let's walk and talk."

An hour later, Reginald had submitted his resignation as well and signed on to Tricia's dream.

"Hey, Reg," Tricia said, putting her notes aside. She stretched her arms over her head and inhaled deeply. "Coffee?"

"Hmm, thought you'd never ask." He crossed the room, filled a mug then turned and sat on the edge of Tricia's desk. "The Allendale campaign?" he asked, taking a peek at the notes.

"Yep. I think I found the right angle. I'll show it to the crew during the morning session."

"We have a lot on the agenda, Tricia. The way business is going we may need to look at hiring an additional person."

Tricia stood and suddenly felt light-headed. She swayed and gripped the edge of her desk.

Reginald jumped up and put his arm around her waist. "You okay?"

Tricia emitted a nervous chuckle. "Just stood up too fast that's all. It's nothing."

Reginald gave her a skeptical glance. "You sure?"

"Yes, yes." She shooed him away. "I'm fine." She

tugged in a breath, thought about getting another cup of coffee but changed her mind and slowly sat back down, hoping to still the sudden racing of her heart. She made a mental note to really make that doctor's appointment. "Let me get these notes into a Power-Point presentation for the meeting," Tricia said, hoping to deflect Reginald's concern for her toward more important matters—their clients.

"Need any help?"

"No, I have it covered. How many items on the agenda?"

"Eight agenda items, five of which are new projects, and Jean and Chris are working on a new ad campaign for the bridal designer."

Tricia nodded. For the most part she let her crew do their creative thing, but she always kept her eye on each and every project and put her stamp of approval on anything that had her company's name attached to it. She would never be accused of not knowing what went on in her business. She reviewed every piece of film, every line of text, every bill and met one-on-one with every client. She availed herself to her staff and pretty much maintained an open door policy. She gave credit where credit was due and rewarded her loyal staff with everything from flexible hours to extra paid vacation days, bonuses and spontaneous office parties—just to say thank you. If it was one thing she never wanted to be, it was a boss like those she'd walked away from.

"Well, I'd rather complain about too much work, than not enough," Tricia commented, clicking on the PowerPoint icon on her computer screen.

"True, especially with the economy being what it is. But Tricia," Reginald lowered his voice and looked her square in the eye. "You really don't have to work so hard. You have an excellent team who knows what they're doing and they do it well."

Tricia heaved a sigh. "I know Reggie, but—"

"But nothing. When was the last time you took a vacation or even a day off? You've been on the job nonstop since we opened. That can't be good for you."

Tricia leaned back in her seat and folded her arms beneath her ample breasts. "The first thing I learned before jumping into my own business was that it took at least five to seven years to truly get established and show a profit."

"But you've done that in four!"

She pursed her lips. "I'd rather err on the side of caution."

Reginald shook his head. "And the one thing I remember my father always telling me, don't argue with a woman. Even if you're right you can't win."

They laughed.

"Your father is a very wise man."

Reginald took his coffee mug and headed toward the door. "See you at the meeting."

Tricia gave him a finger wave and turned back to the tasks at hand. But as much as she tried to focus, she couldn't keep her thoughts from straying to how odd she was feeling, and the frightening dizzy spell of moments ago.

Chapter 2

When Tricia walked into the presentation room everyone was already inside.

" 'Morning, everybody," she greeted, carrying her ever ready portfolio beneath her arm.

A chorus of "hellos" and "how was your weekend" greeted her in return.

"New hairdo, Leslie?" Tricia asked as she took a seat. "I like it."

Leslie patted her new bob and grinned. "Thanks."

"How's your wife, Lloyd? She should be ready to go in any minute now."

"She's hanging in there, but getting impatient. Thanks for asking."

"Just keep us posted."

Tricia greeted each staff member in turn, singling them out with a personal question or observation. If one didn't really know Tricia the belief might be that her apparent interest in her staff was all part of a game. But for Tricia it was from the heart. She truly cared about her staff. They were all like family to her.

"Ready to get started folks?" she asked.

Everyone settled down and took seats along the eight-foot conference table.

"Jean and Chris, you're up first," Reginald said, assuming his role of moderator.

Jean stood and walked to the wall switch and shut off the light. Chris took his position behind the slide carousel. Jean began with her presentation for the African bridal ad.

Tricia watched the presentation begin to recede as the room grew darker and a wave of heat consumed her. The next thing she knew she was looking up into seven terrified faces. Reginald was kneeling at her side.

"Don't move. You took a nasty spill out of the chair."

"The ambulance is on the way," Jean said, a bit breathless.

Tricia tried to sit up and Reginald put a restraining hand on her shoulder.

"I mean it, Tricia, stay put."

Tricia never felt so humiliated in all her life. Here she was, the president of a thriving business, sprawled out on the floor smack in the middle of a meeting. Not to mention that everyone's expression vacillated between terror and pity. Two emotions she did not want associated with her.

But what was truly scary was that she didn't think she had the energy to get up even if they told her the place was on fire.

The ambulance arrived moments later and the EMS workers hovered over her like a scene out of *Third*

Watch. Once she was stabilized they hoisted her onto a gurney and got her into the ambulance. Reginald insisted on riding along with her. He held her hand all the way to Midtown Memorial Hospital amid the blare of the ambulance's siren.

"Everything is going to be fine," Reginald soothed, trying but failing to sound reassuring. In all the years he'd known and worked with Tricia he'd never seen her so much as miss a beat. When he saw her lying on the floor it was surreal.

Tricia tried not to read between the worry lines etched across Reginald's brow or the tight lines that bracketed his mouth. Reginald was the most optimistic person she knew and when he was worried it could only mean trouble.

"What happened?" Tricia finally dared to ask, as the ambulance bumped and ground its way down the street.

"You fainted . . . or something. How are you feeling?"

She gripped his hand a bit tighter. "Scared," she whispered as tears slowly spilled over her bottom lashes.

"Sssh. Don't get yourself all worked up. Try to relax."

Tricia swallowed hard and nodded.

When they arrived at the hospital, Tricia was taken directly to triage where she was further evaluated and much to her dismay ordered to be admitted.

"Admitted! I can't be admitted," she cried out to Reginald who was summoned from the waiting room.

"Hon, if they think you need to be in the hospital just do what they say." He squeezed her hand.

Tricia blinked back tears. "The ER doctor said I need tests on my heart. Some kind of irregular rhythm." She glanced up at him with wide, frightened eyes.

"All the more reason why you need to be here so they can get to the bottom of it and get you well."

"We're ready to take her upstairs now," the nurse said, stepping into the exam room.

"Call Phyllis for me will you, Reg? Let her know what's going on," she said, as the nurse and orderly wheeled her out of the room.

"I will. I promise," Reginald said, as he watched Tricia being wheeled away.

"I'm really feeling better," she insisted as they went down the narrow corridor to the elevator.

The nurse gave her a patronizing "I've heard it all before" glance. "I'm sure you do, but why not let the doctor make that decision. You just try to take it easy." She pressed the button and the elevator door swooshed open.

Tricia huffed and looked around at her draped quarters that were in a dull shade of what tried to pass for green. How did they ever expect anyone to get better with such depressing colors, she absently mused. The walls could use some work, too, she added as an afterthought. All she knew at the moment was that she wanted to get the hell out of there and back to work. She could only imagine what her staff must be thinking. Her head began to pound. The last thing she needed was any of her clients finding out that she'd collapsed in the middle of a meeting. There were already rumors abounding that her company was growing too big, too fast and there were those who wanted in on the action. She'd been approached on more than one occasion to sell portions, if not all, of her company to "investors." She'd always turned them down. Well, once she saw this doctor, she was sure she'd be out of this joint one, two, three.

"Ms. Spencer?"

Tricia glanced up toward the image in the opening of the curtain and she wasn't sure if her heart was racing because of her recent ordeal or because Mr. FINE dressed in white stood in front of her.

Never at a loss for words she suddenly couldn't respond. Her mouth was as dry as a bag of sand.

He let the curtain fall behind him as he stepped inside, lowering the chart he held in his hand. He walked over to the bedside. The nurse walked in behind him and stood in the background.

"I'm Dr. Evans, the cardiac resident on call. I'll be taking over your case." He took out a miniflashlight and pointed it at her eyes. "Look up," he commanded in a way that made you want to obey his every word. "To the right. Left. Very good." He shut off the light and slipped it back into the pocket of his smock. He consulted the chart again. "Your blood pressure is in the danger zone. Were you aware of that?"

"No," she squeaked, and wondered where her gospel-sounding voice disappeared to.

He pulled up a chair. "Have you ever fainted before?"

18

She shook her head. Damn she could almost count his eyelashes he was so close. And he smelled good, too.

"Any history of heart trouble or high blood pressure?"

What did he say? She shook her head again just in case. His skin was the color of smooth dark chocolate. Without thinking, she ran her tongue over her lips.

"I want to run some tests and keep you here for evaluation at least two days, possibly more."

Her eyes widened in alarm and she finally found her voice. "I can't stay in the hospital that long."

When he smiled down at her and his eyes crinkled and a dimple flashed, she nearly fainted again.

"That's what all my patients say. It's best to check everything out Ms. Spencer. It's apparent that this episode you had today is an indication that something is wrong. Don't you want to know what it is? I'm sure you do," he answered before she could. He stood. "I've put in the order for your tests. The nurse will take some blood and get additional information from you. I'm sure everything will be fine. But we need to be certain." With that he turned and walked out.

The nurse handed her a set of papers on a clipboard. "I need you to sign where it's marked."

Tricia blinked several times and absently took the clipboard. "Is he always so abrupt?"

The nurse laughed. "It may seem that way, but Dr. Evans is one of the best doctors on staff. You're lucky you got him. I'll be back shortly to get some blood from you."

Tricia nodded. Dr. Evans. Hmmm. She wondered

what his first name was. Not that it really mattered, she quickly corrected herself. Someone like him would never be interested in someone like her. That had been made clear to her for years. Why should things be any different now?

She really must not be well, she thought. The whole notion of her and Dr. Evans was beyond ridiculous. But wow, if only. She rested her head against the flat hospital pillow and dared to dream of the possibility.

Chapter 3

"How long did they say you were going to have to be in here?" Phyllis asked as she snatched up a chair next to Tricia's bed and sat down.

"The doctor said he wants to run tests and keep me a few days for observation."

Phyllis pursed her lips. "I don't want to have to say this but—"

Tricia held up her hand. "Then don't. I know . . . you told me so." She rolled her eyes and tried to get comfortable in the bed without ripping the IV out of her arm.

"When Reginald called me, I could only imagine the worst. Girl you scared me half to death."

"You couldn't have been any more afraid than I was. One minute I was sitting in my chair, the next I was sprawled out on the floor."

"Oh, Tricia." She patted her arm. "Well, I'm sure everything will be fine."

"So do I." She forced a smile.

"Did they start the tests yet?"

"After taking about ten pints of blood I should hope so."

Phyllis bit back a chuckle. "Yeah, hospitals have a thing for drawing blood." She looked around. "At least you have a decent room."

"I'd rather be home in my own bed."

"You will be. For once just do as someone else tells you to do."

Tricia pursed her lips.

"Good afternoon ladies."

Both women turned toward the door and Tricia could have sworn on a stack of Bibles that she heard Phyllis gasp.

Dr. Evans walked toward Tricia's bed and his casual, sexy stroll put Tricia in mind of Denzel Washington. She never thought anyone on earth had the walk, but damn if the good doctor didn't.

"I came to check on my patient. How are you feeling?" He looked down into her eyes.

"Good enough to go home." Her voice came in a throaty whisper and she could have kicked herself.

"We'll have to see about that." He turned to Phyllis. "Would you mind excusing us for a minute?"

Phyllis stuttered something unintelligible and eventually left the room.

Dr. Evans sat down in Phyllis's vacated seat. "I've ordered an EKG and some stress tests. I'm pretty sure you're going to need some medication to get your pressure under control. And I want you to talk with our nutritionist."

Tricia pushed herself up in the bed. "Why?"

"One primary cause for high blood pressure in addition to stress or heredity is weight and eating habits."

Tricia swallowed.

"What do you do for a living?"

"I'm president of my own advertising agency," she said with pride.

He nodded seemingly unimpressed. "Must be hectic," he murmured. He lifted her wrist and listened for her pulse. "I want to check your heart." He placed the stethoscope beneath her breast and it took all she had not to shudder. His face grew serious as he looked off into some distant place. "Hmmm."

"What does that mean?"

Dr. Evans focused on her face. He wrapped the stethoscope around his neck and sat back. "My preliminary diagnosis is that you have dysrhythmia."

"Dis-what?"

He grinned. "Dysrhythmia. It's a condition characterized by abnormal rate and rhythm of the heartbeat, called arrhythmias or impaired condition."

Her mind started to swim. Was she going to die?

"In your case, I believe it's relatively harmless. At least for the time being. But it can become serious if some life changes aren't made." He stood and checked his watch. "I'm going off duty now, but if anything should happen they will contact me directly. Try to get some rest in the meantime. I've put you on a low-salt diet. Your dinner should arrive shortly."

She frowned. Low-salt. Yick. "Doctor?"

"Yes." He stuck his pen in the top pocket of his smock.

"Are you telling me the whole truth? You're not

23

hiding anything because you think I can't take it, are you?"

"I'm always honest and up-front with all of my patients, Ms. Spencer. Everything I've told you is what I believe from seeing hundreds of cases such as yours. No matter how dire a situation may be, the patient has the right to know so that they can make appropriate decisions. Don't you agree?"

Tricia swallowed over the lump in her throat and nodded, not trusting her voice.

"I'll see you in the morning." He turned, did his Denzel thing and was gone.

An instant later, Phyllis was back in the room.

"Damn girl, that's your doctor?" she squeaked, taking a quick glance over her shoulder. "If I was you I'd think up some other stuff to be wrong just so he could work on me."

"Phyllis you need to stop. Dr. Evans isn't paying me a bit of attention other than as a patient."

"You could change that with a new attitude," Phyllis said with a huff.

"All I want to do is get these tests over with and get out of here," she said, not sounding as convincing as she did earlier. Maybe a few days around the good doctor wouldn't be so bad after all, she thought.

"Can I get you anything?" Phyllis asked.

"No. I guess at some point they will bring me some delicious hospital food. Dr. Evans said I'm on a low-salt diet."

"Yummy," Phyllis teased.

Tricia rolled her eyes. "Do you really think he's cute?" she asked, trying to sound nonchalant.

"Cute! He's off the scale, my sister." She examined her nails. "I wonder if he's married."

"What difference would that make?"

"A lot since you're going to make a play for him."

"I'm not going to do any such thing."

"If you say so. But I saw that look in your eyes and heard the way your voice got all girly."

"What look?" She couldn't debate the girly part.

"Like you wanted to have him for dinner."

"As usual, your imagination is working overtime."

"If you say so. But I know what I saw and what I heard. And to be truthful, I don't blame you. I sure wouldn't kick him out of bed."

They giggled.

"Phyllis, you are terrible. You have a great husband."

"Sure, Frank is a doll, but that doesn't mean that I've gone blind. A girl can still look and wish wonderful things for her best friend." She gave Tricia a wink.

"Umm, I was just thinking. If you have some time, would you mind stopping by my place and bringing over my makeup bag and my silk scarf?"

Phyllis arched a brow. "Sure. Need anything else?"

"And maybe that really nice gown you got me last Christmas. It's in my bottom drawer."

Phyllis bit back a smile. She reached in her purse. "I have this great new lipstick. I think it would be perfect for you." She handed Tricia the tube.

Tricia opened the tube and smiled. "Perfect."

Chapter 4

As promised the next day was filled with one test after another. Tricia felt like a science project by the time the nurse brought her back to her room.

"When will the results come back?" Tricia asked, once she was settled in her bed.

"Some will take a few hours—hopefully. That depends on how busy the lab is."

"Will Dr. Evans be coming in today?"

The nurse checked the IV and slipped Tricia's chart in the slot at the bottom of her bed. "I'm sure he'll stop in when he makes his rounds. He's not on duty until later this afternoon. He has his private patients in the morning."

Private patients . . . hmmm. Tricia didn't respond but wondered if Phyllis would be back with her gown before the good doctor arrived. Not that she was hoping for anything to jump off between her and the doctor—that was ridiculous of course—but she did want to look decent if she had to sit around the hospital.

"I'll check on you later. They should be bringing lunch soon." The nurse smiled and left the room.

Tricia heaved a sigh and settled back against the pillow hoping to get comfortable. She didn't spend the greatest of nights, barely sleeping for more than a few minutes at a time. Her mind wouldn't shut down as she went over and over the events of the previous day. She knew she'd been pushing herself lately, more so than usual. But the last thing she expected was to collapse.

But her main concern was getting out of the hospital as quickly as possible. She could not depend on her sister Lena to look after their mother. Lena was too busy chasing behind that no good man of hers and keeping up with her raunchy, grown kids. No matter what Tricia may have needed Lena for, she'd never come through. What she did come through with were excuses—one after another.

It had been that way between them for as long as Tricia could remember. She longed for an older sister whom she could rely on, get advice from. But it seemed as if fate had reversed their roles. From the time they were kids, it had always been Tricia who took charge while her sister was involved in one escapade after another. What made it worse was that their mother always made excuses for Lena. Lena could do no wrong. Even when she became pregnant at seventeen with her first child and had her second by the age of twenty, with no marriage in sight, their mother, Maxine, simply said, "Lena has wild ways but a good heart and look at these two beautiful children." Humph, Tricia thought, children that were basically raised by their grandmother—until she had her stroke. An unfortunate turn of events, but if one thing did come out of it, Lena was forced to take care of her own kids, which left Tricia to take care of their mother and try to keep a roof over her sister's head.

Tricia shut her eyes. Now with *her* down for the count what was going to happen to her family?

"Good morning, Ms. Spencer."

Tricia looked up and she knew this time that the sudden racing of her heart had nothing to do with anything other than pure excitement.

"Hi." *Damn where was Phyllis with her gown?* She pulled up the stiff white sheet almost to her chin.

"How are you feeling today?" Dr. Evans walked over to her bed and looked down at her.

His smile was soft and engaging and, for a minute, Tricia forgot what he'd asked her—again. She cleared her throat and her thoughts. "Uh, I'm feeling pretty good." She shifted her weight in the bed and wished she'd at least put on some lipstick.

"As soon as the test results come back I'll be better able to discuss a plan of action with you."

She nodded. "The, uh, nurse was telling me you have a private practice."

"Yes, I do, in Brooklyn."

"Really? Then why do you work here?"

He grinned and Tricia felt her stomach muscles flutter. "I like the energy of the hospital. I get called in for consultations on cases that I may never see in my private practice. It keeps me fresh and up-to-date on new treatments."

"Do any of your hospital patients become your private patients?"

"From time to time. Not often." He angled his head. "Why?"

28

Tricia shrugged slightly. "I was only wondering who I would see if I needed follow-up . . . stuff like that."

"I'm sure the hospital will recommend a doctor here on staff or in the clinic that you can see. Or your own doctor can recommend someone."

Suddenly she felt as if she'd been slapped. It was pretty clear he had no interest in having her as a patient. He'd as much as said so. Either that or he believed she couldn't afford him.

"I suppose you're right," she said, her voice tight and controlled.

He tapped the side of the bed. "Well, get some rest. We hope to have you out of here by tomorrow or the next day at the latest." He turned and walked out.

The news should have had her jumping for joy. But instead it was a letdown. She knew that once she left the hospital her contact with Dr. Evans would come to an end. It didn't really matter. She was getting her hopes up for nothing. She shouldn't have let Phyllis put the silly notion in her head in the first place. Dr. Evans had no interest in her. What she needed to concentrate on was getting better and staying well.

Tricia reached for the bedside phone and dialed her mother's number. She tugged in a breath. She'd speak with the housekeeper and let her know what had happened but would warn her against telling her mother. The last thing her mother needed was to be worried about her. Lena was enough of a headache.

The phone rang five times before someone finally picked it up and it wasn't the housekeeper.

"Hello," said a very groggy-sounding Lena.

"Lena? What are you doing there?" Tricia asked, sitting straight up in bed.

"Sleeping until you woke me up," she grumbled.

Tricia blinked several times and shook her head. "What? Why are you there, Lena? You have your own place. Is Mom okay?"

"Yeah, Mom is fine." She yawned loudly. "I lost my place so I had to camp out here."

"Lost your place? Just like that? Lena!"

"Relax will you." She muttered something under her breath. "I'll be out of here in no time."

"That's not really the point, Lena. You shouldn't have to be there in the first place."

Lena sucked her teeth long and hard. "Always preaching. Always preaching. Look, I'm living my life the best I know how and yeah I make mistakes but so does everyone. The least you could do is say you're sorry about what happened, but no, you just want to lecture like you always do."

Tricia squeezed her eyes shut and counted to ten. She couldn't name one person on the entire planet who could upset her the way her sister did. She tugged in a calming breath.

"Where's Mom?"

"She must be cooking 'cause I smell bacon."

"Lena, can you do me a favor," she said, her voice syrupy sweet.

"Sure."

"Get the hell up out of the bed and see what Mama's doing in the kitchen!" she screamed so loud her head began to vibrate. "You know good and well she's not supposed to be in there." Her voice rose to new heights. "Where is the housekeeper?"

A nurse came rushing into the room. "Ms. Spencer, are you all right?"

Tricia raised her hand to wave the nurse away, even as the furrows deepened in her forehead.

The nurse came to the side of the bed. "You're really going to have to calm down, Ms. Spencer. Perhaps you should have the conversation later." She stood in front of Tricia with her arms folded, looking as if she would not hesitate to snatch the phone from Tricia in a wink.

Tricia stole a glance at the nurse. She lowered her voice, and hissed out the words between clenched teeth. "Listen to me Lena, I don't know what's going on over there, but for once in your life would you attempt to do the adult, responsible thing and go and see about Mama? Make sure she's okay and not in the process of burning down the house! The number for the housekeeper is posted on the fridge. Please call and find out what happened. I'll check back with you later." With all the calm she could muster, she gently hung up the phone.

The nurse gave her a stern look and took her wrist to listen for her pulse. Her brow arched as she listened then slowly put Tricia's arm down.

"Well?" Tricia asked.

"A bit fast but not dangerously so. But that doesn't mean that you're free to push it off the charts. You're here to get your health under control not out."

Tricia tried to look contrite, but all she could think

about was her sister. Now she really needed the green light so she could go and see what in the world was going on with her family.

Dr. Evans returned to his small stuffy office tucked away on the third floor of the city hospital. He closed the door behind him in the hopes of stealing a few minutes of quiet time before heading back out into the trenches. He turned on the small boom box on the windowsill and adjusted the tuner to his favorite local jazz station. The strains of John Coltrane filtered through the room. Michael smiled. Nothing like good music to soothe the savage beast he thought, taking a seat behind his paper-strewn desk.

He picked up the file on top and flipped it open. *Tricia Spencer.* When he'd walked into her hospital room and saw her for the first time, he'd felt a flash of déjà vu. She looked enough like Christine that it nearly stopped his heart. He still had nightmares about what happened to Christine. His colleagues had consoled him and told him he'd done everything he could. But his best wasn't enough to save her. For months he watched her struggle until she finally lost the battle. A part of him went with her. It took months for him to regain his confidence. Her death had compelled him to open his own office.

Michael glanced at the framed photograph on his desk: he and Christine during happy times, the early years of their marriage. He tugged in a deep breath. He'd do what he could for Tricia while she was under his care and he would move on to the next patient. He would not allow himself to even for a moment imagine that she could be any more than what she was—a patient who needed his care. He wouldn't let the sudden stir of emotions, feelings that had become unfamiliar, resurface and cloud his judgment. Not again.

He made some notes in her case file just as one of the nurses tapped on his door.

"Come in."

"Hi, Dr. Evans." She handed him a stack of paper. "These just came in on Ms. Spencer."

"Thanks." He took the reports. "How was she?" He glanced over the results while he listened.

"She seemed fine. But something upset her earlier. Some kind of phone confrontation. I told her she was going to have to take it easy."

Michael's head slowly came up, his gaze resting on the nurse. "Confrontation?"

The nurse shrugged slightly. "She was arguing, rather loudly, at someone."

"I see. How were her vitals afterward?"

"I took her pulse. It was a bit fast but nothing to be overly concerned about. She seemed fine, more annoyed than anything else."

Michael nodded. "Thanks."

She turned and walked out.

So she had spirit, Michael mused. He shouldn't be surprised. She was direct with him from the moment they met. He always liked that in a woman. But he wasn't going to entertain what he liked in a woman especially if it had anything to do with a patient—this one in particular.

Chapter 5

When Phyllis and Reginald arrived at the same time to visit with Tricia, they halted dead in their tracks when they walked in on her putting on her shoes.

"What in the world are you doing?" Phyllis demanded, tossing her purse on the vacated bed.

"Have you been discharged?' Reginald asked.

Tricia looked from one to the other. "Getting dressed and getting the heck out of here. And no I have not been discharged."

Phyllis and Reginald started running their mouths at once.

Tricia held up her hand. "Just hold on one minute," she commanded, raising her voice just enough to let them know she meant business. "I'm checking myself out. I took all the tests I intend to take and either I'm fine or I'm not, but whatever it is, I'm not going to spend the rest of my time in the hospital."

"Tricia this is crazy! You didn't just have a little dizzy spell. You passed out on the floor," Reginald said.

"I'm perfectly well aware of that. But I can't stay

here a minute longer. If I do I'm liable to have a real heart attack or worse." She reached into the nightstand and took out her purse.

"Tricia, what happened?" Phyllis asked with a deep frown creasing her brow.

Tricia snapped her head toward Phyllis. "Lena is what happened." She grabbed her bag, tucked it under her arm and marched out.

Phyllis and Reginald took one look at each other and both of them knew that with Lena it could be nothing but trouble. They followed behind her.

Tricia stopped at the front desk, thinking that it was only right that she tell them she was leaving. She tenderly rubbed her arm where the IV had been.

The nurse looked up from her notes. "Ms. Spencer! What in the world are you doing?" She got up and immediately came around the front desk.

"I'm checking out," Tricia said simply.

"But you can't do that." She looked her up and down. "What did you do with your IV?"

"I took it out." Tricia inhaled deeply. "Carefully," she added.

"I need to call the doctor."

"Fine. But I'm still leaving." Tricia tapped her foot with impatience while the nurse had Dr. Evans paged on the hospital intercom.

"Dr. Evans, Dr. Michael Evans, please come to the nurses station immediately."

No sooner than she'd hung up the phone from paging the doctor that the second line rang.

"Yes, doctor. Right here doctor." She pursed her lips and handed Tricia the phone.

35

Reluctantly Tricia lifted the receiver to her ear. She wanted to act tough, but truth be told, the sound of Dr. Evans's smooth voice right up in her ear was almost more than she could pretend she didn't care about. She started feeling warm all over as she listened to him calmly chastise her then advise her she was not to leave until he arrived, which would be almost immediately.

For the benefit of her audience, Tricia put an "I'm doing him a favor by waiting" look on her face as she handed the phone back to the nurse. "The doctor said he's on his way," she said in a voice barely above a whisper.

"I hope he can talk some sense into her," Phyllis hissed through her teeth, then marched over to a row of chairs lined up against the wall.

Tricia followed suit, not letting on that her head was feeling kind of light, but she attributed it to having been in the bed for so long.

Three heads turned in the direction of the swinging door and Dr. Evans burst through, looking more than a little annoyed. He cut a look in Tricia's direction then went right to the nurse's station, mumbled something, then turned to Tricia. "Would you come with me please?"

On the short hop from his office to the ward, Michael couldn't dismiss the mixed feelings he experienced when he got the call that Tricia was signing herself out of the hospital. There was a small part of him that was relieved, but a much bigger part that knew he still wanted to find a way to see her—at least long enough to ensure that she was solidly on the road to recovery. At least that's what he told himself.

Michael opened the door to an available office, stepped aside and let Tricia past. Her breast inadvertently brushed against him and a jolt of electricity jettisoned through his body. He snapped his head to clear it and he would have sworn he'd heard her gasp. But that must have been his imagination.

"Did you say something?" she asked, turning to face him and realized this was the first time she'd been in a room with him and not flat on her back. He was taller than she thought. Nice.

"No. Did you?"

She looked curiously at him and shook her head.

Michael cleared his throat and extended his hand toward an empty seat. "Please," he said.

Tricia huffed but sat down anyway seeing as that her knees were wobbling after that brief brush of ecstasy. *Lordhammercy.* She crossed her legs, glad that the cheap pantyhose she'd had on when EMS brought her in didn't have runs.

"Now, do you want to tell me what's on your mind, signing yourself out like that? All of your results are not back in yet."

"That's all fine and dandy Doc, but I have really pressing family matters that I need to take care of, and staying in this hospital and not knowing what's going on first-hand is only going to make me sicker than I already am—or not." She looked at him with a question in her eye and her voice.

Michael leaned back in the chair then folded his

hands on top of the desk. Tricia noticed the well-manicured nails and the long sinewy fingers. Her stomach did a little flip.

"Is it something that can be taken care of by someone else? You really should take it easy at least for the next few days and definitely until all the results come back."

Tricia leaned forward, not caring that the dip in her navy suit offered a nice little peek at her abundant cleavage. "Dr. Evans, I have a sick mother, and a sicker sister, not sick as in ill but—anyway, things aren't right at home. I'm the one who looks after my mother and now I find out that my sister has moved in." Instinctively she rolled her eyes. "That can only be trouble and I'm not going to lay up in some hospital bed while who knows what is going on in my mama's home. It's as simple as that and there is nothing you can say that is going to change my mind. I'm leaving here today with or without your permission." She bobbed her head sharply for emphasis.

It was pretty clear that there was nothing he could do to keep her, short of having her committed for mental instability. Tricia Spencer may be a lot of things, but in need of psychiatric observation wasn't one of them. He didn't have any options. It was a patient's right to sign themselves out of the hospital and there wasn't much he could do but advise strongly against it.

He tugged in a breath. "Okay, look, you can leave, although in my medical opinion you shouldn't. But I will agree on the following terms."

Tricia arched a brow. "And what might the terms be?"

"You are to come to my private office no later than tomorrow for me to check you out. And you will continue to come until I give you clearance. I'll even work around your schedule."

She worked hard at not looking utterly delighted. "Hmmm," she murmured as if she were really mulling it over. "Fine." She folded her arms.

Michael reached into the desk and pulled out a notepad. He wrote down the address of his office and handed it to her. "What time can I expect you tomorrow?"

"Will two o'clock work for you?"

"I'll see you then. And take it easy. If you feel strange or weak, you call me immediately. My number is on the paper."

She glanced at it again then tucked the square sheet of white paper in her purse and stood.

He scribbled something else on a prescription pad. "Get this filled right away and take one pill per day with plenty of water. It's for your blood pressure."

Tricia nodded and took the prescription. "I'll see you tomorrow." She headed for the door and this time her heart really was racing—with anticipation. A meeting tomorrow in his private office. She couldn't have done better if she'd planned it herself. But first things first: She needed to see exactly what her slick-as-oil sister was up to now.

Chapter 6

"Take me straight to my mother's house," Tricia instructed the instant she was seated in Phyllis's car.

"Don't you at least want to go home first?" Reginald asked from the backseat.

Tricia whipped her head around. "No." She folded her hands in her lap.

Phyllis shook her head. "All you had to do was call me. I could have gone over there."

"This is something I need to take care of."

"So what did the doctor tell you?" Reginald asked.

That hot flush ran through her again at the mention of the good doctor. "I have to see him tomorrow . . . at his private office."

Phyllis snapped a look at her and slapped Tricia's thigh. "When were you gonna tell me?"

Tricia held back her smile. "I was. It's no big deal."

"No big deal," Phyllis squealed.

"Am I missing something?" Reginald asked.

"Tricia has a thing for Dr. Evans and—"

"Phyllis you need to stop."

"It's the truth and she knows it. And I think he has a thing for you, too. I saw the way he was looking at you when you weren't looking."

"Really?" Tricia asked before she could stop herself.

"You go, Tricia. Only been in the hospital barely three days and hooked a doctor," Reginald teased.

Tricia gave him a nasty look from over her shoulder. "Just remember I still sign your check."

"No need for threats."

"So are you going? Well of course you're going. Do you know what you're going to wear?"

"You're really making too much of this. The only reason he has me coming to his office is because I signed myself out and he wants to be sure I'm doing okay."

"Right," Phyllis said, the one word dripping with sarcasm. "He could have easily referred you to the clinic—not his *private* office."

"That's true," Reginald chimed in.

"The both of you are making too much out of this, I swear."

"Hmmm," they murmured in unison.

Tricia rolled her eyes and tried to concentrate on what she was going to say to her sister, but images of Dr. Evans, the sound of his voice and the gentle smile was playing havoc with her head. She was trying to play it cool and hoped he had no inkling that she had an interest in him. And she hoped she'd be able to continue to play it cool when she went to see him the following day.

When they pulled up in front of Tricia's mother's

house, Tricia immediately spotted her sister's boy-friend's white Escalade, and she knew her pressure just shot through the roof.

Tricia was already pulling off her seat belt before Phyllis came to a complete stop.

"Just take it easy," Phyllis warned, feeling the flames fanning from Tricia. "Maybe he's just visiting."

Tricia tossed off her seat belt and grabbed her purse. "Not for long." She got out and marched toward the house just as Lena pulled the door open looking as if she was ready for a long night out on the town. As usual she was dressed like a fashion model and just as sleek and trim, her Halle Berry haircut and her honey-toned skin absolutely flawless.

Lena grinned. "Tricia, what are you doing here?" She came down the steps with Graham, her current boyfriend, following behind her.

Tricia gritted her teeth. "Where's Mama?"

Lena hitched her thumb over her shoulder. "Up-stairs resting." She tucked her purse under her arm.

"Is the housekeeper here?"

"No. I sent her home early."

"I'm not even going to ask you why."

"I'll be back in a couple of hours." She breezed by Tricia and headed for the Escalade.

"Good to see ya again," Graham said.

Tricia grumbled something under her breath. "We need to talk, Lena."

Lena gave her a finger wave. "Later."

Tricia watched the couple get into the gas guzzling vehicle and speed off. For a moment she lowered her head, hoping to get her thoughts in focus. Why was it always Lena who could turn people's worlds upside down and walk away unscathed? It was Lena who won the games, had all the friends, male and female, and their mother's undying love.

There was a part of Tricia that resented her perfect sister. Lena never had to struggle for anything, just lift a finger to get what she wanted. Tricia was the one who had to work hard at everything, from her looks, and her weight, and men, to vying for her mother's affections. She worked twice as hard to feel half as valuable.

Slowly she took the stairs and stepped inside.

Chapter 7

Michael pulled his Benz into the driveway of his single-family house in the Canarsie section of Brooklyn. Another night alone, he mused, as he stuck his key in the door. Most times he didn't mind. He'd grown accustomed to his own company. But as he stepped inside, for the first time in quite a while, he wished he had someone to come home to, to share his day with.

He shut the door behind him and turned on the hall light. Strange he should feel this way out of the blue. His thoughts switched to Tricia Spencer. She was the reason. Without any effort she'd inadvertently resurrected those old buried emotions. Was it the fact that she reminded him of his wife or was it simply Tricia herself? He knew he could have easily recommended that she have her follow-up in the clinic like most patients. But the truth was, he wanted to see her again, and having her come to his office would ensure that he would.

Michael walked down the narrow hallway that led

to the kitchen. He pulled open the fridge and peeked inside, hoping to find something worthwhile to fix for dinner. He pulled out some cold cuts, not really in the mood to fix anything more complex than a sandwich.

He took his sandwich, put it on a plate and took out an icy cold bottle of beer to go with it and went into the living room to catch up on the news. He ate and stared sightlessly at the tube, but he kept thinking about Tricia. Had she made it home okay? What was the big family emergency that compelled her to leave? Did she have a relapse? He got up, went to the phone and called the hospital.

"Yes, this is Dr. Evans. I, uh, need some information on a patient that was discharged today," he said quickly before he changed his mind. He knew he was taking his medical responsibility a bit too seriously, but it couldn't hurt just to check. "Yes, do you have a contact number for Tricia Spencer? She was my patient. I need to make sure she . . . picked up her prescription." He waited a few minutes until the duty nurse found the information he requested. "Thank you."

He hung up the phone, debated for half a minute as to the veracity of calling her at home, but decided to go with his gut. He dialed her home number and waited. After four rings her voice mail came on. The simple sound of her voice affected him more than he realized it would. His heart beat just a bit faster as he listened to her smoky voice.

"Ms. Spencer, this is Dr. Evans. I wanted to make sure that you arrived safely and are still feeling well. I hope you're resting and I'll see you tomorrow at my office. If you begin experiencing any problems, don't hesitate to have the hospital page me." He cleared his throat. "Have a good evening."

As he hung up the phone, he suddenly felt like a fool having called a patient like that. He wished he could take the call back, but it was too late for that. He inhaled deeply. What was done was done. What he needed to do was regain his professional perspective and shake these feelings about Tricia Spencer aside. Come tomorrow, that is exactly what he would do. Tricia Spencer was a patient, nothing more.

Much to Phyllis's and Reginald's annoyance, Tricia went through the house from top to bottom getting it in order, cussing and fuming the entire time. And every time they tried to help she found something wrong with the way they did it. She fixed dinner for her mother and got her settled in bed before finally flopping down on the couch.

"I haven't been gone a full week and Lena has turned this place into a dump," she fumed. "And of course, Mama thinks nothing of it." She sucked her teeth and shook her head.

"Tricia, you can't do this to yourself," Phyllis scolded. "We don't want you back in the hospital. What will your mother do then?"

Tricia tossed her a look and then her expression softened. "I know," she conceded. "It's just that Lena is so irresponsible. I gave her money last month to help cover the rent. Obviously she used it for something else—probably a new outfit or a night out on the town with that trifling man of hers," she grumbled. "I just don't understand it."

"You can't keep cleaning up Lena's messes, Tricia," Phyllis said. "She's a grown woman and she needs to learn to handle her own business. As long as you keep picking up the pieces for her she'll never do it on her own."

"What choice do I have? As much as she's a pain, I can't see her out on the street."

"Well you better figure something out or else your discharge from the hospital will be very short-lived."

They were all silent for a moment.

"Did you speak with the housekeeper?" Reginald finally asked.

"Yeah. Lena told her she wasn't needed anymore since she'd moved in. Can you believe that?"

"So what did you tell her?"

"That she needed to be back here tonight. And that she was not to take any more instructions from Lena, especially since I'm the one paying for her to be here."

"Well at least you know your mom will be looked after," Phyllis said. "And then you can go home and get some rest." She paused. "What are you going to do about Lena?"

"I wish I could kick her to the curb, but I know Mama would have a natural fit." She sighed heavily. "I don't know at the moment."

The doorbell rang and Tricia pulled herself up from the chair and went to answer the door.

"I'm so sorry, Ms. Spencer," Jean the housekeeper said. "I didn't know what to do when your sister showed up and told me to leave. I tried to reach you at home and at work. They said at your job that you were in the hospital. Are you all right?"

Tricia patted Jean's shoulder. "I'll be fine. Come in."

Jean gave her a tentative smile. "How is your mother? I've been so worried." She stepped in and set her suitcase on the floor.

"She's fine. She's upstairs resting."

"I'll go right up and check on her."

"Thank you."

Tricia exhaled a breath of relief and smiled for the first time in hours. She returned to the living room. "That was Jean. I'm going to go up and say good-bye to my mother. Would you mind driving me home?"

"Of course not," Phyllis said, "whenever you're ready."

"Okay, I'll be right back." She left the room.

After Phyllis and Reginald got Tricia safely home with a list of warnings and instructions, Tricia finally made it up to her bedroom. She was exhausted, both physically and mentally. She'd been so worried about getting to her mother's house she'd totally forgotten to get her prescription filled. It would just have to wait until tomorrow, she thought, as she sat down heavily on her bed and heard the telltale squeak.

She glanced at the flashing light on her phone noting the messages waiting. Well they would have to wait, too, she decided, then got up and headed to the bathroom. All she wanted to do at that moment was sit in a hot tub and unwind.

Emerging an hour later, Tricia padded to her bedroom, her lids heavy and her body totally relaxed. She crawled under the smooth sheets and was just about to turn out the light when she remembered the messages waiting for her.

She reached over to the nightstand and pressed the button. The first two were from bill collectors, the next from Jean and the last nearly took her breath away. She sat straight up in bed as she listened to Dr. Evans's voice. A slow smile spread across her wide mouth and grew until her jaw began to ache. She pressed the button and replayed it three times. She didn't want to read anything into the very professional sounding call—yes she did. She wanted it to mean that he thought a little more about her than just a patient. But that was silly, she realized. He was just doing his job. Nothing more. Sighing, she reached for the light and turned it out, and as much as she tried to put him out of her head she couldn't, and her mind was filled with images of Dr. Evans giving her a real physical exam. She turned on her side, then on the other, then on her back. If she was a different kind of woman she'd take him up on his offer to call him if she began experiencing any difficulties—because she was certainly having difficulty getting to sleep with him on her mind.

The following morning, Tricia was up with the sun. Her night had been plagued with scenarios between her and Dr. Evans. In one dream she'd passed out in the street and he'd been called to give her mouth-to-mouth resuscitation. In another he'd invited her to the beach for a picnic on the boardwalk under the moonlight. The last one got her out of bed. In that dream she was in his office and he'd asked her to disrobe so that he could examine her, but when she did, she saw the look of disappointment in his eyes when he really looked at her naked body. And then Lena appeared, gorgeous and slim. Dr. Evans smiled at Lena with the kind of appreciation that only a male look can project to a woman. Tricia ran crying from the room with the exam gown barely covering her girth.

Tricia puttered around the house until the hour was decent enough to call her mother's house and tried to keep the nightmare out of her thoughts. Thankfully, Jean answered and assured her that her mother had rested well during the night and was having breakfast. She'd seen no sign of Lena, which meant she'd spent the night out. She should be thankful that Lena was missing in action, but the reality was, as always, Lena assumed that Tricia would take care of everything, even though Lena had discharged the housekeeper. And knowing her sister, she was bound to turn up at some point.

As Tricia sat at the kitchen table sipping a cup of tea, the phone rang.

"Hello?"

"Good morning, may I speak with Tricia Spencer please?"

Tricia frowned at the unfamiliar female voice. "Speaking."

"I'm calling from Dr. Evans's office."

Tricia swallowed. "Yes."

"I was calling to confirm your appointment for this afternoon."

Tricia immediately thought of her dream and the look of disappointment on Dr. Evans's face.

"I'm so glad you called. I'm going to have to cancel my appointment. Please tell the doctor that I . . . that I'm sorry." She hung up before the woman could protest.

For several moments, Tricia stood there with her hand still on the phone. That was the best thing, she told herself before finally turning away.

Chapter 8

Michael breezed through his rounds at the hospital, completed his charts and signed out. Generally he enjoyed his work as a private practitioner. He'd been able to really know and care about the patients that he treated, sometimes for years. But today was special. As much as he tried to beat down his feelings, he was truly looking forward to treating his new patient. Even if it remained platonic, which he knew that it must, seeing her again and perhaps often would be enough. At least he hoped so.

He'd reviewed her chart and her family background. She wasn't married, didn't have children and while she'd been at the hospital he didn't notice a significant other turning up to see her. He wondered if she was the kind of woman that was consumed by work with no time in her life for a relationship. She did say she ran her own business. She was probably good at it, too. What was he thinking? She's just a patient, Michael, he reminded himself. Just a patient—one that he wanted to know better.

* * *

When he arrived at his office, three of his patients were already there waiting. He greeted each in turn and went to the front desk to get the lineup from his secretary.

"How are you today, Leslie? Looks like we'll have a full house."

"Pretty good. All the patients for today confirmed, except for a new patient." She pulled out the appointment sheet. "Tricia Spencer? When I called to confirm she said she had to cancel."

Michael hoped that his surprise didn't show in his expression. "Did she say why?" he asked as casually as he could.

"No. Just that she had to cancel." She shrugged slightly.

"Thanks." He tugged in a breath. "Well, give me about five minutes and send in the first patient."

"Sure thing, Dr. Evans."

Michael walked into his office and closed his door. He felt oddly disappointed. All the energy and adrenalin that had been pumping through his veins all day in the hope of seeing Tricia evaporated. The zest he'd had only moments ago was completely gone. He sat down heavily in his seat. Why had she changed her mind? Then he thought about his phone call. He tried to recall everything he'd said. Had she heard something in his voice that sounded more than a medical interest? He hit his head with the heel of his palm. "Idiot." She probably figured he was being *too* concerned. "Idiot," he sputtered again.

His intercom buzzed. He stabbed at the flashing light. "Yes," he snapped.

"Are you ready, Dr. Evans? You have a full schedule today."

Not quite, he thought. "Yes, send in Mr. Mason." He slipped off his jacket and put on his white smock. With any luck the day would fly by and he could go home.

Short of actually going into the office, Tricia had done everything in her power to keep her mind off of her missed appointment with Dr. Evans, from tossing a load of laundry in the machine and emptying out the refrigerator to calling her job five times just to check on things, to which Reginald advised her if she called again he was going to quit. In between she made a trip to the pharmacy to get her prescription filled.

She glanced up at the kitchen clock. One thirty. She still had a half hour. But even if she'd left twenty minutes earlier she'd never make it to Brooklyn in time for her appointment. Besides, she'd canceled and that was that. She'd get a recommendation from her own doctor for someone else to see. No sense in setting herself up for disappointment. She looked at her prescription bottle, opened it and shook out a pill. No time like the present she thought as she filled a glass with water and swallowed the pill. With nothing left to do she decided to do something she hadn't done since she couldn't remember when—relax and read a book.

She headed into her living room and scanned the bookcase filled with books that she purchased out of a sense of loyalty to black writers, but didn't have time to read. She pulled down Jill Nelson's *Sexual Healing*.

Just as she got settled on the couch with her book propped up on her knees the doorbell rang. She frowned. Who knew she was home? Probably someone selling something. She reluctantly got up and went to the door. The last person she expected to see was Lena.

Tricia propped her hand on her hip and looked her sister up and down. "What is it, Lena, and how did you know I was home?"

"I called your job. They said you weren't in."

"And? That still doesn't explain why you're here." She looked past her sister to see if Graham's behemoth of a ride was parked on the street.

"I came alone," Lena said, answering the unasked question. "Can I at least come in?"

Tricia huffed and stepped aside.

Lena went straight to the kitchen and the refrigerator. She pulled open the door and peered inside. "Whatcha got cool to drink?"

"Water."

Lena closed the door and turned to her sister. "Does it always have to be this way between us?"

"What way, Lena? You mean you skating through life, using everyone and everything to get what you want for the moment and moving on, regardless of whatever chaos you may have caused in the process? Is that what you're talking about?"

Lena at least had the decency to look contrite, even if only for the moment.

"That's not the way it is at all," she countered and plopped down on a stool at the island counter.

"Then maybe you care to explain, beginning with

how you lost your apartment after I gave you the money you asked for last month to pay your rent. And what happened to the temp job you had?"

Lena twisted her scarlet lips. "I didn't just owe the two months rent," she confessed. "It was more like four and I was sure I could get the rest together but . . ."

"So you wind up moving in on Mama, and firing the housekeeper! What is on your mind, Lena?" Tricia's head began to pound.

"Just take it easy. I just figured since I was there, you could save some money if you didn't have to cover the housekeeper."

Tricia tossed her head back and laughed. "Oh, so you were thinking of me, is that what you want me to believe? That's a bit much even for you, Lena."

"It's true whether you want to believe it or not." She opened her purse and pulled out a white envelope and shoved it across the table. "Here, it's not much, but I want to start paying you back." She glanced away.

Tricia looked at the envelope and then at her sister. "Do you really think it's just about the money, Lena?" Tricia asked.

"I owe you. You remind me every chance you get that I owe you. So I'm trying to pay you back. You have a problem with that, too, huh?" She shook her head in frustration. "I'll never get it right when it comes to you." She stood and pushed away from the chair.

"Wait a minute. Don't walk out. That's what you're best at, walking away. And I get stuck picking up behind you, ever since we were kids, and I'm sick of it, Lena. I'm sick and tired of it."

"You never understood."

"Understood what? Make me understand." Her head pounded a little more and she began to feel a little dizzy.

"You were always the one who got it right. You were the smart one, the one who knew how to get things done. You were better at everything. And I'm your older sister," she shouted, pointing to her chest. "But you and your perfect self, your perfect life always made me feel like I never measured up. I was the one who should have been taking care of you, looking out for you. But I never could. You never needed anyone but yourself."

Tricia's vision began to grow cloudy. It seemed like Lena was moving in and out. She swayed in the chair and gripped the end of the table.

"Tricia?" Lena grabbed her sister's arm. "Trish, what's wrong?"

"Dizzy."

Lena put her arms around her sister's waist and braced her weight. "Come on, let me get you to the couch. Can you walk?"

Tricia nodded.

Lena helped Tricia to the couch then knelt down in front of her. She looked into her eyes. "What is going on?"

Tricia leaned her head back and the room continued to spin. "I don't want to go back to the hospital," she said in a weak voice.

"I'm calling 911." Lena jumped up to go to the phone.

"No."

Lena spun around. "I'm not going to stand here and let you pass out. Let me take care of you for once!" She picked up the phone and dialed the emergency number. Lena quickly explained what happened. "An ambulance is on the way." She came back to Tricia's side and sat next to her. "Try to relax, Sis." She stroked her brow.

"I'll be okay. Just . . . a . . . little dizzy that's all."

Moments later the sound of sirens could be heard followed shortly by a knocking on Tricia's front door. Lena got up to answer it.

The EMS workers went straight to Tricia and began their evaluation.

"We're going to take you to the hospital just to be sure," the paramedic said. "Have you taken any medication?"

Tricia nodded and pointed to the bottle on the table. The worker took a look. "Blood pressure meds. Have you had an episode like this before?"

"Yes. A few days ago."

He nodded. "Okay, let's get you out of here." His assistant came and opened the stretcher and they placed Tricia on it.

"I'm coming with her," Lena said.

"Sure, you can ride in back."

"This is a nightmare," Tricia murmured, as she lay on the exam table in the triage room.

Lena took her hand. "It will be okay," she said. "It will."

"Ms. Spencer."

Lena turned toward the male voice and her eyes immediately lit up.

Tricia glanced away.

Michael came to her side. "What happened?"

"I got dizzy."

He flipped open her chart. "Did you take the medication as instructed?"

"Yes."

He unwrapped his stethoscope from around his neck and placed it on Tricia's chest. He listened for several moments then stepped back. "You had a bad reaction to the dosage of medication. I wish you had stayed in the hospital so that we could have monitored your reaction. But . . . that's a moot point now." He took a breath and looked down at her. "Why didn't you come for your appointment today?" he asked softly.

"I . . . felt fine."

"Not a good reason. I want to keep you here overnight."

"Again?" she wailed.

"Yes, again. I want to see for myself how you respond to the new medication."

"Fine."

"I'll see you up on the ward." He turned to leave.

"Uh, doctor, can I talk with you for a minute?" Lena asked sweetly.

Michael glanced at her, then at Tricia.

"She's my sister," Tricia murmured. "It's okay."

Michael nodded. "I'll see you shortly." He extended his hand toward the door to allow Lena to leave the room first.

Tricia watched them walk out and knew without a doubt that any dream she may have had about her and the good doctor was a thing of the past. She never could compete with her sister and she couldn't imagine that things would change now.

Chapter 9

"Thank you so much for taking time to speak with me," Lena said, looking Michael over. "I'm so worried about my sister. She's always such a superwoman it's scary to see her like this." She sniffed.

"Your sister will be fine, if she follows my instructions and takes her medication."

Lena folded her arms. "So exactly what kind of doctor are you?"

"A cardiologist."

"A heart doctor? Something is wrong with Tricia's heart?"

He smoothly sidestepped her question. "Is your sister under a lot of stress at home or at work?"

She thought about how upset Tricia had been with her about moving back into their mother's house, her dismissing the housekeeper, all the money she owed her and who knew what else. "Nothing out of the ordinary," she said.

"Hmmm, well she's definitely going to have to make some life changes." His pager went off. He checked

the number then looked at Lena. "I've got to go. I'll
see your sister when she gets upstairs. And if you have
any influence on her at all, tell her she really needs
to listen to me this time."

"I will. And thank you."

Michael nodded and hurried down the corridor.

Lena watched him until he got on the elevator. Dr.
Michael Evans. Handsome, successful . . . everything
a girl could want.

After checking on an emergency admittance, Michael headed to his hospital office before going up to
see Tricia.

When he'd gotten the call that she'd been readmit-
ted, at first he was terrified that something tragic had
happened, something that he had not foreseen. He
nearly shouted with relief when he realized that her
latest dizzy spell was brought on only by a bad reaction to the medication. An adjustment in her dosage
would fix that.

He took a seat for a moment. This time he would
have to convince her to follow his instructions to the
letter. Although her condition wasn't critical, there
were no guarantees that she wouldn't take a turn, especially if she was hell-bent on not keeping appointments and signing herself out of the hospital before it
was advisable.

But all that aside, he had her back at least for the
time being. He knew it was ethically wrong for him
to approach her in any way other than as her doctor.
But he was willing to make do with the time he had
with her. And maybe, just maybe, after it was all said

and done, he could take it a step further—if she was even interested.

He signed off on several charts then headed back out to the elevator. Hopefully, Tricia's sister could convince her to do the right thing. She seemed genuinely concerned. Funny, they looked nothing alike. Lena resembled a runway model, the kind you had to keep your eye on 24/7, while Tricia was the kind of big beautiful woman you wanted to come home to and stay there.

The elevator doors opened. He stepped inside, and reminded himself once again that Tricia was his patient and nothing more.

Tricia stared up at the ceiling, not wanting to believe that she was right back in the hospital again. She'd hardly ever been sick in her life and now this. She felt so weak and vulnerable, feelings that were foreign to her. A tear slid down her cheek. She felt a hand on her arm. She turned.

"What's wrong, Sis?" Lena asked, sounding genuinely concerned.

Tricia sniffed hard and shook her head. "Nothing," she muttered.

"That doctor of yours seems really nice."

Tricia watched her sister's eyes sparkle for an instant and her stomach knotted. "As long as he's a good doctor, that's all I'm interested in," she said, trying to sound uninterested.

"Humph, if he was my doctor . . . well—"

"We're ready to take you to your room," the nurse said, interrupting Lena.

Tricia took a deep breath and looked at her sister. "There's no need for you to stay. Thanks for everything, but you should go." She looked away.

Lena pressed her lips together and straightened her shoulders. "Some things never change," she said with a heavy breath. "If that's what you want, Tricia, fine. When am I going to get it into my thick head that superwoman doesn't need anyone." She spun away and walked out.

Tricia wanted to call her back, tell her that she was sorry. But the truth was, she and Lena had been at odds for so long she wouldn't begin to know how to apologize to her. Besides, Lena was always so wrapped up in Lena that she probably didn't care one way or the other. Her brief moment of revelation, Tricia was sure, was an aberration, and certainly not because Lena was changing her stripes—maybe a momentary bout of conscience but nothing more.

There was an instant when Tricia almost let down her guard—when Lena opened herself up in the kitchen. But it quickly passed and her guard was way up once she saw Lena respond to Dr. Evans. She wondered how long it would take Lena to weave her spell on the doctor.

She folded her arms across her stomach and closed her eyes as the nurse wheeled her to her room.

"I see they've gotten you all settled," Michael said, walking into Tricia's hospital room.

"As settled as I'm going to get, I suppose," she replied, inching the sheet higher.

Michael stepped closer and Tricia drew in a tight breath and tried to swallow over the dryness in her throat.

"I've changed the dosage on your medication," he began. "Apparently it was too strong for you and that's why you had the reaction." His eyes ran over her near-perfect face. "I'm sorry."

Instinctively, Tricia reached out and touched his hand and the shock of the sensation registered in both their eyes. For a hot instant Michael's nostrils flared as he drew in a sharp breath. Tricia blinked rapidly as if her vision had suddenly become cloudy, but she couldn't seem to move her hand and neither did he.

"As long as it was nothing more serious than that," she said in a faraway voice.

"It was one of the reasons why I wanted to keep you here . . . so that I could take care of . . . monitor your reactions," he said, inwardly flinching at the flub.

Tricia's chest rose and fell a little too quickly for her tastes, but she couldn't help it. He had the most extraordinary eyes.

Michael cleared his throat. "Um, I should let you get some rest. I want to review the rest of your test results."

"When do you think I can go home?"

"I'm sure we'll have you out of here in a day or so. But this time"—he wagged his finger—"you need to stay put until I say you can go."

The corner of her mouth curved up into a half smile. "If there's one thing that raises my pressure it's a man who tries to tell me what to do."

"Is that right?" he countered. "Well, in this case, I think you need to listen to *this* man. Have a good evening."

Tricia didn't realize she was holding her breath until he was out the door and out of sight. Her breath came out in a gush and she pressed her hand to her chest.

"Lawdhavemercy. Was that man just flirting with me?" She giggled. If only it were true.

"I gotta tell you, Trish, I don't like hospitals," Phyllis said the following afternoon as she sat next to Tricia's bed. "You have got to take care of yourself or we might mess up a really good friendship."

Tricia laughed. "Phyllis you don't have good sense."

Phyllis tried not to laugh. "I'm serious, girl." She pulled her chair closer to the bed. "Did you see him?" she asked in a hushed voice.

"See who?" Tricia asked, playing dumb.

Phyllis popped her on the arm. "You know who. Dr. Love."

"That's out of the question."

"Why? You got yourself back in here, so you better make the most of it."

"Any remote chance that there could ever be anything between me and the doctor went out the door the moment Lena walked in," she said, even as she remembered her easy banter with the doctor and the shared hot looks from the previous day. But it was best that she didn't dwell on the impossible. She needed to be realistic, no matter how he'd looked at her or the things he'd said.

Phyllis snapped her head in Tricia's direction.

"Look, you know I never push my opinions on you or try to talk you into doing something that will hurt you. But I'm not going to sit back and watch you turn him over to your sister on a silver platter like you've been doing all your life."

"Phyllis, Phyllis, I appreciate your zeal but let's face it. It is never going to happen. So just leave it alone. Okay?"

Phyllis rolled her eyes. "I think you're making a mistake."

"I don't. Now let's drop it."

Lena stood outside her sister's hospital room. Her intentions had been to return today, after Tricia had gotten some rest, and apologize to her—that was until she caught snatches of the conversation between Phyllis and Tricia. So big sis had a thing for the doctor and didn't think she stood a chance. A slow smile slid across Lena's lush mouth. She turned away and headed back down the corridor.

"Good afternoon, Ms. Spencer."

Lena looked up into the eyes of Dr. Evans.

"Good afternoon." Lena flashed him her hundred-watt smile. "How is my sister doing today?"

"Didn't you go in and see her?" he asked, noting that she was coming from the direction of her sister's hospital room.

The light seemed to dim around her. She lowered her gaze for a moment. "My sister and I . . . well . . . we aren't really on the best of terms. I . . ." She shook her head. "Never mind." She hugged her purse to her chest. "I should go." She looked up into his eyes.

"Tell her I stopped by," she said, her voice suddenly as fragile as spun glass. She hurried off down the hallway, leaving Michael very curious about the relationship between the two very different sisters.

Chapter 10

"How's my patient today?" Michael asked, stepping into Tricia's room.

Phyllis gave Tricia a stealthy wink. "I'd better get going. You need me to bring you anything?"

"No, I'm fine. Thanks."

Phyllis leaned down and kissed her cheek then turned to the doctor. "How much longer?" she asked.

"The test results look pretty good. I'm planning on discharging her in the morning. I want one more night to see how she responds to the medication."

Phyllis turned to Tricia and beamed. "Isn't that wonderful? I'll bring your things in the morning."

Tricia smiled. "Thanks."

"I'll see you in the morning." She walked out.

Michael stepped up to the bedside. "As I mentioned, I've gone over your tests. Your heart is strong, but your pressure is high. You will definitely need a diet and exercise plan to maintain your pressure."

Tricia nodded. "Do you see a lot of cases like mine?"

He pulled up a seat, thankful for a few minutes to spend with her. "More often than I would like, unfortunately. Stress, bad eating habits, lack of proper rest and exercise are major contributors to what can lead to potentially dangerous consequences." His voice lowered. "I wouldn't want to see that happen to you. You're young, beautiful and have a full life ahead of you."

Did he just call me beautiful? She felt warm all over.

"So what are you suggesting?"

"That you make time out of your busy schedule to see me . . . at my office," he added quickly. "That you follow my instructions and take your medication."

"I will. I promise." A slow smile spread across her mouth and lit up her eyes.

"Good." He sat there for a moment, taking her in and wondering what she was like outside of a hospital room. "Um, you mentioned that you had your own business . . . advertising?"

"Yes." She beamed with pride. "ImageNouveau Advertising. It really keeps me busy. We have to work twice as hard being a minority-owned company."

"I can imagine. What type of advertising do you do?"

"Hmm, wow, everything from small business advertising to corporate clients. We've done some television ads as well. The company is growing by leaps and bounds." She went on to tell him about some of the clients she had, the current projects she was working on. Michael seemed totally interested in her every word, Tricia thought, as she rambled on about her passion—her work. She laughed lightly. "I was in the middle of a staff meeting for a new client when I . . . passed out."

Michael nodded. "It was certainly a warning, one that you can't ignore."

"I won't."

"Your job sounds really exciting. You get to meet all kinds of people and find a way to make their dreams come true. That can't be easy."

"It's not easy, but it's the challenge that I love. What about you? Why medicine?"

"I guess you could say I was a nerd in school." He chuckled and lowered his gaze for a moment. "I was always 'cooking' something up in my mother's kitchen, taking things apart. I had this need almost to see what was going on inside of things. When my dad died of a heart attack in my second year of med school, I knew that I was going to specialize in cardiac medicine."

"You're living your dream, too, and making others' dreams come true—life and longevity. That's a powerful thing," she said, a hint of awe in her voice.

He smiled a shy smile. "We both are. I guess we have that in common."

"Yeah, I guess we do." Tricia nodded and before she knew what she was doing the words spilled out of her mouth. "Are you married?"

Shock widened his brown eyes for an instant. "Uh . . . no. I was." He took a breath. "My wife died of heart failure in our second year of marriage."

"Oh . . . I'm so sorry. I—"

He shook his head. "No, it's okay. It's been almost eight years." He smiled sadly. "You find a way to get past it. It's one of the reasons I started a private practice, so that I could really give my patients the personal care that they need and deserve."

"I'm sorry. I . . . that was none of my business." She wished the floor would open up and swallow her.

"Not a problem. Don't worry about it. You're not," he said, "married I mean."

Her chest tightened. "No."

They stared at each other in an awkward moment of silence.

He tugged in a breath and stood. "I could talk all day—apparently." They both laughed. "But I have other patients to see before taking off for the rest of the day. But I'll be in to see you in the morning. And if everything still looks good I'll sign you out."

Michael looked at her for a long moment and then his pager went off, breaking the spell. "I'd better go."

All she could do was nod her head, not trusting what fool thing would come out of her mouth next.

When he was out of sight she slapped her forehead with her palm. "Idiot! He must really think you're desperate to ask a dumb question like that," she muttered. She turned on her side. How was she ever going to look him in the eye again? But then she thought about the soft expression on his face when he asked if she was married. Was he asking to be nice? Was it just reflex? He had to know from reading her file that she wasn't married.

Oh, why was she even entertaining the idea? He was a handsome, successful doctor who probably had women making fools of themselves over him all the time. And she'd just added her name to the list. She sighed heavily. Plus she was certain that knowing her sister the way she did, it would be only a matter of time before Lena got her grips on him anyway.

But then she thought about what Phyllis said about handing him over on a silver platter. Why did she believe she was so unworthy, never able to compete with her sister? She was the one who was successful, dressed well, not bad to look at, had a giving spirit, good friends, and was financially secure. She'd make an excellent catch, she mused.

She sat up in bed as an idea began to form in her fertile mind. For once in her life she wasn't going to turn a man over to her sister. She liked Dr. Evans and wanted to have the opportunity to know him as a woman and not as his patient. And she knew just how she was going to do it.

Chapter 11

When Tricia walked into her office less than a week after her discharge, she was nearly brought to tears by her staff. They'd prepared a welcome back banner and an array of flowers fit for a queen, not to mention the spread of food that was laid out in the conference room.

"Oh my goodness!" she cried as she walked in to shouts of "welcome back," hugs and kisses. "You guys are too much," she said, her voice thick with emotion.

"We missed you," Reginald said, slipping his arm around her waist. "We haven't gotten a thing done since you've been gone," he teased.

Tricia cut him a look. "I know better than that with you in charge."

The group laughed in agreement.

"So how are you feeling?" Leslie asked.

"Pretty good, all things considered." She took a seat at the table. "But I've been gone long enough. It's time to get back to business. We can eat and work." She reached for a bowl and filled it with fresh fruit.

A groan went up from the staff. Tricia rolled her eyes and waved her hand toward the chairs instructing them all to sit down.

"First bring me up-to-date and then I'm going to tell you about a very special advertising campaign we're going to be working on." She smiled brightly at each one in turn.

Reginald took the floor first, followed by Christopher and Jean and then Lloyd and Renee, then Leslie and Jessica. By all accounts the current projects were coming along fine. They were ahead of schedule and on budget.

"We need to schedule a meeting with Mr. Hayes," Reginald said.

Tricia looked up from her laptop where she was taking notes. "Everything okay?"

"He needs a little more hand-holding than most. The twice weekly phone calls and weekly reports don't seem to be sufficient," he said, his tone dripping with sarcasm.

Tricia laughed. "I'll call him when we're done here and make an appointment for one day next week. You and Leslie can handle him from there."

Leslie twisted her lips. "He's such a whiner," she complained.

"But the customer is always right," Tricia said, "especially when they help to pay the bills. You know you're doing a dynamite job with his ad campaign for his new line of haberdashery. He's just nervous that's all. Before you know it this will all be over." She looked at Lloyd. "When do you think all the pieces will be finished?"

Lloyd flipped open his notes and slid his glasses up his long nose. "We're scheduled to start shooting the print ads in two weeks. If all goes well, the taping for the commercials will begin the following week. They are doing the final casting now."

"Good." She turned to Leslie. "Make an appointment to pay a visit to the studio and take the casting director to lunch tomorrow. Get a feel for what is going on. This way when you have your meeting you'll be able to answer every single one of his innumerable questions." The corner of her mouth curved into a grin. "Now." She let out a long breath. "On to our next project." She waited for everyone to settle down. "As you may have guessed, this hospital bout really threw me for a loop and gave me some time to do some serious thinking about my life, this business . . . a lot of things. And what I've decided to do . . ."

Michael stretched his long legs out on the couch and aimed the remote at the television. It was his one day off and he intended to make the best of it by doing as little as humanly possible. He had a bowl of chips, a bucket of ice with three beers on chill and a remote control. What more could a man want?

He tucked a hand behind his head and leaned back. It would be great to have someone to spend the afternoon with, he thought, as he surfed through the stations. It had been so long since he'd had someone in his life and anything other than his job and his patients, he probably wouldn't know how to act. Actually it would be great to have Tricia Spencer around.

Yesterday when they sat and talked he'd gotten an

opportunity to see how intelligent and funny she could really be. She was not only a good talker she was a wonderful listener as well. She enjoyed music, old movies and seemed genuinely interested in what interested him. How was he ever going to get the chance to spend time with her outside of his office without breaking the code of doctor-patient relations?

He sat up. The hell with it, he thought. He was tired of being the good guy, following the rules. For once he was going to do something for Michael. He got up and darted upstairs to the bedroom. Quickly he went through the notes that he always carried around with him and found Tricia's home number. Not giving himself enough time to talk himself out of it, he dialed. He spirits slowly sank when her answering machine picked up. He started to leave a message but changed his mind. He returned the receiver to the base. It was probably just as well, he decided. He had no real reason to believe that Tricia had the slightest personal interest in him.

He pushed himself up from the bed and started to walk away then stopped. Why the hell was he giving up so easily? With the little that he knew about Tricia, she was probably back at work. He looked at his notes, found her office number and quickly dialed.

"ImageNouveau Advertising. How may I help you?"

"Good morning, this is Dr. Evans. I was wondering if I could speak with Ms. Spencer."

"One moment, please."

Tricia was at her desk, excited about the staff's enthusiasm about her latest endeavor and it gave her the perfect opportunity to work with Dr. Love—Dr. Evans—on a long-term regular basis. A big, bright smile broke out across her mouth in concert with her ringing phone.

"Yes?"

"There's a Dr. Evans on the phone for you. Line one."

Tricia's hand started to shake and a rush of heat darted to her head. "Uh, okay." She tugged in a deep breath and pressed the flashing button. "Hi Dr. Evans, this is Tricia. Is something wrong?"

"No, no, everything is fine. I know this may be out of the ordinary but I was . . . calling to check on you, see how you were doing?"

"So far so good." She waited.

"Good, glad to hear that." He cleared his throat. "Listen I was wondering . . . if you're not busy . . . maybe you might like to have dinner with me."

Tricia squeezed her eyes shut and then quickly opened them. She pinched her thigh until it stung. Nope, it wasn't a dream. "Dinner . . ." She tried to keep from squealing. "That sounds really nice. Sure. Did you have a day in mind?"

"How about this evening if you're not busy. It would have to be a bit early since I'm due back in the hospital at six tomorrow morning."

"Early is fine. I usually finish up here at four." That was a lie. She couldn't remember the last time she'd left the office at four. Well, actually the last time was on a stretcher.

"Can I pick you up at work, or would you rather I pick you up at home?"

"Uh . . . home is fine. Let me give you the address."

"I have it."

"Oh . . . I forgot you have quite a bit of information on me. I have a lot of catching up to do."

"Yes, you do. I'll see you about six."

Slowly Tricia hung up the phone. She couldn't believe what just happened. Dr. Michael Evans asked her out on a date—*her* not Lena. She leaned back in her chair and stared sightlessly across the room. Then reality stepped in and knocked her in the head. She had to call Phyllis!

Chapter 12

"You need to wear the emerald green suit," Phyllis insisted as the two women rifled through Tricia's closet.

"It's too tight in the waist," Tricia said, panic beginning to well inside her. "The red wrap is perfect." She pulled the silk dress out of the closet and held it up in front of her. "You don't think it's too provocative do you? I mean it is cut kind of low in the front. He may think I'm trying to come on to him or something."

"You *are* fool! Put the dress on. And let me work on your hair. You have about forty-five minutes."

"Oh lawd! Maybe I shouldn't go."

"What?"

"Suppose I make a fool of myself."

"You will if he shows up at the door and you're still running around in your slip. Now let's go."

"Okay, okay," Tricia agreed as she fanned herself with her hand.

"I want to see how you look and be gone before he gets here."

Tricia spun toward her friend. "Why?"

Phyllis put her hand on her hip and cocked her head to the side. "He doesn't need to think that you have your girl checking him out on the first date."

Tricia pushed out a breath. "Fine." She stomped off toward the bathroom. "Abandon me." She shut the door.

A few minutes later Tricia stepped out fully dressed with an expression of expectation on her face. "Well . . . does it work?"

Phyllis got up from her perch on the side of the bed and walked in a slow circle around Tricia. Suddenly she stopped, threw her hands up in the air then began to clap.

"You are going to knock him dead in the dress. It is working, girl."

Tricia beamed with delight. "Are you sure?"

"Do I ever lie to you? Now come on and let me work on your hair."

While Phyllis used the flat iron on Tricia's shoulder-length hair, Tricia told Phyllis all about the bedside conversation that she and Michael had before she was discharged.

"Although I heard the story before," Phyllis said, turning under the ends of Tricia's hair, "I love to see your eyes sparkle and hear that funny, girly thing that happens to your voice."

Tricia covered her mouth, mildly embarrassed. "I guess I have told you the story more than once."

"Listen, it's fine. It's good to see you excited about something beyond work. It's good to see that you're not going to let go of a perfectly good opportunity because you've convinced yourself that only Lena is worthy. Michael Evans would be damned lucky to have you, not the other way around."

Tricia giggled. "I think you may be a bit prejudiced."

"And I'm not ashamed to admit it!" She came around to the front of Tricia seated on a stool and took a look at her handiwork. With a critical eye she seemed to examine every hair, every dip. Finally she stood back, and a haughty look of satisfaction danced across her aquiline face. "I done good!"

Tricia peered in the mirror. She turned her head from side to side. "If you ever want to give up your day job, you would never be broke."

"Thanks," Phyllis grumbled good-naturedly. She checked her watch. "Well, twenty minutes to count down. I'm out of here."

Tricia grabbed her hand. "Don't go. Suppose he doesn't show up?"

Phyllis twisted her lips. "Of course he will show up unless you intentionally gave him the wrong address." She picked up her purse and car keys from the dresser. She leaned down and kissed Tricia's cheek. "Just relax, be your wonderful self and have a good time."

Tricia released a breath. "I'll try."

"You will. And call me the minute you get in the house and give me the blow-by-blow."

Tricia giggled. "I will. And thanks, girl."

"Hey, what are sister friends for?" She winked and walked out.

Tricia sat in front of her dressing table mirror, her thoughts running a million miles a minute. What was she going to say? What if he hated her dress? What if he was asking her out only because he felt sorry for her?

"Stop it!" she said aloud. She stood and looked at her reflection. "He asked you out because he wanted to, because he wants to get to know you better." She fortified herself with those thoughts just as the doorbell rang and her convictions flew out of the open window.

Nerves locked her in place. He's here, she thought. Her pulse began to race. She checked her makeup in the mirror, took a cleansing breath and headed for the door.

"Lena! What are you doing here?"

Chapter 13

"I hope that greeting means you're glad to see me," Lena said, stepping around her sister to come inside.

Tricia turned. "You still didn't answer my question. What are you doing here?"

Lena tossed her purse on the couch and plopped down beside it. "I came to see how you were doing." She took a good look at her sister and frowned. "Why are you all dressed up?"

Tricia shut the door and walked into the front room where her sister sat. "I'm going out."

"Do you think that's wise? You've barely been out of the hospital a week."

"I'm fine. I went back to work today."

"Tricia, did the doctor say it was okay?"

She planted her hand on her hip. "Yes. As a matter of fact—"

The ringing doorbell cut her off. A look of panic crossed Tricia's face. The last person she wanted Michael to see was her sister—especially looking the way she did—gorgeous as usual.

"Want me to get that?" Lena asked as she started to get up.

"No! I mean . . . no, I'll get it." She spun away and went to the door. She plastered her best smile on her face and pulled the door open.

"Hi," Michael said in a voice so smooth and sweet the single word was almost edible.

"Hi." Her throat was suddenly as dry, almost raspy. "Uh, I'm ready. Let me just get my purse."

Michael's dark eyes cinched for a moment. "Are you all right? You seem—"

"Dr. Evans!"

They both looked in the direction of Lena's smoky voice. She walked toward them and the image of a preying panther leaped into Tricia's mind.

"Well, good to see you again. Came to check on your sister?"

"Yes. I wanted to be sure that she was taking care of herself, but I see that she has that covered." She gave him a long, smoldering look.

Tricia stepped aside and walked into the kitchen. Things couldn't have worked out worse, if all the planets and the stars were misaligned simultaneously. She sat down at the counter and felt like crying.

She wasn't sure how long she'd been sitting there until she saw Lena pull up a stool next to her.

"You want to tell me why you're sitting in here when that fine specimen of a man is sitting in your living room waiting to take you out?"

Tricia looked at her sister for a long moment. "What?"

"He's waiting for you, Sis."

"But—"

"I know, you figured Lena was going to be her usual trifling self and move in on your date. Right?"

"Well . . ."

"Look, I know I've been a real pain in the ass all these years. I know I've done everything I could to get through life the easy way including using you. But when I saw you get sick in here and sat with you in that ambulance, I realized just how much you really mean to me. When I came over here to pay you back that money"—she paused a moment—"it was for real. I wanted to clean the slate between us, show you that I wasn't as worthless as you thought and leave it at that—until you got sick. I've been so selfish all these years. I made it hard for you because you were always better at everything. All I had was my looks. You have looks, personality, smarts. I could never compete with that so I tried to make your life miserable. But the thought of losing you . . ." Her eyes filled. "I'm so sorry." She reached for Tricia's hand.

"Lena." Slowly she shook her head as she looked into her sister's hazel eyes. "I've been so busy being pissed off at you all these years, I never even thought about how you were feeling."

Lena sniffed. "I would have felt the same way if I were you." She gave her sister a tight smile. "Now come on, that man is waiting on you."

"Yeah, he is." Tricia pushed up from the stool. "We'll talk soon. Okay?"

"Sure." She followed her sister out of the kitchen.

"Ready?" Tricia asked as if her disappearance for the past ten minutes or more was nothing unusual.

"Absolutely."

"Well, you two have a nice time," Lena said.

"You're more than welcome to join us," Michael offered.

Lena's hand flew to her chest. "Really? That's so sweet of you." She looked at her sister. "I'll take a rain check. Maybe some other time."

Tricia's heart settled back to its natural rhythm.

Michael opened the front door and the sisters walked out. Tricia stopped and turned to lock the door and found herself breast to chest with Michael. She gazed up into his eyes and silently prayed that she didn't look as thrilled as she felt at that moment.

He smiled slyly. "We have to stop meeting like this," he said in a husky whisper.

Tricia swallowed hard. No we don't, she thought, as she stuck her key in the door and locked it behind them. "That's up for discussion," she countered in the same hushed whisper.

Lena watched the exchange from the bottom of the steps. Humph, her sister with a doctor—not on her watch. "Good night, folks," she sing-songed as she sashayed to her car. It was only a matter of time before she slipped him away from Tricia just as she'd done with all the other men who even remotely became interested in her.

"There's this great place in the Village," Michael said as he helped Tricia into the car. "The Pink Teacup."

She smiled. "Yes, I've heard of it, but I've never been. I heard the food is incredible."

87

"Yes, it is."

"Do you go often?" she asked, as she fastened her seat belt.

Michael adjusted the mirror and put his belt on. "My wife and I used to go there often."

"Oh." She stared straight ahead.

He turned to her. "I hope you don't mind."

"Uh, no, not at all."

He turned on the CD player and pulled off.

For several moments the music was the only sound in the car.

"So how was the first day back at work?" Michael finally asked.

"Busy." She chuckled lightly. "I walked in on a welcome home party from my staff. That was really nice."

"I'm sure they missed you, but I hope you didn't try to overdo it."

"No, not really. But it was good to be back in action again. I missed my work."

"Yes, I understand how you must feel. It would probably drive me crazy if I couldn't work—even as exhausting as it can be sometimes."

"Exactly!" she said, excitement lifting her voice. "But you get a different kind of energy when you see everything coming together or get a new concept to actually work the way you envision it."

"That's the way I feel when I see a patient gain a full recovery, even the little steps along the way, and you know you are a part of the success."

Tricia nodded in agreement. "That's not what happened with your wife?" she asked.

Michael gripped the wheel, and slowly shook his

head. "Nothing I tried, none of the specialists we took her to, could help her." He paused. "I felt as if I'd failed her."

"But I'm sure you did all you could."

"Yeah, that's what all my friends said. But it's hard watching someone you care about drift away from you and there's nothing you can do to stop it."

She reached out and touched his hand. "I didn't mean to bring up something painful. I guess my nosiness got the best of me."

"You remind me of her," he said quietly.

"What?"

"You remind me of her. Your face, sometimes the way you smile. When I first saw you I was stunned for a moment. I thought the Fates were playing a trick on me." He laughed with self-deprecation.

She blew air through her nose. "Is that why you've taken such an interest in me?" she asked, her voice hitching a notch.

"I don't want you to think that this is some macabre fantasy of mine. The truth is . . . well the truth is when I first saw you I wanted to run in the opposite direction."

"Why?"

"Because just looking at you brought back all kinds of memories. Some good, some not so good."

She lowered her head. "Oh, I see."

"No. I don't think you do. Not really. After talking with you, spending some time with you—it was Tricia Spencer that I was interested in—not a memory. What held me back was the fact that you were and still are my patient."

"So then why are you taking me to dinner?"

"To get to know you outside of a hospital room for one thing."

"And . . . you said one thing. That sounds like there's more."

"There's something I need to talk to you about."

"What?"

"Let's discuss it over dinner."

Chapter 14

Lena kept a safe distance behind Michael's blue BMW as they wound their way around Manhattan traffic. She wasn't even sure why she was following them or why she even cared what her sister did or who she did it with. But she did care. For as long as she could remember she'd been jealous of her younger sister. Everyone always said how responsible and smart Tricia was. All they ever said about her was that she was pretty. Tricia was the one that would amount to something. She was the one who had their mother's love.

Sometimes she got so scared when she looked in the mirror she would start to shake. What was she going to do when her body was no longer firm in all the right places and her perfect features began to sag and Clairol no longer did the trick? All she had was her looks. She knew that. Men told her that all the time. Tricia had everything else. But . . . if she could get the doctor, show him that she was a much better catch than her overweight sister, then all her worries would be over. She'd make him love her, take care of her. Tricia would get over it. She always did. Besides, she had a business, friends. She'd be fine.

Lena slowed to a stop when she saw Michael get out of the car then help Tricia. A tight line formed between her brows. She looked so happy. A twinge of guilt momentarily knotted her stomach. But only for a moment. She waited until they were inside the restaurant then pulled up behind Michael's car. She pulled out a pen and paper from the glove compartment and jotted down his license plate number. Never know when she was going to need it.

"This place is really nice," Tricia said as she was assisted into her seat by Michael. She smiled as she looked around at the quaint but cool setting. She folded her hands on top of the table and looked at him once he was settled. "Let's make a deal."

He grinned. "Already?"

"Yeah, already." She tugged in a breath. "I'm not sure where things are going with us, or if they are going anywhere at all. But if they do, then we need to build our own memories." She glanced around then looked him in the eye. "You know what I mean?" she asked gently.

His eyes grew soft with images that Tricia couldn't see. His mouth slowly curved upward on one side. By degrees he focused on her. "You're right." He paused. "The truth is, since my wife died I think I've been on an official date twice." He chuckled and shook his head. "Doesn't say much for my social life. So I guess there was a part of me that wanted to recreate something and that's not fair to you."

"It's okay. All of us carry baggage around; some is just heavier than others."

They laughed.

"Tell you what, let's skip this place and start over. I mean really start over."

Tricia grinned. "Are you serious?"

He stood. "Yes. I think I would like to start creating some new memories, beginning tonight." He extended his hand and she placed hers in it and stood.

"I like that idea a lot," she said softly.

He placed his hand at the small of her back and they walked out.

"You said you liked jazz," Michael said as they headed back to his car.

"Yeah, I do. Why? What do you have in mind?"

"There's always something going on at the Blue Note or even Smoke. Food is edible, but the music makes up for it."

"Sounds good to me."

"Great."

When they arrived at the Blue Note, they were thrilled to see that Kirk Whalum was on the bill and that there were seats available for the next set.

"Oh my goodness. He's one of my favorites," Tricia squealed in delight.

Michael grinned. "Couldn't have worked out better if we'd planned it." This time he put his arm around her waist as he ushered her inside.

She glanced up into his eyes when his arm pulled her in close contact with the hard lines of his body. Damn that feels good, she thought, as she stepped into the dim confines of the club. If they were going to begin creating their own memories, they were off to a great start. She didn't even want to imagine how the evening would ultimately end, but she hoped it had something to do with connecting with those lush lips of his.

It took a big chunk of self-control not to turn her around in his arms and kiss her right there in the lobby of the club. She felt so good beneath his fingertips. Her gentle scent stirred his senses, her laughter was like music and her voluptuous body set his into overdrive. He was definitely going to have to keep his cool and take it slow. He needed to be sure, not only for himself but for Tricia, that what he was starting to think and feel was not some leftover fantasies about his wife. He wanted to be sure before he took it too far.

Tricia didn't pay much attention to what she was eating; it could have been tofu for all she knew. She was having such a good time it didn't matter. Michael was not only too good to look at, he was funny, knew a little bit about a lot of things, hopping from one topic to the next with the ease of a dancer. And he could dance, too! When they got up on the tiny dance floor she was sure her knees were going to buckle and she was going to make a pure fool out of herself. But he held her so close, his arms were so protective around her, that she would have been a fool to fall out of them. They danced to several tunes then returned to the table.

Michael held her chair. "Thank you," he said, bending down and whispering in her ear. A shiver of delight ran up her spine.

"My pleasure."

Kirk Whalum finished up his set to rousing applause.

"Ready?" he asked.

Tricia nodded.

.

"Thanks, I really had a great time. That was such a treat," Tricia said as they headed back to her house in Harlem.

"I had a ball. And I'm glad it was with you," he said, turning briefly to look at her.

Tricia felt her face flush. "Me, too," she admitted.

"I know you mentioned you had an early morning," Tricia said when they'd pulled up in front of her door. "But you're welcome to come up for coffee if you want."

He grinned and her stomach did a little dance. "I was hoping the night wouldn't end just yet."

Hopefully her expression remained in neutral, because she was screaming and hollering inside. She almost did a dance up the stairs.

"Make yourself comfortable," Tricia offered, once they were inside. She flipped on the light in the living room. "Regular or decaf?"

"Actually at this hour I probably need to stay away from coffee. Some juice would be fine if you have it."

"Coming right up."

*   *   *

When Tricia returned, Michael had turned on the stereo and the "KISSing After Dark" DJ Lenny Green was on the radio wooing his listeners with his rich, deeply sexy smooth voice.

"I always wonder how hard he must have to work to sound like that," Tricia quipped as she handed Michael a glass of juice.

Michael chuckled. "Thanks." He took a sip and patted the space next to him on the couch.

Tricia hesitated for a split second and sat down.

He cleared his throat. "Listen, before we went out to dinner, I told you there was something I wanted to talk to you about."

She nodded. "Yes."

"We were having such a good time, I'd almost forgotten. But I want to get this out of the way." He reached for his jacket on the back of the couch and pulled out a business card from the pocket and handed it to her.

Tricia took the card, looked at it and frowned. "I . . . don't understand. This is a card for a cardiologist."

"I know. He's a good friend of mine and an excellent doctor."

"But, why? You're my doctor."

He inched closer. "The truth is I can't continue to treat you, Tricia, not the way I'm beginning to feel about you. I'd lose my objectivity. Besides, it goes against my medical ethics to date my patients."

"Michael . . ."

"When I see you, from now on I want to see you

only as a woman. When and if you allow me to undress you, I don't want it to be a hospital gown."

Where was a fan? It was getting mighty hot!

"Are you sure?"

"When can I see you again?" Michael asked without beating around the bush.

Tricia's eyes widened. "Uh . . . when do you want to?"

"How about this weekend?"

"The weekend sounds fine."

"Great." He stood. "Listen, I'd better get going. You need your rest and so do I." He picked up his jacket and started for the door.

When he reached the door he stopped and turned. "Make sure you give the doctor a call. I'll let him know to expect you." His eyes ran over her face for a moment.

Tricia felt the pulse in her throat beat like a tom-tom as she watched in rapt fascination as his head lowered.

The first sensation of his lips on hers was like an electric charge and she was sure she moaned. He slid his arms around her waist and tenderly pulled her closer to him as he pressed her lips with his just a bit more and then more until her lips parted to accept the tentative exploration of his tongue. This time it was Michael who moaned and Tricia's spirit soared to seventh heaven.

When he finally eased away and looked at her it was with utter fascination in his eyes. He cupped her chin in his palm and tipped her face slightly upward. "I sure like how these new memories are being made," he murmured. He kissed the top of her head and stepped back. "Can I call you at work tomorrow?"

"I thought you would never ask."

Michael chuckled. "Have a good night." He turned and trotted down the steps.

Tricia watched from the door and waved as he drove away. Somehow, maybe she floated, she wasn't sure, but she found her way to bed and had the most incredible dreams of her and Michael all night long.

The following morning, Tricia was up with the sun and had an extra little bounce in her step. She checked the meal sheet she'd posted on her fridge and fixed a bowl of oatmeal, fruit and herbal tea. She forced it all down with a smile and took her medication with a full glass of water just as the instructions indicated.

After breakfast and a shower she called Michael's colleague and made an appointment for the following week, then she called and checked on her mother and was surprised to hear that Lena had already left the house. Maybe she was job hunting, but Tricia didn't say that to her mother.

"Is the housekeeper there, yet?"

"Yes, she's been here since seven. When are you going to stop by and see me so I can be sure you're okay? Lena told me what happened at your apartment. Thank goodness she was there. You know I would have come to see you if I could."

"I know, Mama. Don't worry yourself. I'm going to be fine."

"You make sure you take care of yourself."

"I will. Talk to you soon, Mama."

Feeling assured that most things were right with the world, Tricia finished dressing and headed for work. If she wanted to be ready to make this presentation to Michael, she wanted everything to be perfect. She knew it would take a few weeks to pull together, but with the help of the staff she knew she could do it. And in the meantime she had the weekend to look forward to.

"Oh no!" She slapped her forehead with her palm. She'd forgotten to call Phyllis and give her all the juicy details. She'd call when she got to the office. Maybe they could get together for lunch or dinner. There was so much she wanted to share with her friend. She had to pinch herself to make sure this all wasn't a dream.

For the first time in longer than she could recall, she was truly happy, bubbly inside and it had nothing to do with work.

Who would have thought that passing out on the floor of the conference room would have such great results.

The weeks flew by and each day was highlighted by a phone call from Michael. During the day, they could talk for only a few minutes at a time. But at night, when she lay in bed with the lights low, under the comfort of her cool sheets, she could listen to his voice whisper in her ears for hours. On his day off they always went out to a movie, jazz or comedy club and one night they drove out to the water at Flushing Meadows Park and talked until the sun came up.

Tricia thought it was all so magical as they pulled up in front of her house. She was so happy and feeling good inside and out. The diet and exercise plan that the doctor had her on gave her more energy and she looked better in her clothes, so much so that she'd splurged on two new suits and some sexy underwear—one never knows, she'd thought, when she stood in line in Victoria's Secret. Their cuddling sessions and passionate kisses were becoming more intense each time they were together. Michael was taking his time and it was driving her wild.

"Come on in, I'll fix us a smoothie. I've gotten pretty good at those." She giggled.

"It doesn't take much to tempt me you know." He closed the door behind them and followed her inside.

But before she could get halfway across the room, he grabbed her arm and turned her around.

"I don't know about you, but I like what's been going on between us," he said, his voice thick and intense.

"So do I." *Did she sound as breathless as she felt?*

"It's taken all of my good home training not to make love to you every time I see you." He stepped closer and put his arms around her waist. "But I wanted to be sure that you wanted me as much as I want you." He waited a beat. "Do you?"

"Yes," she whispered, the single word sounding like a hiss. She swallowed hard.

He took her hand. "Show me the way."

Chapter 15

Tricia led Michael to her bedroom and prayed that he didn't hear her knees knocking. She pushed open the door with her free hand and stepped inside.

In all the times he'd been to her house, he'd never set foot in her bedroom. For him it was a matter of protocol and principle. When he came in here he wanted it to be right and he truly felt in his heart that it was.

Tricia turned and casually turned up her palms. "Well . . . this is it," she said with a nervous smile, suddenly thinking that maybe this wasn't such a good idea.

"Lovely, just like you. Warm, soft and delicate." He tugged in breath, suddenly feeling like an awkward teen, but when he looked and saw the same uncertainty in her eyes he stepped toward her. "Only if you want to. Really want to," he said, taking her face in his hands.

She nodded, afraid to speak.

A slow smile moved across Michael's mouth as he

lowered his lips to meet hers. There was no hesitation, no testing or teasing this time. He knew what he wanted and wanted it badly.

He felt her shudder against him when he pressed his throbbing erection between her thighs, so he pressed a bit harder. He wanted her to know how much he desired her. He eased her jacket from her and was delighted to find warm brown, pulsing flesh and the sexiest bra he'd seen in a long time. He moaned deep in his throat as he dipped his head to run his tongue along the full rise of her cleavage.

"Ohh," Tricia cried out.

He slipped a strap from one shoulder and then the other. Then reached behind her for the zipper of her skirt.

Suddenly panic set in. The lights were on, Tricia realized. She didn't want him to see her naked in the light.

"Wait!" she said, startling them both.

"What—what's wrong?"

"I . . . uh, need to turn out the light. It's too bright in here." She pulled out of his embrace and headed for the wall switch.

Michael stopped her with his hand over hers. He shook his head. "No. I want to see you, every glorious, gorgeous inch of you."

"But . . ."

"No buts . . ."

He kissed her long and hard and suddenly she'd totally forgotten what she'd been so panicked about moments ago. The only things that mattered were Michael's kisses, the way he whispered her name like a man starved for a good, hot meal and the way his hands ran across and scorched her body.

When he eased her back to the bed and lowered her down she knew that the moment she'd dreamed of was a breath, a touch, a look away. Was she ready? Was he? And would they respect each other in the morning?

She didn't give a damn! All she wanted at that moment was Michael. She wanted to feel every inch of him and give him all that she had to offer in return.

"You're everything I could want in a woman," Michael said as he teased a taut nipple with his teeth.

Tricia's body involuntarily arched.

His hands stroked her curves. Her heart hammered in her chest. What did he really see when he looked at her, she worried, even as the heat of his touch seemed to scorch her skin with longing.

"You're so beautiful," he whispered, as his tongue trailed along her stomach. "I want to taste you first."

For an instant she stiffened. She'd never done that before or had anyone who'd even suggested it. But the instant she felt his mouth suckle the hard pearl of her sex, she prayed it wouldn't be the last time.

She grabbed the sheets in her fists as he teased and taunted her, stroking her wetness like a cone of ice cream. And just when she thought she couldn't take it anymore, he pushed the envelope to the next level. Her body was no longer her own and her throat felt raw from crying out as wave upon wave of shuddering spasms gripped her.

"I want to feel you now," he murmured as he braced his weight above her. "And I want you to feel me." He leaned over, pulled his wallet out of his pants pocket and took out a condom, then dropped the pants back to the floor.

"Let me do it," she said, looking up at him.

He handed her the packet, which she opened. Inch by tantalizing inch she rolled the condom over his shaft and he never knew this simple act could be so erotic. He nearly came just watching what she was doing and anticipating what was to follow.

She glanced up at him when she was done, still holding him in her hand. "All finished," she whispered.

"Not quite."

He eased her down on the bed and slowly spread her thighs.

"Oh . . . my . . . God," he groaned when he eased himself into her heat.

"Michael," Tricia cried when he pushed into her and she finally experienced what she'd only imagined.

They played with each other, whispered hot words, teased with fingertips and hungry mouths even as their needy bodies bumped and ground against one another, almost desperate in their desire to experience every inch, every crevice, leaving nothing unscathed.

This was more than she imagined. More than she could have hoped for. Michael was . . . there was no word to explain what he was doing to her body, how he made her feel about herself. If this were to end tomorrow, she knew that she had at least experienced true joy.

As Michael moved slow and steady inside her, cra-

dling her body against his, he knew not only ecstasy
but fear. He was scared. Afraid of the overpowering
raw emotion that Tricia brought out in him. No one
had gotten anywhere near his heart since the loss of
his wife and, without even trying, Tricia had stolen it.
It was hers to do with as she wished. There was no
doubt about that. And all he could hope for was that
she would treat it with care.

Then all of a sudden, she did something with her
hips—a little twist kind of move and he nearly lost his
mind. A shock went up his spine so intense that all
of its energy pushed through him in an orgasm that
made him see stars.

The intensity of it shot through Tricia. She could
feel deep within her his release and that set off a chain
reaction in her, and her body gave in to the blinding
pleasure that consumed her like a fire raging through
dry woods. She held him, calling his name over and
over as the shudders flowed through her again and
again until she wept.

"I could get very used to this," Michael whispered
against her damp hair.

"So could I."

"We'll have to really talk about making other ar-
rangements. It's not easy living with a doctor."

Did he say living with? She turned on her side to
face him. "Living with?"

"Does that bother you?"

"Uh . . . I—"

"Don't think for a minute that my plan is to have

us simply live together. I'm an old-fashioned guy at heart. I just want you to understand that I'm serious about us. Very."

"Girl, I'm still tingling," Tricia confessed to Phyllis as she balanced the phone between her shoulder and her ear.

Phyllis giggled. "It's about damned time. That stuff will dry up if you don't use it you know."

Tricia busted out laughing. "Girl, you need to stop." She went on to tell her about the living together part.

"Oooh, my man is serious. You go, girl. I'm so happy for you. You deserve it. You've been taking care of folks and carrying the weight long enough. It's time you got to share it. And he ain't bad to look at either."

Tricia cracked up again. "You got that right. Well, listen girl, let me get back to work. Besides, Michael usually calls about this time."

"You go work your show. I have to tell you girl, this is the best advertising campaign you've ever put together. You are the product and Dr. Love is the very happy client."

"How about that. Talk to you later." She hung up the phone and flipped open her laptop to the presentation she'd been working on to show to Michael. She'd never really thought about it until Phyllis mentioned it, but she guessed she was putting together a campaign—a campaign to win his heart and shed her inhibitions. And so far she was pretty successful.

She scrolled through the computer menu until she found the program and pulled it up. It just needed some final touches and it would be ready. Now this was something that she could truly be proud of.

Michael checked his watch as he hurried down the corridor. He'd had no less than three emergencies this morning, and he still had rounds to complete. He checked his watch. He hadn't called Tricia. Their daily phone calls were what got him through the day. He looked forward to them and now he was in a foul mood because he hadn't heard her voice. He reached for his cell phone and stopped. He couldn't use it inside of the hospital. He quickly glanced around and figured he could steal a few minutes without disaster striking.

He pushed through the hospital doors and stepped outside only to run into Lena as he was dialing Tricia's number.

"Dr. Evans." Lena put on her Colgate smile and jutted her breasts out just a little bit further than necessary.

Michael instinctively lowered the phone. "Lena. Hi. What are you doing here? Is someone sick?"

"No. Nothing like that." She stepped a little closer and the rush of people into the building pushed her full against him. Instinctively he grabbed her to keep them both from tumbling backward. Her lips were suddenly inches from his. "Sorry about that." But she didn't move.

Michael stepped away. "Not a problem. You didn't say why you were here."

"I was hoping you had a few minutes where we could talk."

"I do have rounds but I can spare a minute. Let's move out of the doorway." He led her over to a bank of benches. "Now what can I do for you?"

"I'm going to get right to the point, Dr. Evans. For as long as I can remember I've been jealous of my sister. But I've never been more jealous of her as I am now."

He frowned. "Why are you telling me this?"

"Because you need to know. I don't take losing lightly, especially to Tricia. So if you think you really have a thing for her and she has a thing for you, I suggest that you make it work. If not, I'm coming after you myself and I don't play to lose. Ask Tricia, she'll tell you. Tricia can make you happy. I can make you . . ." She grinned wickedly. "Just treat my sister good."

He stood and shook his head. "That's my intention. I'm in love with your sister."

"Good. 'Cause I love being bad, Dr. Evans. And I know I would have a ball being bad with you. Ciao." She gave him a finger wave and switched down the walkway and out to the street.

For several moments Michael simply stood there, not believing how bold Lena Spencer actually was. But he had to give it to her, she was honest and she was trouble. He chuckled and walked back toward the entrance, then realized he had yet to call Tricia. He raised the phone to dial the number and frowned when it showed that a call was connected. He lifted it to his ear. "Hello?"

"I love you, too," Tricia said into the phone.

"Trish?" Then it hit him. He'd dialed the number

and put the call through when Lena showed up. Tricia heard the whole conversation.

"Do you, baby? Really?"

"Yes, really."

He took a look at the hospital. "You know what, the heck with rounds. I'm coming to get you, right now. I'll tell them I had an emergency." He clicked off before she could protest.

Tricia was practically giddy when she hung up the phone. She'd said it, and so did he. It was official—they were in love. She tossed her head back and squeezed her eyes shut. They were in love. "Well let the choir say 'Amen!' "

"What choir?" Reginald asked, peeking his head in the doorway.

Tricia chuckled. "The amen choir. Come on in."

Reginald stepped inside. "When do you think you'll be ready with the presentation?"

"Actually, I think we're good to go. As a matter of fact, we can do the presentation today."

"Today?"

"Yep." Her eyes sparkled with mischief. "Get everyone together in the conference room in about an hour."

Reginald frowned. "Woman, you are crazy."

"Just go."

Reginald left and Tricia put the finishing touches on the presentation, saved it on her computer then darted into the bathroom to freshen up before Michael arrived. She started to giggle again. She was in love! And for once Lena couldn't get what she had.

* * *

"Tricia, Dr. Evans is here to see you," her secretary said into the intercom.

"Send him in."

Tricia quickly patted her hair and smoothed her suit just as a knock came on her door.

"Come in." She waited for him behind her desk.

"Hey gorgeous."

Tricia blushed. "You're not too shabby yourself."

He crossed the room and swept her into his arms and kissed her long and slow. "That's what I needed to confirm everything."

"Everything like what?" she asked, breathless and lightheaded.

"That I am truly, honestly, deeply without a doubt in love with you, Tricia Spencer. And it was your wild sister that actually got me to say the words I've only been playing with in my head all these weeks." His gaze danced across her face. "I love you."

"I love you back."

He held her tighter. "Does this door lock?"

Her eyes widened in alarm. "Lock?"

"Yes. I won't wait until tonight."

She tugged on her bottom lip with her teeth. Here in her office? Oh yesss.

A half hour later, Tricia emerged from her office as cool and as well put together as always. Except for the extra bounce in her step or the flush of her cheeks she looked the same as she led Michael down the corridor to the conference room.

What a woman, Michael mused as he watched the

sway of her hips. He needed to play hooky from work more often.

Tricia opened the conference room door and was glad to find everyone already seated.

"Thanks for coming on such short notice everybody." She put her laptop on the table and connected it to the projector. "Leslie, could you get the lights please?" She turned to Michael. "ImageNouveau is proud to present the *Living for Life* campaign."

For the next twenty minutes, Tricia put on a slide show of slogans, visuals and commercial concepts to promote healthy living from nutrition to exercise to finding the right doctor or hospital, along with a moving commentary from her about her own health scare. The campaign was complete with Web site information for a variety of health resources as well as phone numbers and addresses.

She walked to the wall and turned on the lights. "When I had my episode I realized for the first time just how fragile life can be, and how much we take for granted. I was lucky. And I want to share my experiences with others."

Michael leaned back, momentarily awed by what he'd seen. He knew the kind of powerful impact that kind of presentation could have.

"What can I do to put this everywhere?"

"I was hoping we could start with the hospital. Maybe run it on a loop inside of some of the clinics."

Michael stood and walked over to Tricia. "And that's only the beginning. I can tell you that," he said to her. "I am so proud of you." He leaned down and kissed her right in front of her staff. She nearly fainted for real. Then he turned to everyone who was staring wide-eyed at them. He put his arm around Tricia's waist.

"Did I mention that I'm in love with this woman?"

The room erupted into a roar of applause and Tricia dissolved into tears of joy.

Chapter 16
Six Months Later

Tricia and Michael had just stepped out of the shower and were busy drying each other off when Tricia suddenly squealed and pointed to the television. "That's me!"

Michael looked at the screen and sure enough, there was his baby. He smiled with pride and squeezed her close.

"I thought I had it all together," she was saying, "great business, good friends, clothes, a car. But none of that matters if you don't have your health. It took a frightening experience for me to realize what was truly important . . ."

"You did it, Trish," he said after the commercial concluded. "You have no idea how many lives you will touch and change. The possibilities are limitless."

"If it does one person some good, I'll be happy."

He gently began to massage her shoulders. "Remember way back when I told you I was an old-fashioned kind of guy?"

"Hmmm," she murmured, relishing the feel of his fingers.

He slowly turned her around. "I have a campaign that I want you to run for me."

"What is it?" She looked up into his eyes.

"I want you to put together the biggest, most lavish wedding of your dreams, and then I want you to work out a plan where you and I will love each other for the rest of our lives." He smiled at her tenderly. "So what do you say to that?"

Her eyes filled with tears of unabashed joy. "Yes. Yes. Yes."

He lowered his mouth to meet hers. "I was hoping you would say that."

The Perfect
Seduction

Brenda Jackson

Acknowledgments

This story is dedicated to all the beautiful full-figured women, and to businesses like SelenasSecrets.com who continue to make it sexy for all of us.

And to all my avid readers who are celebrating ten years of reading romance novels by Brenda Jackson. Happy Anniversary!!

I opened to my beloved, but he was gone. My heart stopped. I searched for him but couldn't find him anywhere. I called him, but there was no reply.
—The Song of Solomon 5:6
(*The Living Bible*)

Chapter 1

Megan James's heart slammed against her sternum as she watched the tall, good-looking, well-built man get out of the SUV and close the truck door behind him. Despite the distance separating them she recognized him immediately.

Tyler Savoy.

Even now at the age of twenty-nine, it was hard to forget the man she had fallen in love with at fifteen, and the memories just wouldn't go away. Emotions were swirling inside of her and strange as it seemed, it appeared that the feelings she'd always felt for Tyler were still there.

She continued to study him and decided that time had only enhanced his looks. While a teenager growing up he spent a lot of time on her grandfather's ranch, working after school and during the summers as his assistant. Dr. Matthew James had been the area's only veterinarian and had encouraged Tyler—who'd had a strong love for animals—to go after a career in that same profession. She would never forget the day Tyler left Alexandria, Virginia to attend Tuskegee University in Alabama to pursue a degree in veterinary medicine. To her he had been moving millions of miles away and not just a couple of states over.

They had been two teenagers in love and she'd known that the intensity of their attraction for each other had worried her parents and grandfather. Out of respect for their concerns for their budding romance, Tyler had always tried to keep a tight rein on his passionate side, although she had known and understood that he'd wanted more from their relationship than hand-holding and the kiss they would share every once in a while.

And she had wanted more, too. It seemed that as a teen she had encountered all kinds of overzealous hormones. On many nights, instead of sleeping, images of Tyler would flood her mind. He would be with her in bed, with his arms wrapped around her tight, kissing her, whispering all kinds of sweet words in her ears, touching her in ways she had never been touched before. Those images had been good and they had been locked safe and secure in her dreams where she could be as naughty as she wanted to be. But during the day-light hours, she had to behave the way she knew her parents and grandfather expected.

Until that one prom night.

Inhaling deeply she pulled her gaze away from the window and headed for the door, not wanting to remember that night and the way it had ended.

Webb Conyers, her stepfather's foreman, would see Tyler and escort him to the barn where one of the horses had taken ill. And since she was in charge of things for three weeks while her mother and stepfather were away on their honeymoon, she would be the person Tyler would need to talk to.

As she opened the door and walked out she wasn't sure if she was ready to come face to face with Tyler again, but it seemed that she really didn't have a choice in the matter.

"Hey, boy what's the matter?" Tyler soothingly murmured to the huge bay as he entered the stall and gave him a gentle pat on the rump. He and Moonshine were old friends and Tyler quickly recalled that this particular horse had been his first patient over ten years ago.

"Like I told you on the phone, Tyler, Moonshine's been acting funny for the past couple of days. He's barely eating and everybody knows what kind of appetite he has," Webb Conyers, the foreman of the Triple Circle Ranch, was saying.

Tyler nodded as he opened his vet bag. "Then let's see what's bothering him."

A few minutes later, after giving Moonshine a complete checkup, Tyler couldn't find anything wrong with the horse. "Do you still let him out into the yard to get an adequate amount of exercise?" he asked. At one time Moonshine had been a well-trained competitor and had received numerous awards in horse shows. He was still a good horse and a real beauty.

Webb nodded. "Yeah, everyday, but because he's been acting so ornery lately, we've been keeping him off to himself."

Tyler lifted a brow as he leaned against the stall gate. "Ornery? How?"

Webb shrugged as a smile touched his lips. "You know how horses can get this time of the year, Tyler."

Tyler nodded. Yes, he knew. It was spring, which meant mating for most animals, even humans—especially humans who found time to do it any season of the year and not just spring. Unless you were like him and were too busy working to become involved with anyone. He couldn't remember the last time he had slept with a woman. Probably eight months ago, maybe longer. "Then that's probably your problem. Moonshine might be old but he isn't dead. Does Winston intend for him to die of old age without ever mating again?"

Webb chuckled. "Now that you mention it, Moonshine started acting funny ever since Sarabelle arrived."

"Who's Sarabelle?"

Webb smiled. "She's a docile mare Winston purchased for his wife so she can have an even-tempered horse to ride."

Tyler nodded again. He remembered when he'd returned to work after visiting his cousin Blake and his wife Justice for a couple of weeks in Canada. One of his colleagues had mentioned that Mason Winston, the owner of the Triple Circle Ranch, had married Susan James. Susan's deceased father-in-law, Matthew James, had been Tyler's mentor for years and was instrumental in his decision to pursue a career in veterinary medicine.

"I heard Winston had gotten married," Tyler decided to say.

Webb had to smile again. "Yeah, and it's about time. Susan is a wonderful woman and just what Winston needs. Now he can stop being lonely and start enjoying life."

Tyler glanced around. He knew that Winston had been a widower for over twenty years and that Susan James's husband had died a few years back. "Where is Winston, by the way?"

"He's still on his honeymoon. After the wedding he and Susan took off in one of those huge camper things and headed out West. They won't be back for another three weeks."

"So you're the one running things while they're gone?"

"More or less, but they left Susan's daughter here since I'll be away in Florida next week to check out some horses we're contemplating buying."

Tyler, who had been putting his supplies back in his medical bag, paused. He glanced up at Webb, surprised. "Susan's daughter is here?"

"Yeah. Do you know her?"

Tyler slowly nodded. "Yes, I know her."

Thoughts and feelings that Tyler hadn't encountered for several years invaded his consciousness. Yes, he knew Megan James. The memory of their two year love affair suddenly flooded his mind. God, how he had loved her and how easily he had foolishly let her go. But at the time he had done what he thought was the right thing by heeding her parents' and grandfather's wishes to move aside and allow her to go after the future they'd always wanted her to have: a college education at Harvard. With a grandfather who'd been a highly respected doctor in veterinary medicine and parents who possessed PhDs, it stood to reason that she would have such a high IQ and be selected to be a part of an accelerated program to graduate from high school two years ahead of her peers. The last he'd heard she was a professor at some university in California. He'd also heard that like him, she was still single and hadn't married. But that had been a couple of years or so ago when he had run into her mother at the county fair and he'd asked about her. He couldn't help but wonder if Megan's marital status had changed since then.

Tyler allowed his mind to wander back a bit. He doubted if he would ever forget the day he'd first set eyes on Megan. He had been seventeen, a long way from his present age of thirty-one, and had stopped by her grandfather's ranch to apply for a job. She had been the one to open the door. And for a moment he had been more interested in the fifteen-year-old Megan James than he had been in the job he'd come applying for. Months later, on her sixteenth birthday, he had kissed her for the first time, and even now he could remember the sweet taste of her innocent lips.

"Well, she's the one you'll need to talk to if you're having ideas of getting Moonshine and Sarabelle together," Webb said, interrupting Tyler's wandering thoughts. "I don't think Winston would care one way or the other but in his absence it will be Megan's decision."

Then after a brief pause he said. "You'll get the chance to talk to Miss Megan. Here she comes now."

Tyler glanced around and watched with a leveled steady gaze as the woman he once loved to distraction walked toward them. He blinked as a torrid sensation settled in his gut. Megan was no longer pencil thin but had spread out over the years and acquired a voluptuous figure with an abundance of curves that were in all the right places.

She walked like a woman who was comfortable with her full-figure and confident in her appearance, and he could easily see why. In his opinion she was looking mighty good in a pair of jeans and a pullover top. Her hair was still long in length, almost reaching her shoulders. He remembered how often he had wanted to take a fistful of the glossy strands while holding her mouth hostage under his. But he'd never been able to put all the passion he'd felt into their kiss for fear of losing control and not wanting to stop, and worse yet, wanting to carry things further—like he had been tempted to do on her senior prom night.

A gust of July wind lifted her hair back away from her face and he saw more of her features. The Megan James he once knew had grown into a very beautiful woman and had a gorgeous sexy body to match. He bit back a groan and steeled himself when suddenly all the suppressed desire he had tried not to feel for her all those years ago took over his body.

He inhaled deeply, wondering why he was suddenly

swamped with such lusty feelings. Now he understood just what Moonshine must be going through. Sexual frustration, no matter what type of animal you were, was definitely one hell of a thing to deal with.

He frowned, wondering why his grandmother, Thelma Savoy, who had a reputation of keeping up with everything and everybody and knew what was and what was not happening in the Alexandria area, hadn't told him something as important as this.

Why hadn't anyone as informed him that Megan James was back?

Chapter 2

"Hello, Tyler, it's good seeing you again after all these years," Megan said, extending her hand in a greeting when she came to a stop in front of him.

Tyler returned the handshake. His response was slow in coming since any words he wanted to say died on his lips the moment their hands touched and his gaze locked with hers. Up close she was even more beautiful than he remembered. Had it actually been thirteen years since he had last seen her?

He drew a slow breath thinking that adulthood suited her. Her complexion of chestnut brown looked even smoother than it had been back then, and her dark eyes could still hold him spellbound. "Same here, Megan," he said finally, hearing the deep, throaty sound of his voice as he spoke and wondering if she heard it as well.

He continued to stare at her, thinking they'd known each other too long for such a formal greeting when what he wanted to do was to pull her into his arms and kiss her, giving her one hell of a welcome back home greeting. But he knew he had lost his right the same night he had broken her heart by not showing her how much he had loved her and wanted her.

"So, what's wrong with Moonshine?" she asked, breaking eye contact and turning away to glance over at the horse, and at the same time effectively derailing his memories of that particular night so long ago.

Tyler cleared his throat. Why did he find it hard to tell her there was nothing wrong with Moonshine that a good amount of mating with Sarabelle wouldn't cure? He opened his mouth to answer her question but Webb, bless his soul, beat him to the punch and answered.

"There's nothing wrong with Moonshine other than he has it bad for Sarabelle. It's that time of year and he refuses to be denied."

A smile touched Tyler's lips when he saw a blush appear in Megan's features. Her grandfather had been the area's vet for years and being familiar with animals she knew exactly what Webb meant.

"Oh," she said clearing her throat. "Then I guess we need to make sure his problem is taken care of," she said softly. She then turned and met Tyler's gaze once more after watching Webb lead Moonshine out of his stall, leaving her and Tyler alone. "How's your family?" she then asked. "I saw some of them at Mom's wedding last weekend."

He lifted a brow and folded his arms across his chest. "Really? And just who did you see?" He was curious since no one had mentioned seeing her and just about everyone in his family had known how he'd felt about Megan years ago.

"I saw your grandmother Ms. Thelma, your cousin

Tonya, as well as your cousins Ben, Nash and Morgan." She smiled. "Tonya told me about her Internet sales lingerie company. I think it's wonderful how well her business is doing and to think she finally snagged Bryan Manning. She's been in love with him forever."

He smiled. The family was proud of the success of Tonya's business and yes she had loved his best friend Bryan Manning forever. Everyone was glad the two had finally gotten married.

"And I also heard that your cousin Blake married Bryan's sister, Justice. Right?"

Megan's words interrupted his thoughts. She had definitely heard a lot. He couldn't help wondering if she had heard anything about him? Had she even inquired? He sighed deeply. He could understand Tonya not mentioning anything to him about seeing Megan since Tonya and Bryan had left to go out of town before he'd gotten back from Canada. And he could even overlook Ben, Nash and Morgan's failure to inform him of anything since they happened to have gone out of town as well. But there was no excuse for his grandmother not mentioning it when he'd had dinner with her last night.

He blinked when he noticed Megan was staring at him with a lifted brow as if she was waiting for him to respond to something. He racked his brain trying to remember the question. He then remembered. "Yes," he responded finally. "It was a double wedding with Blake marrying Justice that day as well. It was quite a feat for two Savoys to marry two Mannings. I think my grandmother cried through the entire ceremony."

Megan grinned. "I can see Ms. Thelma doing that."

Tyler tipped his head back and studied her. He had forgotten just how beautiful she was when she smiled. He felt the muscles knot in his stomach as he tried to remember the last time a woman had had such an effect on him. But then when it came to Megan James, she'd always been able to get next to him in ways he didn't want to think about.

He watched as she glanced around as if trying to avoid eye contact with him, and wondered if she had picked up on the sudden tension in the air that surrounded them. It was the same tension that had begun creeping up as they'd gotten older; tension he had worked so hard to control and harness all those years ago. "Megan?"

She swung her gaze back to his and heat radiated from the top of his head all the way to the tip of his toes. He knew the intensity of it was probably making its way to the hard-packed dirt beneath his boots.

Their eyes held for the longest time and he suddenly felt his control slipping as he stared straight back at her the same way she was staring at him. Suddenly he began remembering that night thirteen years ago. Prom night. After taking her to the dance she hadn't wanted to go back home, saying it was too early. She had wanted to go someplace and talk, find out everything about his first year away at college. He had let her talk him into getting a hotel room . . . just to talk.

He should have insisted on taking her home that night but he hadn't wanted the evening to end anymore than she had. It had been his first year away at college and he had missed her like hell, and if she wanted for them to go somewhere where they could talk privately, he hadn't had a problem with it. But talking had been the last thing on their minds once they had entered the hotel room and closed the door behind them.

Alone and no longer under anyone's watchful eyes, he had kissed her in a way he had always wanted to kiss her, filled with two years of wanting and need. The intensity of his desire for her as well as her desire for him had overwhelmed him, leaving him powerless to fight the temptation any longer, and they had quickly gone up in flames.

They had undressed and he had picked her up in his arms to take her to the bed when his sanity had quickly returned, and he'd been hit with the realization of what they were about to do and the enormous risk involved.

He'd suddenly remembered the promise he had made to her grandfather; a promise that no matter what, he would maintain control and never take his relationship with Megan to a sexual level. Her family had plans for her future, plans that didn't include a teen pregnancy. Although he'd had condoms with him that night he still couldn't take the chance.

So he had pulled back, gotten dressed and had silently helped her to redress and then had taken her home, refusing to answer her question as to why he had stopped. The next day he had made the decision to leave town early and return to college, and although they had exchanged a few letters after that—angry letters that she had written to let him know how hurt she'd been with the decision he'd made that night—this was the first time he had seen her since then.

In the distance they heard the sound of a dog barking and the spell was broken. He knew she had been thinking about that night just like he had. "How have you been, Megan?" he asked, clearing his throat.

"I've been fine, Tyler. What about you?"

"I've been fine, too."

She nodded. "Granddad would be proud of you. He always said you would make a wonderful vet and from what I've heard you're doing a fantastic job."

He lifted a brow wondering who she had heard that from. His grandmother? One of his cousins? Winston? "Thanks. I love what I do. What about you? I understand you continued on with your education, got your doctorate and are now a college professor."

She smiled. "Yes. I teach mathematics at Berkeley and love what I do, too, but I was looking forward to this break."

He chuckled. "Students getting on your nerves?"

She nodded. "But even more so are the administrators. They are shoving the *do more with less* policy down our throats. My classes have gotten larger and my work days longer. I don't mind staying busy but all work and no play isn't healthy."

He nodded and glanced at her hand and noticed a ring wasn't on her finger. "You're still single?"

She met his gaze and shoved her hands into the back pockets of her jeans. "Yes, I never married. What about you?"

He leaned back against the railing wondering why

she had never married, but then she would probably wonder the same thing about him. "I'm single, too," he said, thinking of just how single he was. "And I've never married either."

For a long moment neither of them said anything and emotions he didn't want to feel began swirling inside of him. He couldn't help but dwell on the unspoken question that lingered between them. Why hadn't either of them ever married? Did it have anything to do with how they had felt about each other back then? Fourteen years was a long time to be carrying a torch for someone but . . .

The cell phone attached to his belt rang, startling him. "Excuse me," he said to Megan, before answering it. A few moments later he nodded in response to what the caller was saying. The Miller's cat had taken ill. He inhaled a ragged breath as he disconnected the call and hooked the phone back on his belt. He had to leave on another appointment.

"So how long will you be in town?" he decided to ask, not wanting to leave just yet but knowing that he had to go.

"Until Mom and Winston get back; probably for another three weeks. They planned to be gone a month."

He tried not to notice how she had caught her lower lip between her teeth, something that used to turn him on back then and was doing so now. He gripped his vet bag tighter in his hand and quickly made a decision. "I'd like to take you to dinner while you're here, Megan."

He didn't want to think that he could possibly be

asking for trouble. A part of him needed to know if there were any lingering grievances as a result of that night eleven years ago. If so, they needed to come to terms with it. His heart began to pound and a part of him wanted to believe that the only reason he wanted to take her out was for old times' sake; talk to her some more and find out what she'd been doing over the past thirteen years.

But he knew that a part of him needed to know why she'd never married.

Her decision may not have had anything to do with him, but he had to be sure that refusing to make love to her that night hadn't caused the sort of emotional damage she had claimed it would in the bitter and angry letters she had sent to him.

She had written that he had hurt her and that she had believed the reason he had stopped things from going further between them that night was because he hadn't really wanted her as much as she had wanted him. Boy, had she been wrong, but he had decided not to write back and tell her otherwise. It had been best to let her believe that particular lie, forget him and move on with her life.

He studied her. They weren't the same two people, but in the back of his mind he knew there were things that needed to be settled between them, issues that had lasted too long that needed to be resolved.

He watched her, knowing she was considering his invitation. He inwardly sighed when she finally smiled and said, "Thanks. I think dinner would be nice, Tyler."

He nodded. "How about Paddy's Place tomorrow night?"

She smiled as she remembered the popular restaurant. "Do they still serve the best seafood?"

"Yes, it's still the best."

"Then I definitely can't refuse."

He smiled. "Okay, then it's a date and I'll pick you up at seven. It will be nice to find out what you've been doing over the years," he said, gripping his vet bag even tighter in his hand.

"Okay, and I want to catch up on things with you as well." She glanced down and checked her watch. "I'd better go. I left something cooking in the oven." For a moment she stared at him then said, "I meant what I said earlier, Tyler. It's good seeing you again."

"Same here, Megan, and I'm looking forward to tomorrow night."

"So am I," she said before turning to leave.

He watched her go and moments later when she had disappeared into the house he sighed deeply before walking toward his truck. She had agreed to go out with him, which meant she was no longer angry about that night. He was grateful for that. He looked forward to taking her out to dinner as nothing but old friends—talking, eating, dancing . . . kissing.

Kissing?

He stopped abruptly and inhaled even deeper. Megan James was back after all this time, and he was feeling the impact already.

Megan stood at the window and watched as Tyler drove away. Only when she could no longer see the vehicle did her heart slow down its erratic pounding.

The few moments she had stood in front of him,

pretending not to be affected by him, had been hard. Each and every time his hazel-eyed gaze focused on her face, she had felt heat radiating low in her stomach. She had quickly accepted that Tyler had the same effect on her now that he'd had when she was in her teens.

She couldn't help but think about her childhood, which had been a long way from normal. She had begun college at sixteen, gotten a bachelor's degree from Harvard by the time she was nineteen and a doctorate from there by her twenty-first birthday. She had a good-paying job at Berkeley and enjoyed living in California. But still, everything was not completely right in her world, which made her thoughts shift to Tyler again.

The Savoys, and there were a mass of them in Alexandria, had trademark hazel eyes and good looks. There were more guys than girls but all of them were known to be respected and well-liked in the community. Their grandmother, Thelma Savoy, who was considered the backbone of the Savoy family, wouldn't have it any other way, and had instilled into her grandchildren and great grandchildren strong moral values and a deep sense of doing what was right.

Something warm curled up inside of her at the possibility that her presence had affected Tyler as well. And she had meant what she'd said. It had been good seeing him again because doing so had made her realize something deep and essential. You never fully got over your first love. Her mother had been right. A part of her would always love Tyler. For a long time she had thought he had rejected her, and to add insult to injury, when he hadn't answered her letters it became obvious that he had cut her out of his life. She had thought that way until she had discovered the truth.

She would never forget the long talk she'd finally had with her mother a few years ago, less than a week after breaking off her engagement to Jason, a guy she had met in California. Her mother had told her of the promise they had asked Tyler to make, a promise they had felt was needed after her grandfather had found a love letter she had written to Tyler, telling him of her nightly dreams about him and how more than anything she wanted those dreams to come true.

She had never sent that letter, had never entertained thoughts of doing so. She had merely written it to put a lot of her thoughts and feelings on paper, not realizing that it would one day end up in the wrong hands. Upon reading her innermost sensuous thoughts, her family had decided the best thing to do was to take drastic steps to make sure her dreams never became a reality. Instead of deliberately ending things between them, which they knew would be the wrong approach, they had preyed on Tyler's good upbringing, his high sense of integrity, honor and doing what was right. In the end he had made her grandfather a promise; a promise he had kept even under the most arduous temptation.

During the two years of their courtship, she had appreciated all the time Tyler had spent with her. Until he had shown interest in her, her life had been downright isolated and lonely since most of the kids at school had thought because of her high IQ that she was just plain weird. But not Tyler. He had treated her special and not like some overeducated, superintelligent freak. He had convinced her that being smart was something she should be proud of and not ashamed of. And by choosing her as his girl he had shown others that he thought she was pretty as well as smart. Being the girlfriend of one of the most popular guys at school had made her feel extremely special. It didn't take long for other boys to take notice, but then it was too late, because her heart fully belonged to Tyler. Even when he'd left for college, the boys stayed their distance since there were plenty of Savoy cousins around who were intent on protecting their cousin's interest.

Megan sighed deeply as she walked away from the window. It had done her heart and mind good to realize that the reason Tyler had turned away from her in the blazing heat of passion had nothing to do with him not desiring her, but everything to do with keeping the promise he'd made to her grandfather. She wondered what he would think if he knew that she now knew the truth.

A shiver ran through her when she remembered her physical reaction to him earlier. She was amazed that she was still that attracted to him and wondered what he would think to find out that she was a twenty-nine-year-old virgin. Once she had gotten to college she'd discovered that because of her young age, a lot of the guys thought she was easy game. And although she would be the first to admit that her dating skills hadn't been up to speed, she had been Tyler's girl long enough to know what behavior she wanted from a guy. And it definitely wasn't a man who couldn't keep his hands off her for all the wrong reasons.

All that changed when she met Jason. He'd also been one of those individuals who'd accelerated through school most of his life. But his only problem was that, with his analytical mind, he had a tendency to analyze anything to death, which would often drive her crazy. And if that wasn't bad enough, she just couldn't entertain the thought of sleeping with any man other than Tyler. He had been the man whom she thought she would be with for the rest of her life, and their love was one she'd thought would last forever.

Her *forever* had come crashing down with her on that one prom night. Even now she couldn't forget that night, especially all the sensuous foreplay that should have resulted in them making love. He had touched her everywhere and even now her breasts still ached from the memory of his mouth on her. Nor could she forget the sight of a naked Tyler, broad-shouldered, solidly built, masculine and powerful. He had been mere inches of going inside of her body, joining their bodies as one, when he'd pulled back, denying them what they both had wanted.

Over the years thoughts of him had still crept into her dreams, which was why she'd had no other choice but to break off her engagement with Jason. There was no way she could marry one man while still having deep, torrid titillating thoughts of another; thoughts that hadn't completely gone away.

Megan sighed. Seeing Tyler again had resurfaced heated desires and inflamed emotions. They were no longer the desires and emotions of a young girl but a full-fledged woman. As crazy as it seemed, she knew what she needed from Tyler to be set free, and it went a lot deeper than just resolving the past. In her heart and mind she felt that he owed her a "prom night"— one that would end the way theirs had meant to end, with no promises standing in the way. He was to have been her first lover and now she wanted him to still be that.

She still wanted Tyler as her first lover.

There was no way she could move on with her life, put the past behind her, and get Tyler out of her system until they had the night they should have had. It didn't take long after being in Tyler's presence to know he was still an honorable man, someone who still believed in doing what was right. He was raised to treat a woman like a lady. And with that thought in mind she knew what she had to do. He had denied her what she'd wanted once, but she was determined that things would be different this time around. They were now adults and could do whatever they wanted without anyone's interference. There were no promises to stand in the way of having the kind of night together that they were meant to have.

And Megan knew that a night with Tyler was what she wanted more than anything.

Chapter 3

Tyler tucked his hands into the back pockets of his jeans after ringing the door bell. He sighed deeply. More than once since yesterday he had questioned the sanity of his decision to take Megan out, and no matter how many times he asked the question why, the answer would come back reluctantly and honestly. There were issues they needed to finally resolve.

Thirteen years was a long time for misunderstandings. There was a time he could read Megan like a book. He had known she had wanted more from their relationship back then. But she hadn't known of the promise he had made to her grandfather, a man he had highly respected.

Tyler had been aware each and every single time Megan had desired him. It had been there in her eyes, a hunger that was more than a teenage girl should have to deal with. He would never forget the first time she had caught him off guard when they had kissed good night. He had intended for it to be only a chaste kiss on the lips, but she had pulled his head down to hers and had taken over the kiss, inserting her tongue into his mouth, deepening the contact and giving him a glimpse of how things could be if he were to loosen up a little, let go of the reins. Her action had transformed an innocent kiss into a very heated one, and when she'd finally let go of his mouth, she had smiled as if pleased with the response she had gotten out of him.

Tyler shook his head when he remembered the Megan he had encountered yesterday. She appeared friendly yet reserved, but he couldn't read her like he used to. She was different, but then so was he. However, one thing was still the same and that was his all-consuming desire for her.

He straightened from leaning on the column post when he heard the sound of the door opening. He then clenched his teeth at the same time desire struck him solidly in the gut, not stopping there as it plunged deep into his muscles. He would probably begin swearing if such a thing were acceptable in a lady's presence. So he just stood there and stared at her as heat flooded his body, wondering if she had any idea just how good she looked wearing a sundress that practically left her shoulders bare except for thin spaghetti straps.

Everything about the dress was a total turn-on and he couldn't understand why. He had seen women in sundresses before, but for some reason he knew the vision of Megan in this one would forever stand out in his mind. Maybe it was the red color of the dress that meshed so well with the tone of her skin. But then it could have been the neckline and how it scooped, showing the top of creamy and full breasts. They were breasts whose nipples were pressed against the material of the dress; the tips so taunt he couldn't help but wonder if she was wearing a bra, and just the thought that she wasn't made his mouth water.

"Come on in, Tyler. I just need to let Ms. Baker know that I'm leaving."

Tyler nodded as he entered the huge living room. He knew Florence Baker had been Winston's house-keeper for years. He also knew that she was a good friend of his grandmother's, so he didn't doubt that news of his date with Megan would hit the phone lines before they got out of the driveway. He had tried calling his grandmother last night and again that day but both times she had been out doing errands. She was seventy-five and still driving around Alexandria like she had helped put in the streets. Periodically, the family would get together and discuss the possibility of taking her car keys away, but they would quickly dismiss the thought when they would have to admit that she drove a lot better than some of them.

As Megan turned to leave the room, Tyler stared after her, his good intentions getting shot to hell once again. The dress was a decent length, hitting above her knees, and she was wearing the sexiest red high-heeled sandals that totally complemented her outfit. As far as he was concerned, she was taking the word sexy to a whole other level.

A sudden flashback reminded him of the time that he had seen her completely naked—every delectable inch of her—and now since that body had matured a lot over the years—her curves fuller, more voluptuous—his imagination couldn't help but work overtime.

"I'm ready now, Tyler."

Megan's voice broke into his thoughts when she returned to the living room. He breathed in deeply, thinking that perhaps the interruption was a good thing. He needed to keep his mind off Megan's dress and her body. He cleared his throat. "I hope you're hungry."

She smiled. "Oh, I'm starving."

Tyler inhaled sharply. Megan had spoken three simple words but for a quick moment he could have sworn he could read her thoughts again, just like he used to, and there was a hidden meaning behind her words. He tipped his head back and studied her, but the expression looking back at him was blank, unreadable once again.

He shook his head, thinking he must have imagined it. Amazing what little sleep could do. He hadn't rested worth a damn last night. Thoughts of Megan had taken over his dreams just like they had years ago. "I'm glad you're hungry because I intend to feed you," he said taking her hand in his and leading her out of the house.

"Tyler Savoy, I'm counting on it," she said in a low, sultry voice.

He glanced over at her. Again her face was a mask of unreadable expression.

Megan began wondering if she had bitten off more than she could chew as she felt the heat of Tyler's gaze burn through her clothes, and boy was it intense.

Liquid heat was already gathering in her stomach and slowly spreading lower. The nipples of her breasts were beginning to feel achingly hard, and had been since she opened the door to find him standing there and his hazel-eyed gaze had locked on her.

She was momentarily pulled from her thoughts when he led her to a silver gray Jaguar. She blinked. The car was a real beauty. She then glanced up at him and he read the question in her eyes and smiled.

"The SUV is my company vehicle. This is what I usually drive when I'm off work and at play."

She nodded and couldn't help wondering how many women had had the pleasure of sitting next to him in this vehicle while he was at play. "It's nice," she said, forcing the jealous thought from her mind. They had officially broken up years ago and the women he had shared his time, bed and body with over the years was none of her business. Accepting that to be a fact of life, she relaxed the hands by her side that had curled into fists.

"Thanks," she said when he opened the car door for her and waited until she had snapped her seat belt and shoulder harness in place before closing it. She watched as he quickly walked around the front of the car to get in. Tyler could still wear a pair of jeans and draw attention. She remembered how envious the other girls were that she had a boyfriend who had looked so good. But then, all the men in the Savoy family had a reputation of looking good and were considered a good catch. Any parent would have been proud for their daughter to bring a Savoy home to dinner.

A few seconds later, they pulled off. Megan only

hoped that she could survive an evening out with the much older and sexier Tyler Savoy.

"Are you ready to order, ma'am?"

The waitress's question made Megan glance up. The last time she had eaten at Paddy's the menu consisted of a half page of items. Now the menu consisted of five pages. It seemed they not only served delicious seafood but other full course, mouth-watering meals as well. Although she'd had a taste for fried shrimp earlier, she couldn't help eyeing the baby back ribs. The couple sitting at the table across from theirs had ordered a plate and they looked simply delicious.

"May I make a suggestion?" Tyler spoke up, evidently understanding her dilemma. "How about if you order the fried shrimp plate and I order the baby back ribs and we can share."

She knew Tyler couldn't help but see the gratitude that was shining in her eyes. "Are you sure?"

He chuckled. "Yes, I'm positive."

"Thanks."

"You're welcome."

After writing down their orders, the waitress collected their menus then left them alone.

Tyler forced his gaze away from Megan and glanced around. The last time he had come here was when the male Savoy cousins had gotten together last summer to celebrate Blake's engagement. They had pushed three tables together to accommodate all ten men. He smiled remembering how much fun they'd had and how they had practically ordered everything on the menu that night.

He couldn't stop staring at Megan. She was avoiding his eyes by studying the flickering candle that sat in the middle of their table. She hadn't brought a jacket, and he wondered if she was cold since the air-conditioning seemed to be set at a low temperature. It was a cool summer evening, not typical for July. But then he had to admit he was enjoying her bare shoulders and how the top part of the dress cradled her firm breasts. He wasn't good at guessing women's sizes but he figured she was probably a size sixteen and definitely a nicely built one.

When she finally glanced up at him he couldn't help but ask. "Are you cold?"

She shrugged and smiled. "No. I'm use to warm days and cool nights. The part of California where I live is known for them."

"Oh."

She placed her elbows on the table and leaned toward him. Her smile widened. "Haven't you ever been to California?"

For a moment he couldn't answer, couldn't utter a single sound. When she'd leaned over, the top of her dress gaped open and he could see more of her breasts. He sat nearly motionless when he realized she really wasn't wearing a bra.

He swallowed when he remembered that one night when his mouth had gone crazy on her breasts by making a feast of her nipples. Boy had he enjoyed himself, he thought, remembering every single detail, especially the purrs that had come from her lips.

"Tyler?"

He quickly moved his gaze from her chest to her

eyes. "Yes?" he asked, barely able to get the word out.

"Have you ever been to California?" she repeated the question.

He shook his head, trying to concentrate on what she was asking him. "No."

"Then I'm issuing an invitation for you to come and visit me one day. I think you would like it. The Pacific Ocean looks a whole lot different from the Atlantic. Both are beautiful but I think the Pacific is even more so."

"Yes, that's what I heard from Blake," he said, settling back in his chair so looking down the top of her dress wouldn't be so obvious. "And thanks for the invitation. I might take you up on it."

"I'm hoping that you will."

Tyler lifted a brow as he watched Megan pick up the glass of water she had ordered and take a sip. There was something in the way she'd just spoken, a sexy tone that had made his breath catch and had him thinking that she'd been flirting with him.

It then struck him that other than the time he'd taken her to the prom, the two of them had never officially gone out on a date. When they had been in high school she had been an advanced student: a senior at sixteen. Although her fellow classmates were dating, her parents felt that she was too young to do the same; however, since they approved of their relationship they did allow them to take part in supervised activities around her grandfather's ranch or at his grandmother's house. He had never taken her to the movies, a sports event or a drive through the countryside. To say her parents had been rather strict would be an understatement.

He took a sip of his own water as he waited for her to look at him. Was she nervous about them being together? If that was the case he intended to get her relaxed.

Avoiding Tyler's gaze, Megan set her water glass down. She then glanced around again noticing how crowded the place had gotten since they had arrived.

"Megan?"

She glanced up and met his gaze. "Yes?"

Whatever words he was about to say died on his lips when the waitress returned with their meal, setting both platters in the middle of the table. "Let's dig in," he said instead.

Chapter 4

Tyler set down his fork and glanced across the table at Megan. Like him she had finished eating but was studying the lit candle again, seemingly in deep concentration. Something warm and tender touched him as he continued to study her. She'd always been special to him, and he remembered feeling on top of the world just knowing he'd been the guy in her life.

He doubted that she knew just how much he had loved her back then. When he'd first shown interest in her, she'd seemed surprised that any guy would go for the brainy type. But there had been more to her than just a high IQ. She had been a caring person and there hadn't been a pretentious bone in her body. And more importantly, she had a special way with animals, especially those that had been in her grandfather's care.

Again sensing her nervousness and not understanding the reason for it, he decided to break the silence. "Did you enjoy everything?" he asked quietly, not wanting to startle her to attention.

It seemed that he did anyway when she snapped her head up and her gaze met his, held it and locked into it. Parts of him began simmering, a slow, low heat. As a young girl Megan James could break through his every defense and now it seemed that since she had become a woman she was effectively sending every defense he had tumbling.

Over the years he had missed her. He had thought of her often, wondering if she was happy. What had made their relationship so special was that they'd been friends before they had become lovers.

Lovers.

He quickly reminded himself that they had never been lovers, not in the true sense of the word, although they had come close that night. So close his body ached just thinking about it and the memories were starting to overwhelm him.

"Yes, I enjoyed everything," Megan spoke, breaking into Tyler's thoughts. "Nothing has changed. As usual the food here is excellent." She leaned back in her chair. "I was just thinking a few moments ago that not counting prom night, this is our first real date."

He smiled. "Yes, I was thinking that same thing earlier myself."

She sighed deeply. "My family's overprotectiveness didn't help me, Tyler. When I got to college I was like a fish out of water and quickly became a target for guys who had only one thought on their minds."

Tyler eyed her steadily as his lips thinned to a hard line. Her family had thought that all her problems would be solved once they got her off to Harvard, but even schools like Harvard had guys who were intent on getting inside a girl's panties. "Did you handle them?" he heard himself asking in a low voice, inwardly hoping and praying that she did.

She chuckled. "Oh, yeah, I handled them. I may have been naïve in some things but not in all. Besides, the first strike against them was that they weren't anything like you. You had spoiled me."

Tyler's brow lifted. "Had I?"

"Yes. Being your girlfriend taught me to expect a certain behavior from a man and it helped to instill total confidence in myself. It also taught me not to sell myself short. In my book you were a tough act to follow for any guy."

He smiled. If her intent was to stroke his ego, then she was doing a pretty good job, Tyler thought. At that moment the one question he had been asking himself since seeing her again yesterday resurfaced and he couldn't help but want to know the answer. "Why aren't you married, Megan? All you used to talk about was getting your education and getting married one day."

Megan took a swallow of her water, deciding not to remind Tyler that at the time the man she'd thought she was going to marry was him. "I almost got married."

That definitely got Tyler's attention. "You did?"

"Yes. Jason and I met while in grad school and were engaged for almost a year."

Tyler broke off one of the cookies that had been served as a complimentary dessert. He tried to savor it but all he could do was think about Megan in the arms of another man, and a bitter taste crept into his mouth. "What happened?" he asked, chewing slowly.

"Although we thought we were well suited, we later discovered we weren't. Jason was a walking genius and could analyze anything to death. After a while it wore on my nerves. I couldn't imagine spending the rest of my life with him."

She decided not to add that Jason's kisses hadn't stirred her, his touch hadn't filled her with desire and there was never a time she was tempted to rip his clothes off.

Tyler stopped chewing and met her gaze intently. "So you broke off your engagement?"

"Yes."

"What about love?"

A long pause. Not that Megan had to think about the answer but she knew he needed to understand. "Like I said, Jason and I were well suited. He figured that with our intelligence our kids would be little geniuses. All I could see were kids growing up being too smart for their own good." And she decided not to add they wouldn't be Savoys, inheriting their father's hazel eyes the way she always dreamed about.

"So you didn't love him?"

Megan wondered if he was asking a question or making a statement. But she decided to answer anyway, wishing that she could tell him that he'd been the only man she had ever truly loved. "No, I didn't love him," she finally answered. "So, what about you?" she decided to ask, shifting the focus from her love life to his.

Tyler shifted in his chair. He knew what she was asking. Eleven years was a long time not to be in a serious relationship with someone. "No engagements, not even close," he said as a half smile tilted the corners of his mouth. "I date occasionally but that's about it." But even as he said the words, he knew that wasn't about it.

Although he had spent a lot of time working it hadn't been like he'd had to build up his practice. The persons whose animals he took care of were the same ones Dr. James had cared for, and since he had been his assistant, it had been fairly easy for him to come back home and get established in his private business. Also, the name Savoy had helped. His family was well known and respected around these parts.

It suddenly occurred to him just how intimate their setting was. The lights were low, jazz music was playing and the candles on every table were lit. He enjoyed the easy conversation he and Megan were having and decided that he liked the new grown-up version of Megan James too much. The transformation was startling and definitely pleasing to the eyes. And speaking of eyes, she still had a turn-you-on pair. He would never forget how those same eyes had darkened as he moved over her in bed that night just moments before he was to enter—

"It's hard to believe you don't have a steady girlfriend."

Tyler swallowed. Glad her words had intruded into his thoughts when they had since they'd been headed for dangerous territory. He leaned back, hearing the implied message in Megan's words. "I can say the same for you. It's hard to believe you don't have a steady boyfriend either."

He took his statement one step further and said, "You're a very beautiful woman, Megan." He hoped she believed that he wasn't just giving her a line but had meant every word he'd said.

"Thank you." Megan nervously glanced around. She didn't want him to take note of the effects his words had on her. From other men she would consider them just words a man would say in an attempt to score, but Tyler had always been different.

She noted that most of the people who had been sitting around them had either left or were in the other room where a jazz band was performing, which was another new addition to Paddy's since the last time she'd been here. She sighed deeply, knowing she had to get things out in the open and make her request to Tyler. Now that she knew that he wasn't involved in a serious relationship with anyone, she didn't have any misgivings about what she was about to say to him.

"Tyler?"

He met her gaze. "Yes?"

She swallowed past the lump in her throat. "We've always had this special bond, haven't we?" she asked, reaching across the table and squeezing his hand.

Tyler nodded, feeling tension, and something pretty close to desire creep into him. "Yes, why?"

"Because I need to ask a big favor of you."

She removed her hand but that didn't stop Tyler's heart from pounding. "Sure, what do you need?"

She smiled. "My birthday is in a few months."

He nodded. Knowing exactly when it was and how old she would be. "October tenth, and you'll be thirty."

Her smile widened. "You remember?"

"Yes."

She leaned over the table, closer to him. "Do you also remember prom night?"

Tyler lifted a brow as he swallowed deeply. "Yes." He wondered why she was bringing that night up and what one had to do with the other.

"Things didn't go the way I had wanted and planned," she admitted softly.

That was an understatement, he thought. He had known what was on her mind when she had suggested they go somewhere private to talk, since he could always read her like a book. She had sent out signs, big ones, all during the dance, and the smiles she had given him that night had meant to seduce. At sixteen she had decided she wanted to take their relationship to another level if he was ready or not. And unfortunately, he had played right into her hands.

Almost.

At the very last minute he had come to his senses. Pulling away from her had been the hardest thing he'd ever had to do.

"For a long time I was angry with you, Tyler, for what you did," she said, interrupting his thoughts.

He nodded. "Your letters said as much," he replied, trying to ignore the look in her eyes that had him thinking of things that he shouldn't be thinking about.

"After I broke off my engagement with Jason my mother and I had a long talk, and although she had no idea what almost happened between us that night, she did tell me the truth."

Tyler was about to pick up his glass to take a sip of water, then hesitated. "The truth about what?"

She eyed him steadily. "She told me about the promise my grandfather convinced you to make after finding that love letter I had written you."

Tyler lifted a brow. He hadn't known anything about a love letter. All he knew was that Dr. James had spoken with him privately, and the old man's request was to promise that he would never touch his granddaughter in an inappropriate way. Tyler had known just what way the man had meant.

"Do you deny you made my grandfather a promise involving me?"

Tyler shrugged. "No, I don't deny it," he said, thinking there was no reason not to be honest with her now since it was water under the bridge. He watched as her gaze took on a determined glint just seconds before she began focusing on the candle once again.

"Hearing you confirm that makes what I'm about to say a lot easier," she said in a slow breath before lifting her eyes to meet his. "You owe me something, Tyler, and it's something I want."

He looked at her in surprise. "I owe you something?"

"Yes."

Silence filled the space between them as he racked his mind trying to figure out what he owed her. If it was an explanation of why things had ended the way they had that night, then she already had her answer

157

to that. He had admired and respected her grandfather too much not to do what the older man had asked. Besides, a part of him had known that Megan wasn't ready to become sexually involved with him, although she'd thought otherwise. He had been her first and only boyfriend, but their relationship wasn't like the normal one for a couple.

He then wondered if perhaps she felt he owed her an apology for taking her to the hotel room in the first place knowing that he wouldn't carry through with anything. The sad thing about it was that his control had gotten shot to hell the moment he closed that door and she had turned around, caught him off guard and kissed him.

Knowing that there was only one way to find out just why she thought he was in her debt, he finally broke the silence, asking quietly. "And just what is it that I owe you, Megan?"

Resting her cheek on upraised hands while her elbows rested on the table, she held his gaze. When he was unable to bear the tension a minute longer she finally spoke.

"You owe me a prom night, Tyler. One that will end the way it should have ended thirteen years ago."

Chapter 5

Tyler stared at Megan thinking he had clearly misunderstood what she'd said. "I owe you a prom night? One ending the way you think it should have ended?"

"Yes."

Tyler quickly glanced around for the waiter. He needed something stronger to drink than water, but then he remembered he was the one driving. His gaze latched on to Megan again and he could tell from her expression that she was dead serious. "B—but why?" he stuttered, trying to make sense of her request.

"I have my reasons, Tyler."

He watched as she picked up her water glass, took a sip then lowered it again. He could tell she was nervous. It hadn't been easy for her to make that request so why had she? "Then you're going to have to share those reasons with me, Megan, because I don't understand why after thirteen years you would want to go back."

She set her elbows on the table and leaned toward him, making sure she had his attention, which wasn't necessary because she definitely had it. "For me it's not about going back, Tyler, it's about moving forward. I'm well aware it's been thirteen years, but I've been unable to get on with my life the way I should."

Tyler leaned away from the table and from her. Megan James was too much temptation, and at the moment her request definitely had him remembering the way she had wanted their night to end, which meant . . .

Shivers moved up his spine and he felt heat rising through all parts of his body. Did she really expect them to . . .

He studied her gaze and knew that she did. "You haven't been able to get on with your life in what way, Megan?" he asked, still not understanding. She was insinuating that that night had left some sort of a scar on her, and he wanted her to explain what she'd meant.

Megan glanced around. She was glad everyone had left and she and Tyler were alone in this particular section of the restaurant. She met Tyler's gaze. He was waiting for her to answer, intently, attentively.

"I told you about my relationship with Jason and I also mentioned the guys at Harvard."

"Yes."

"Well, evidently you didn't understand the depth of my problem."

Tyler lifted a brow. "And what problem is that?"

She inhaled deeply before answering. "Years ago I convinced myself you were the one; the person I would love the rest of my life, till death do us part. You can call it foolish and you can even call it a young girl's fantasy, but I never thought of what we shared as short term even after you left for college. And although I knew my parents had my life mapped out as far as me attending Harvard, in my mind I was going to return here whenever I finished all my schooling. I was going to return here to you."

He nodded. For a long time he had thought the same way she had. At nineteen when he had thought of getting married, Megan had always been the person he assumed he would marry. But that one night had changed everything. She had tested his control to the limit, and he knew if they continued to see each other when he came home from college that it would only be a matter of time before he broke the promise he had made. Her angry letters had been the excuse he'd needed to end things, so he had.

"Things didn't work out that way, Megan," he decided to remind her.

"Yes, but still, although you may have gotten on with your life, I was left with issues."

She'd been left with issues? He didn't know what to say. Curiosity took over at that point. "What sort of issues?"

Nervously rubbing her arms with her hands, he watched as she focused on the candle again, as if using it to gain the strength and courage for what she needed to say. She then met his gaze. "I have sex issues."

Tyler swallowed. He then picked up his glass of water, needing the cool liquid to wash down the lump that had suddenly formed in his throat. "Sex issues?" he repeated, barely above a whisper. Her words sent alarm bells ringing in his head. And it didn't help matters the way she was looking at him.

"Yes." She sighed deeply, and for some reason he knew whatever she was about to say, he wouldn't like it.

"I'm still a virgin, Tyler," she whispered. "I'm a twenty-nine year old virgin and it's all your fault."

She was still a virgin? Tyler struggled to ignore first the shock and then the quick jolt of intense heat that surged through him with her blunt statement. Emotions, basic and primitive, stirred to life within him. Why did the thought that no other man had touched her fill him with so much desire, so much lust? Especially when he knew it meant so much trouble.

Then the implications of everything she'd said slowly began sinking in. He realized just what she wanted from him. "Surely you don't mean . . ."

"Yes, that's exactly what I mean, Tyler. I want you to be my first, the way you should have been."

For a long moment he couldn't look away from the intensity of her gaze; however, his eyes did drop a little lower to rest on her lips—lips he had feasted on that night until he'd had her purring.

He sighed deeply as he pulled his thoughts out of the past and back into the present. "What you're asking for is impossible, Megan," he said, breaking into the silence and trying to ignore the hot memories that wanted to once again take over his mind. "It's been eleven years. Yesterday was the first time we've seen each other since that night. People don't just pick up and—"

"Yes, they do, Tyler, and you know it. Total strang-

162

ers meet and sleep together on the same night. Not that I would support that sort of behavior, but it's been done. I'd like to think that although we hadn't seen each other over the years that we're still friends. If you have a problem thinking of it as a debt you owe, then consider it as doing me a favor."

Tyler frowned. He didn't like the thought of either one. He looked at her again. He couldn't help doing so. She had basically lived a recluse life growing up. Her parents had picked her friends and had limited them to only those individuals who they felt were safe. And he could even grudgingly admit they had even picked him. He had been someone they had approved of and had given him the okay to see their daughter with their blessings . . . and also with their limitations. She was at dating age and they had wanted her to date someone they could manipulate into doing what they wanted in order to preserve their daughter's virtue. Then to top it off, they had used the old man, the one person he had admired and trusted, to come to him to solicit a promise.

Now, Megan James had more than a high IQ. She had a tremendous amount of sex appeal. It was there in the way she moved and dressed. And he didn't want to think about her body: full-sized and stacked in all the right places. Something else he'd picked up on tonight was that there was a rebellious streak about her, something wild yet feminine. She was the one taking charge of her own life and doing those things she felt she needed to do to bring a sense of normalcy into it. And it appeared that the first thing on her agenda was becoming a nonvirgin.

What if he turned her down? Did that mean she would approach some other guy since she seemed hell-bent on having the job done? Did she know what she was asking for?

Silently he stared at her and she stared back. Even with the soft lighting he could see the hardness of her nipples against the smooth fabric of her dress: a tell-tale sign of a woman aroused, or getting there. His mind was suddenly filled with memories of taking those luscious hard buds in his mouth and feasting on them. That night she had been so responsive, so filled with fire and so wet for him. A shiver ran through him when he remembered how much she liked kissing. He wondered if she remembered the kissing lesson he had given her that night.

He could feel tension vibrating across the table, touching both of them, and as he watched he saw her lips tremble and he knew that at any moment she would take her tongue and nervously lick across them. Moments later when she did, he felt a quick tightening in his gut that moved lower, causing a lot of pressure against the zipper of his jeans.

"So what have you decided, Tyler?"

Although every part of his body seemed to be in turmoil, his eyes were perfectly calm as he continued to look at her. "Do you need an answer tonight?"

She shook her head. "No, but I'd like one by the end of the week."

He nodded. That was only three days away. To say she was rushing things would be putting it mildly. There were a lot of things that he needed to think about. First of which was getting his head examined for even contemplating the idea. But as he sat there staring at her he knew one thing hadn't changed. He still wanted Megan James. Always had and probably always would. After all this time she was still under his skin. "I'll have an answer by then."

She smiled. "Thanks, Tyler."

He laughed softly. "Hey, don't thank me yet. You don't know what my answer will be."

She held his gaze intently. "No I don't," she agreed. "But at least you were willing to listen and I appreciate that," she said, reaching across the table and taking his hands in hers. "I refuse to celebrate my thirtieth birthday still a virgin. It's bad enough that I'm unmarried and childless."

She looked down at their joined hands. His were big compared to hers: big, hard, clean. His grip on her hands was gentle in contrast to the feel of his palm and calluses, which felt rough. But more than anything, she knew these hands could give her pleasure. They had done so before in a way she hadn't thought was possible. She might still be a virgin, but thanks to his hands she *had* experienced an orgasm.

"Ready to leave?"

"Yes." She made an attempt to tug her hands free but Tyler held tight as he continued to hold her gaze. Then he said, "And I want you to think about things, too, Megan. I want you to make sure you know what you're asking for. One night together can cause a whole lot of complications you might not be ready to deal with."

She frowned. What sort of complications was he referring to? If he meant birth control she planned to have that taken care of. Although she did want a child later, first things first, and her main objective was to become a full-fledged woman in Tyler Savoy's arms.

"Promise me that you'll think things through."

She sighed deeply. "I've already thought things through, Tyler. I didn't come to Alexandria with the intent of sleeping with you, but when I saw you and accepted how you still made me feel, then I knew. My reaction to other men with whom I've tried to develop relationships, emotional or physical, has proven that for my first sexual experience, I need it to be you."

He let go of her hand and slowly stood. "But still, I want you to take the next three days and be sure that you totally understand what you're asking for."

After throwing more than enough bills on the table to cover their meals, he took her hand in his again and together they left the restaurant.

Megan shot Tyler a quick look after he'd started the car to take her home. He wasn't saying much and his mouth was set in a grim but determined line. She had a sinking feeling that in three days he would turn her down. A man like Tyler probably wasn't into affairs and that's basically what she was offering him . . . a one night affair to finish what they had started eleven years ago.

When he turned on the CD player and music began, she drew in a deep appreciative breath. She couldn't stand the silence, but there hadn't been anything left to say. She had made him an offer and it was up to him to either accept or reject.

"Would you like to go out with me Saturday night?"

Megan turned and tilted her head to one side to look over at him. The car had come to a stop at a traffic light, and he was staring at her with those gorgeous eyes of his and she felt her face tint under his fierce scrutiny.

"Saturday night?" she asked, as her heart thudded against her ribs. Saturday night was three days from now . . . the day he was to give her his decision.

"Yes. Bryan and Tonya are having a party to unveil Tonya's Temptation's fall line of lingerie."

She nodded after taking a deep breath. "Sure. I'd love to go."

"Great. I'll pick you up at seven."

"All right."

She turned to stare out of the window again, letting her hands relax in her lap. She had never realized before just how much man Tyler was. When she was sixteen she had thought he was built with plenty of muscles, but now there seemed to be more of them, which meant he probably worked out a lot. That would be understandable since his cousin Nash owned a fitness center in town.

She moved her gaze over to him, glad his attention was on the road, which gave her a chance to study his broad shoulders, wide chest and flat stomach. Everything about him appeared powerful, masculine and solid.

Her heart suddenly thumped in a panic. Would she be able to handle a man the size of Tyler? Although she was no longer pencil thin like she used to be and was now wearing a size sixteen, she couldn't help wondering if her body would be able to adjust to his. Megan jerked her gaze back to the scenery out of the window. It was too late to worry about that now.

Tyler briefly took his eyes off the road to glance over at Megan. She had been staring at him moments ago, he had felt it. In fact her eyes had thoroughly skimmed his body. He had felt that, too. Even across the distance that separated them, he was beginning to feel everything about her although he wished he didn't. A woman like Megan was one that men were supposed to marry and not have affairs with. She should be engaged or married. Heaven help him, but he was glad she was neither.

He inhaled deeply knowing he needed to do some heavy-duty soul-searching and come to terms with a lot of things. In just one day Megan James had come back to town and sheathed herself in his life like she had a right to belong there, and a part of him refused to acknowledge that she didn't.

It was something that he couldn't explain when it came to the first with a man. And she had been the first woman he had ever loved and he would take his honesty one step further and admit she had been the *only* woman he had ever loved. Over the years no other female had been able to take her place in his heart, although some had definitely tried.

When Tyler finally reached the Winston ranch, he couldn't help but appreciate how the full moon cast a beam of light across the sprawling land. This is what he wanted, land and plenty of it, and if things worked out the way he hoped, he would be signing the deed to the old Palmer ranch real soon. He had talked to Keith Palmer earlier in the week and the man had no interest in moving back to Virginia to run the ranch that used to be his home. Keith had made another life for himself in Chicago, and that's where he wanted to stay, and now with both parents gone he was glad to sell it.

"Thanks for a wonderful evening, Tyler. I enjoyed myself."

He brought the car to a stop in front of the house and turned off the ignition. His gaze went over to Megan. "And I enjoyed myself as well and I'm looking forward to seeing you again Saturday night."

She smiled warmly. "Same here." She began unbuckling her seat belt. "I guess I'd better go inside."

"Hey, not so fast," he said, reaching out and touching her arm.

As soon as he touched her, a quick sizzle seemed to zap through every part of her body. With all the effort she could muster, she tried catching her breath. She was discovering that sexual chemistry was some pretty strong stuff. "Yes?" she asked, barely getting the word out.

He leaned over slightly, his eyes just inches from hers, and even in the car's darkened interior, she could see the intensity of his gaze. "I'll have an answer for you on Saturday night. And while I'm this close and personal, I might as well do what I've wanted to do all night."

Megan swallowed as Tyler inched his face a little closer. "Which is?"

"Taste you."

With that said Tyler captured her lips in his, effectively ensnarling her gasp of surprise. He needed to let her see that he was no longer the young laid-back, hands-off guy she had been involved with eleven years before. He was a full grown man who had man-size needs. If she wanted them to sleep together, then she needed to know they would probably sleep only ten percent of the time. Ninety percent would be devoted to him giving her the pleasure she had gone so long without.

Tyler heard a moan. Whether it had come from him or from Megan he wasn't sure, but it was as if the moment their mouths had touched a floodgate of pent up desire had come cascading through. He loved the way she tasted and the way he was devouring her mouth indicated that fact. Their kiss, a slow-burning, deep-in-the-gut kind, was taking him on a sensuous journey, a very passionate ride, and all he could think about was the fact that he couldn't seem to get enough of her. She didn't stand a chance against the onslaught of a greedy tongue that belonged to one hungry male. His tongue traveled the area of her mouth from top to bottom, licking, sipping and seducing.

And then something happened. Following his lead, she began seducing him back with an assault of soft lips. She wanted his taste as much as he wanted hers. He made the kiss harder, then took it deeper as everything about what they were doing incinerated his brain cells, making logical thought impossible. Never mind that they were parked in the main yard right outside the house and, even with the lateness of the hour, a ranch hand could stroll by at any time. He had to get as much of her as he could tonight, and when she continued to make whimpering sounds of pleasure, he knew that he wanted to be the only man to ever hear those sounds.

That thought restored some of his common sense, and he reluctantly pulled his mouth away from hers while she breathed his name hotly against his lips. Tyler's gaze fastened on her moist lips and he was tempted to take them again, but he pulled back, away from temptation. He watched her as she leaned her head back against the seat as if needing to get her breathing under control. He, on the other hand, was trying to get something else under control. His arousal was trying to burst through the seam of his zipper.

Several tense moments passed before he said. "We shouldn't have done that but I'm glad we did."

Megan's heart was beating so fast she wondered if it would ever slow down. She wet her lips with her tongue, still tasting him there. "Me, too, Tyler."

"And I think you'd better go inside before I decide that we need to do it again. I would walk you to the door but I don't think that's a good idea in my present state."

Megan nodded. Tyler didn't have to explain what he meant. She'd been raised on a farm and could recognize an aroused male animal—even a fine specimen like Tyler.

For the first time in her life, Megan felt naughty. She had just been kissed almost senseless by the man she had once loved and she was feeling on top of the world. A mischievous grin touched the corners of her

171

lips when she reached across his lap and boldly caressed his erection. The sound of him sucking in a deep breath made her smile. "I've been waiting for this, Tyler," she whispered. "Don't make me wait any longer."

Before Tyler could draw his next breath, Megan had opened the car door, raced up the steps and slipped into the house.

Chapter 6

"Hey, man, we're supposed to be playing a friendly game of basketball and not doing tryouts for the NBA. I've never seen you so wired up. What the hell is wrong with you?"

Tyler caught the towel his best friend, Bryan Manning, tossed over to him and wiped the sweat that was pouring down his face. Bryan was right. Instead of playing he was working off frustrations. He glanced over at Bryan who was waiting for an answer. "Megan James is back," he said, as if that explained everything. And due to his and Bryan's long history of being best friends that dated back to elementary school, he knew Bryan understood just what that meant.

"Tonya told me she saw her, and I take it from the way you're acting that you have, too," Bryan said, leaning against the steel basketball pole.

"Yeah, man, I've seen her. We even went out to dinner last night at Paddy's, and I plan to bring her to the party Saturday night."

Bryan lifted an amused brow. "You're working fast, bro."

Tyler sighed. *Not as fast as Megan would like,* he thought, remembering the proposition she had made at the restaurant.

"You use to have it for her bad, man," Bryan said, breaking into his thoughts. "But because of her grandfather, you pretty much stayed in line."

Tyler smiled, remembering those nights when he would leave the James's place and find Bryan, and the two of them would do what they were doing now. They would play a mean game of basketball to help him work off his frustrations. Now his frustrations went a lot deeper and were annoying the hell out of him, and it didn't help matters knowing Megan had offered to take care of them. If she thought she had been waiting for him, then he had news for her. He could reasonably confess that he had also been waiting for her.

He sighed deeply. He was a man whose life was totally under control; a man who knew exactly where he was going and what he was doing. But in less than twenty-four hours Megan had returned to town and had made him realize just how empty his life was. Yes, he had his family and his friends, but there was no one special in his life. He could now admit that losing Megan had left him with a place in his heart that had never been filled.

After a night of practically no sleep, he had reached the conclusion that although the grown-up, curvaceous and more voluptuous version of Megan James stirred his blood, what he felt for her went beyond the physical. She could still stir deep-rooted emotions inside of him: emotions that wanted him to love her forever.

And all she wanted was a night that would be explosive: a no strings attached affair.

"So, what do you plan on doing?"

Tyler glanced up at Bryan when he again claimed his attention. "I plan to see her a lot while she's in town. A whole lot."

He sighed deeply as he studied his best friend. Marriage definitely agreed with Bryan, and he could admit that inwardly he'd always craved his own happy ending. But deep down inside he'd known that only Megan James could give him that.

One thing a Savoy recognized was when he fell in love, and he knew that even with all the time that had passed between them, he still loved Megan James. She had been his first love and would be his last. But it seemed as if he and the woman he loved were not on the same page. She had plans for something temporary, but he could definitely see something more permanent in their future.

"Hey, I don't like that look on your face, Tyler."

Tyler chuckled as he wiped his face with the towel again. "Why? Is it because you recognize it as the same look of determination you wore when you finally came to your senses to go after Tonya?"

Bryan grinned. "Yes. So does that mean that Megan has stolen your heart a second time?"

Tyler nodded. "Yes, that's exactly what it means. I let her go once, but I don't intend on making the same mistake twice."

*   *   *

"If I haven't told you already, you look good tonight, Megan."

"Thank you, and yes, you've told me," she said. Her appreciative smile was warm, and the sudden flare of desire that her smile caused almost made Tyler lose his breath. He had picked her up at exactly seven o'clock, and now they were walking up to Bryan and Tonya's front door.

During the drive over, they had made a lot of small talk. He had come to a decision about her proposition but hadn't told her what that decision was, and she hadn't asked. But he hadn't been able to ignore the sexual chemistry that had been leaping at them, wrenching all kinds of emotions from the past, and hauling him smack into the very tempting and tantalizing present. He needed to pull himself together or he was definitely headed for trouble.

"There seems to be a crowd here tonight," Megan said, breaking into the silence and yanking him from his thoughts.

He glanced down, regarded her for a moment, thinking just how beautiful she looked tonight. The dress she was wearing was slightly longer in length than the one she'd worn the other night and didn't show as much leg and thigh, but it definitely fit her voluptuous body a lot more snugly. "That's not surprising since Tonya has such a huge clientele. But most of the people here tonight you probably know since they're from high school or grew up in the area."

She smiled. "And it will be good seeing them."

When they reached the front door and rang the

doorbell, Tyler slid his fingers down her arm and took her hand in his as if it was the most natural thing to do. The warmth of her hand in his sent those same emotions he was trying to keep a lid on spiraling, making his pulse jump and his blood race. His gaze held hers and as much as he needed to breathe, he suddenly discovered that he needed to kiss her. It was a good thing that the door opened when it did or he would have devoured her mouth then and there.

"Hey, you two, we were just wondering when you would get here," Bryan said, grinning and stepping aside to let them enter. Tyler saw the sparkle of amusement in his best friend's eyes when he noticed that he and Megan were holding hands. "The fashion show is about to begin, so you have just enough time to get something to eat and grab a seat."

Tyler's fingers tightened around Megan as he led her to the kitchen, only to be stopped by two women who remembered Megan from high school. He regarded her for a second while listening to the conversation, thinking this Megan James wasn't the introvert she once had been. She was more friendly, outgoing, and didn't seem as shy of people as she used to be. She now had the qualities of a self-assured woman. The old Megan had been too busy battling with what others thought of her and getting stressed, that she hadn't matched her peers on the level of both physical and emotional maturity. But now at twenty-nine she could definitely hold her own and was doing a damn good job of it. He liked this self-confident and sophisticated Megan.

"It was good seeing Paula and Lisa again," Megan said, breaking into his thoughts and making him realize the two women had walked off.

He smiled. "Yes, it was."

Moments later with their plates filled with a lot of mouthwatering foods, they reentered the living room to find a place to sit. There was only one spot left on the sofa, and without saying anything, Tyler claimed that spot by sitting down then gently pulling her down into his lap.

He smiled at her surprised expression. "We'll improvise and let one spot serve for two," he said.

Megan couldn't help but smile back as she shifted her body to sit comfortably. Knowing that she was sitting in his lap wasn't helping matters. Beneath her his body felt hard, solid, enticing. She kept her eyes straight ahead, wondering what others thought of her sitting in Tyler's lap. There were other women who were sitting in men's laps as well, but she figured they were couples and not two people who *used* to be considered a couple years ago. She wondered if others assumed since she and Tyler were together tonight that they were renewing their romance?

"You okay?" Tyler asked, whispering in her ear. His warm breath, so close to her skin, was making her pulse escalate.

She turned to him, almost touching his lips in the process and sending a whole new type of hunger pangs through her. She swallowed deeply. "Yes, I'm fine."

"Then turn your body slightly toward me so I can feed you."

When she lifted her brow he smiled and said. "With you sitting in my lap it will be easier. That way I can feed both of us without making a mess."

She nodded and slightly shifted her body to give him a better angle of her mouth; a mouth she couldn't help but notice he was staring at real hard.

"Open up," he coaxed in a deep, low, husky tone, and when she did, he placed an egg roll to her lips and she took a bite of it.

Umm, she thought it was delicious and couldn't help but notice how intent he was on watching her chew it, as she savored each bite.

"You like that?" he asked in the same low, husky tone.

Unable to speak, she nodded her head. "Then I guess I'd better try it."

She watched as he bit off that same egg roll and just like she had done, he chewed it, savored it. She wondered if watching her eat had turned him on like she was getting turned on watching him eat. She had her answer when he shifted in his seat and she felt him. His body had been hard before but she now felt a certain part of him get harder. She might be a virgin, but she definitely knew what that particular hardness meant.

Without saying anything he continued to feed both of them until soft jazzy music began playing and she knew the fashion show was about to begin. Megan decided to get her mind off of Tyler for a moment by glancing around to check out her surroundings. She loved the layout of Bryan and Tonya's home. The two-story structure was spacious and roomy and big enough to hold a fashion show for a limited number of guests.

The outfit the first model wore really caught her eye. It was a two-piece zebra print with soft feminine roses. The gasps from the other women meant she wasn't the only one who found the outfit stunning. Megan knew immediately it was an outfit she just had to have.

Another outfit that caught her eye was a three-piece set filled with rich vibrant colors of maroon, orange and gold; perfect for fall and perfect for lounging in at bedtime, and the matching kimono-styled robe that completed the set made it something she definitely wanted. She made a note to purchase that outfit as well.

All the outfits being modeled were simply stunning and Megan couldn't help but appreciate Tonya for having the insight to create a lingerie company whose products included sizes for full-figured women.

"Did you see anything you like?" Tyler asked her when the fashion show ended half an hour later. She slowly stood up, thinking she had used his lap long enough. He automatically took her hand in his again.

"Yes, I liked everything but there are two items in particular I plan to purchase tonight." Again Megan couldn't help but wonder if Tyler realized that being together would cause talk, and the way he was touching her would only double it. But she could handle the talk if he could.

"I'll discard our trash and then talk to Bryan while you go select the outfits you want," he said, releasing her hand.

She smiled up at him. "Okay. It shouldn't take long." And then she turned and walked off, thinking she definitely needed distance away from Tyler for a while before more illicit thoughts rammed through her mind. Her skin was already tingling all over and her lower belly had begun aching.

A need she had never known before had taken root inside of her and was being nurtured each and every time Tyler touched her, looked at her, or breathed on her. The only thing she could think about was that tonight she would get an answer from Tyler. It was destined to be another long hot week in Alexandria, and with two more weeks to go she hoped she could survive the heat.

Chapter 7

Megan raised an arched brow at Tonya. "What do you mean these outfits are already paid for?"

Tonya, who had boxed up the two items Megan had selected, handed them to her smiling. "Tyler mentioned this morning that any outfit you saw and wanted was yours and he would pay for them. If you have any questions about it then I suggest you go talk to him." Tonya then chuckled. "Now scat. You're holding up the line, which means you're standing in the way of my profits."

Megan shook her head grinning, and accepted the two beautifully gift-wrapped boxes from Tonya. "Okay, I *will* go and talk to Tyler about it." She appreciated him wanting to make the purchases for her, but she wasn't used to men buying her sleepwear.

After leaving the bedroom where Tonya, her mother and a couple of the other women in the Savoy family had an assembly line going to take care of everyone's purchases, she went looking for Tyler. She saw him standing across the room doing exactly what he'd said he would be doing, which was talking to Bryan.

Before crossing the room to where he stood, she decided to study him while he wasn't aware he was being watched. A soft warmth flooded her heart and quickly spread to all parts of her body as she recalled that at fifteen, when she had first seen him, she had thought the seventeen-year old Tyler Savoy had been the answer to her prayers, and now as she looked at him she knew he was also the answer to a lot of other things as well.

He was wearing a pair of black slacks and a light colored pullover shirt, and as she took in the well-defined muscles of his broad chest and shoulders, she thought the coloring of the outfit accentuated his dark good looks as well as his hazel eyes. He looked scrumptious and as delectable as that piece of cake he had fed to her earlier.

Something, possibly the suspicion that someone was staring at him, made Tyler glance around the room before his gaze met hers. The moment their eyes locked, a bolt of intense awareness streaked through her and she couldn't help wondering if he'd felt it as well. His hazel-colored eyes were riveting, sexy and at the moment they were intensely holding hers. The moment stretched out between them, and it became obvious that whatever Bryan was saying no longer was holding his attention. The way he was looking at her made her feel like she was the only person in the room. The only one who mattered. The moment stretched and with each passing second she tried catching her breath and worked to slow down her racing heart. And the only thing she could think of was that if Tyler refused to be the first man to make love to her, heaven help her because more than anything, she wanted to get it on with Tyler Savoy.

Tyler continued to watch Megan as his mind raced over the possibilities. He hadn't given her his answer to her proposition, but he knew what it would be. After a less than normal childhood, if anyone deserved unconditional happiness it was Megan. And there was no way he would allow another man to make love to her.

From across the room he felt the strong chemistry radiating between them, and then of its own accord, his gaze moved to her lips and he remembered how the other night he had brushed them lightly with his own before delving into the sweet depths that had awaited him.

"I hate being ignored, Tyler," Bryan said, interrupting his thoughts.

Tyler chuckled, but didn't stop looking at Megan. "Then I think I'd better say good night because I don't see any hope for it. I'll call you tomorrow."

Without giving his best friend a glance, he walked off toward Megan where she stood holding the two boxes firmly in her hands. "Did you get everything you wanted?" he asked when he came to a stop in front of her.

"Yes, but you didn't have to buy them for me, Tyler."

Taking the boxes from her, his fingers curled around

hers. "It's done, so consider them early birthday presents."

He watched as a smile tilted the corners of her mouth. "If I recall, your birthday is in ten days, so what am I supposed to get you?"

He stepped closer to her and whispered. "Another date with you will suffice," he said smiling. "Now are you ready to leave before Tonya decides that two purchases aren't enough?"

When she nodded, still holding her hand as well as her packages, he led her to the door.

"I've never gone parking with a guy before but I used to hear a lot about this place," Megan said as she smiled over at Tyler. After leaving the Mannings he had asked if she'd ever gone up to Lover's Peak, where couples used to go to make out. Unfortunately, it was on private land so there had always been the risk of getting caught.

When Tyler didn't say anything but continued to watch her silently, she decided to keep on talking to ward off her nervousness. The moment he had brought the car to a stop he had turned off the ignition and shifted in his seat and just sat there staring at her. "I heard that Mr. Palmer would scare off any teenagers he would find up here," she said.

When Tyler still didn't contribute his two cents she added. "I also heard Mr. and Mrs. Palmer died last year within months of each other. That must have been hard on their son."

"It was."

Megan blinked, not believing that Tyler had finally said something. "You still keep in contact with him? I remember the two of you were good friends in high school."

"Yes, Keith and I still stay in contact." He decided not to mention that in a week's time this particular piece of land, including Lover's Peak, would belong to him. The only persons who knew about the pending transaction were his family. He didn't want word to get out until the papers had been signed.

When Tyler became silent again, Megan's pulse started racing once more. She searched her brain for anything they could talk about then remembered something Tonya had mentioned tonight. "Canada," she said in an almost quiet voice.

After staring silently at her for several long moments he asked in a deep husky tone. "What about it?"

"I understand that you recently went there. How was it?"

She watched as he leaned closer then reached out and cupped her face into his hands. She began drowning in the masculine scent of him as his finger slowly caressed her cheek. "I'll tell you later. Right now I just want to kiss you," he whispered, before placing a gentle kiss across her lips.

Gentle was only short-term in Tyler's mind, because the moment a sigh escaped Megan's lips, he deepened the kiss and she willingly opened her mouth to his probing tongue. This had to be the most desirable woman he had ever known, he thought, as he continued to make love to her mouth; needing her taste as much as he needed his next breath. But he knew deep down that what he was sharing with her went way beyond the physical. He was falling in love with her all over again and there wasn't a damn thing he could do about it. Except . . . take her down with him. He was determined to make sure she realized what he had come to grips with earlier today. After all these years they belonged together.

He felt the tips of her nipples harden against his chest and felt the pounding of her heart as well. The purring sound she was making was more erotic than anything he had ever heard, and he felt his body getting harder by the minute. Deciding that if he kissed her for even a minute longer he would lose control, he slowly pulled away.

"Why did you stop?" she asked in a harsh whisper as a sensuous pout formed on her lips. He wanted to lean over and kiss her again but knew they needed to talk first.

He suddenly sucked in a sharp breath when she reached out and touched him and slowly began tugging at his zipper. Evidently she had remembered that his one weakness was her hand touching a certain part of him.

"Are you sure you want to stop?" she whispered softly, leaning over and taking her tongue and tracing the outlines of his lips. Tyler's heartbeat accelerated as a thrill of pleasure shot through him. "No, I'm not sure, but unless you want your first time in the back-seat of a car, I suggest you keep your hands to yourself."

"Umm, if I must," she said softly, and all the while

with deliberate slowness she was easing down his zipper . . . or at least she was trying to. The thought of her actually succeeding in what she was trying to do, which would result in her holding his aroused sex in her hand, was too much to think about.

Tyler shook his head. Megan James was becoming a lot more temptation than he ever thought possible. Heaven help him but he was definitely headed for trouble. "Yes, keep your hands to yourself or I'm taking you home for misbehaving."

Megan smiled. Evidently his tone of voice wasn't too convincing. "If that's what you want."

No, that wasn't what he wanted, but he had to make her believe that it was. "Yes, that's what I want," he said, taking her hand off of him and guiding it to her lap and placing it there. He stared at her hand resting in her lap for a moment before lowering his gaze to her crossed legs and especially to where her dress ended, showing the dark, smooth flesh of one of her thighs. He was tempted to reach out and stroke her the same as she had wanted to stroke him.

"If you're not going to let my first time be in the backseat, does that mean you're going to make sure I do have a first time someplace else?"

Tyler raised his gaze from her legs back to her face. The nymph was grinning. She knew she had him tied in knots and was loving every minute of his torture, but he was determined to make her suffer for it. "If that's your way of asking if I've made some rather important decisions regarding us, then the answer is yes. If your offer is still out there then I intend to be your man."

She leaned forward and her lips came within inches of his. "The offer is still out there and I definitely want you to be my man, Tyler."

Damn, he hoped she meant it, because he didn't intend for there to be another man in her life. Ever. But first Megan needed to understand that for the next two weeks she would have to play by his rules and his rules only.

"I'm glad to hear that," he said huskily, tempted, very tempted to capture her mouth and feast on her tongue again. Now that he had decided he would make love to her, how was he going to keep his hands off of her until she realized what he felt was more than physical? At this very moment all he could think about was hot bodies, tangled sheets and very busy hands and mouths.

He watched her lips part and deciding, what the hell, since temptation at the moment was too strong, he inched closer and clamped his mouth over hers in demanding possession. This time the kiss went deeper and was more urgent than before. He was becoming totally intoxicated with the flavor of her mouth and the rich, sensuous texture of her tongue. He could stay here and kiss her all night, but he knew that eventually kissing wouldn't be enough.

Slowly, he released her mouth and pulled away. Seeing another pout on her face, he closed his eyes momentarily and willed himself to regain control. When he opened his eyes she was watching him, and the deep look of desire in her eyes wasn't helping matters.

"Like I was about to say before I became distracted," he said in a low, husky voice. "I have certain rules you need to follow."

He watched her arched brow lift. "Rules?"

He drew in a deep breath and released it slowly before answering. "Yes. For us to make love will be the final step, but before we reach that point there are other things that we need to do."

She eyed him steadily and at the same time he felt her touch a finger to his thigh, no doubt trying to make him lose control again. "Things like what?"

He reached down and captured her hand in his, deciding to stop her from going any further. "A courtship."

Now he watched as both of her brows went up. "A courtship?"

He inwardly smiled. Evidently she'd assumed they would meet at a hotel tomorrow night and just get it on. Well, he had news for her. He had two weeks to prove to her that there was more between them than just the physical. "Yes, a courtship." He could tell by her expression that she was reasonably confused.

"But why?" she asked, clearly not understanding.

"Because technically we've never courted, and I think it should be a prelude to any man and woman sharing a bed. I'm not into one night affairs, Megan. You might have been my first girlfriend but we never got around to doing things most couples did. Now we have a chance to do them and I think that we should. I want to experience things with you, take you places, have fun, and then in the end if you're sure you still want me physically then—"

"I'll still want you," she quickly said, squashing any notion that she wouldn't.

"We'll see." He met her gaze and held it for a long time. "So, are you willing to play by my rules?"

She nodded. "Yes, if you really want to do this courtship thing."

"I do."

Megan told herself not to let the thought that Tyler didn't want to rush them sleeping together bother her. In a way she guessed she should be glad that he wanted to take the time to do other things with her before they actually slept together. Most men wouldn't bother. "Are we through talking?"

"Yes, we're finished."

The hunger she saw in his eyes made her heart race and heat settle right smack in her middle. "It's still early yet, and I'm not ready to go home, Tyler."

Tyler's hand tightened into fists as he tried not to reach out and haul her across the seat and into his arms. Those were the same words she had spoken to him thirteen years ago. "You're not?"

"No."

"Would you like to talk some more then?"

Megan shook her head. "Preferably not."

Tyler's heart began hammering wildly in his chest and he felt his body get harder. "Then give me an idea what you want to do." He flashed a grin when he added. "Excluding going all the way."

She leaned forward. "Is there such a thing as *almost* going all the way?"

He nodded. "Yes, that's what we did on prom night. We came as close as it gets."

She smiled remembering. She also recalled they had gotten completed naked. But more than anything she remembered how she had come apart in his arms while experiencing her first and only orgasm. Even then Tyler's brand of foreplay had been out of this world. She didn't want to think about how it would be now. "Then let's do it again."

Thinking that wouldn't be such a bad idea, he reached out for her a second before his cell phone rang. Giving her an apologetic smile, he answered it.

Megan only heard part of the conversation, but she knew an emergency had come up and she wouldn't be getting the second orgasm of her life tonight. When he hung up the phone she spoke before he could say anything. "Duty calls, right?"

He nodded regretfully. "Right. There's an emergency out at the Bailey's place, so it seems I'll be taking you on home after all."

Disappointed, she settled back in her seat and put on her seat belt, thinking there would be a next time. There had to be and she would be ready.

Chapter 8

"Flowers for Megan James."

Megan stared at the man standing in the doorway. Over the past three days she had gotten flowers every single day. She wondered if Tyler realized that he was plying this courtship thing on a little too thick.

She reached out and took the flowers from the man she remembered as owning a flower shop in town. "Thanks."

The man rubbed his chin as he studied her. "You must be mighty special to Tyler Savoy. I don't recall him ever doing business with us before, and if he keeps this up, he'll become one of our best customers."

She smiled at the man. "Thanks again and here's your tip."

"You're welcome and I'll see you again tomorrow," he said, turning to leave like it was a foregone conclusion that he would be delivering more flowers to her. She sighed as he closed the door.

"More flowers, Megan?"

Megan turned around and met Florence Baker's curious gaze. "Yes, aren't they beautiful, just like the others?"

Florence chuckled. "Yes. Tyler Savoy has good taste and it seems there's more on his mind lately than taking care of animals. Thelma ought to be overjoyed."

Megan frowned. "About what?"

"About the fact that Tyler is evidently interested in you again. From what his grandmother told me the other night at church, the two of you used to be boyfriend and girlfriend some years ago."

"Yes, but now we're just friends and nothing more," Megan said, placing the vase of beautiful cut flowers next to the others on the table after reading the card. The room was filled with a beautiful fragrance.

Florence snorted like she didn't believe her. "Well, it must be some kind of friendship that makes a man send a woman flowers every day."

Megan said nothing as she watched Florence leave the room. When Tyler had first mentioned the courtship part of their relationship, she had become hesitant for this very reason. People would start getting ideas about them. They would quickly assume there was more going on than there really was.

She was about to go outside and check on things when the phone rang. She quickly crossed the room and picked it up. "Hello."

"How's my girl?"

Megan's breath caught. Tyler's greeting was the one he'd always used when he saw her years ago. She *had* been "his girl" and very proud of it.

"I'm doing fine, what about you?"

"I can't complain. We're still on for dinner tonight, right?"

She smiled. "Yes and thanks for the flowers again. You shouldn't have."

"Maybe, but I wanted to. You're special."

"Thanks." And he was making her feel special. In fact that's what he wrote each time on the card that accompanied the flowers. *You're special.* "I'll be ready when you get here."

"Okay, I'll see you at seven."

After hanging up the phone, Megan smiled. She couldn't wait to see him again.

"Sounds like you've been quite busy today at the Richardson's place," Megan said, as she sipped her wine.

Tyler chuckled. "I have and I appreciate this time when I can relax."

Megan smiled. He had picked her up exactly at seven and they had driven into DC for dinner at B. Smith's, a restaurant that was located on the east side of Union Station and that was simply elegant. The huge room that used to be home to US presidents waiting for their trains was now one of the most successful restaurants in Washington. It was well known that the owner was a former model and a friend to nearly every celebrity you could think of. That was evident in the numerous photographs that lined one section of the restaurant's wall.

She and Tyler had enjoyed a wonderful dinner of lemon pepper catfish and a very tasty salad. Since they were still full they had both declined dessert. Tyler leaned back in his chair and looked at her. "So, what are your plans when you return to California?"

Megan shrugged. Already she was regretting having to leave. This was the longest period of time she had spent in Alexandria over the years and she hadn't realized just how much she'd missed being home. It seemed that every time she went out she would run into someone she'd known. "I'll have another month before the semester starts and I plan on taking it easy. I've enjoyed being home."

Tyler nodded. "You ever thought of moving back?"

His question surprised her, but Megan decided not to tell him she had thought about it that very day. "Why do you ask?"

"Because with your credentials I bet you could get a job teaching at any of the universities around here with no problem. And I'd think your mother would want you living closer to home now that your father and grandfather are gone."

Megan smiled. She had thought of that, too. But her mother had Winston now, and she knew he loved her mother very much and would make her happy.

"And then there are the grandkids?"

Megan looked perplexed as she stared at Tyler. "What grandkids?"

"The ones I'm sure you're going to have one day. At some point your mother would want to see them more often than once a year."

Megan frowned, wondering where Tyler was going with all of this. "Tyler," she leaned over the table and whispered. "Let me take care of being a virgin first before you make me a mother."

He reached out and tucked a strand of hair back that had fallen in her face and whispered, his voice low and husky. "Umm, that's not a bad idea."

She lifted a brow. "What?"

"For me to make you a mother."

His words caused the embers that had been smoldering low in her belly all evening to spark into flames and scorch her insides. It had always been her dream to give birth to a son or daughter who had their father's hazel eyes. Her and Tyler's babies. And for him to speak her innermost desire out loud almost made her ache for the possibility. "Would you even consider it if I wanted that to happen, Tyler?" she couldn't help asking. The way his eyes were holding her captive was making all her senses meld together.

Tyler decided now was not the time to let her know that not only had he considered it, he planned to make it happen one day. But she was right. They had to take care of this virginity thing first; however, he wasn't ready to let the subject rest. "Yes, I'd consider it, but what about your husband?"

She blinked. "What husband?"

"Don't you plan on ever getting married? Usually baby making is something a husband and wife do together."

She shrugged. "The same thing can be said about lovemaking. It's something a husband and wife are supposed to do together, too."

He nodded. "Yes, that's true, so what does that

mean? Are you suggesting that to do things right we should get married so we can make love and have a baby?" he asked, as a smile curled his lips."

A sudden and intense pull tugged at Megan's heart. She didn't want to admit it, but over the last couple of days her mind had been playing a game of *what ifs,* and the main thought that kept flowing through her mind was . . . what if she moved back to Alexandria, took a job at one of the universities and she and Tyler reignited their romance, eventually resulting in marriage and babies.

"Megan?"

When he said her name she realized he still had a question out there and was waiting for an answer. She knew she had to be fair to him and stop things right here. It wouldn't be right to place him in a position that would make him feel that on top of everything else, he owed her marriage as well. "Of course not, Tyler. I'm sure you have an idea of what you want in a wife, and I'm sure I'm far from it."

He looked at her strangely, as if pondering what she'd said. "And just what type of woman do you think I'd want?"

She shrugged again. "Tall with a model figure, a perfect ten, all legs, medium-sized breasts, small waist. The way I used to be." Regret burned her cheeks. She hadn't meant to add that last part. Now she would keep her mouth shut for the rest of the evening. Not wanting to look at Tyler, she began studying the wine in her glass.

"Megan," Tyler whispered, leaning forward to make sure he had her attention. "If that's the type of woman you figure I want, then why is my body at the point of losing control for wanting you so much? If you had any idea just what you do to me, you wouldn't be sitting there as calmly as you are knowing I've considered clearing the table and taking you right on it."

He knew his words had probably shocked her, but she needed to know what she was dealing with here. There was no way he would let her think that she wasn't what he wanted. Whispering lower still he added, "I'd do just about anything to take you somewhere and get you naked. You don't know how often I've fantasized about those luscious looking hips of yours, and how those dresses, like the one you have on now, mold to every conceivable crease and curve you have. And if that's not bad enough, I now know your scent. It's distinctive, intoxicating and arousing."

Megan's body responded to Tyler's words, making her feel dizzy, breathless. No man had ever said such things to her before. She was satisfied with her size but had figured a man like Tyler would want a certain type of woman—but he had just let her know that without a doubt he was attracted to her, voluptuous body and all. And she knew he wasn't just saying what he thought she wanted to hear. There was so much sincerity in the way he was looking at her that a special warmth spread all the way through her.

She leaned across the table toward him and whispered, "If you want to take me somewhere and get me naked then what's stopping you?"

"The realization that you're not ready for that part of a relationship with me."

Megan's brow furrowed. As far as she was concerned she was more than ready and had been ready since the first day he had arrived on the ranch. "What makes you think that?"

"Because I do, and that's all I'm going to say on the matter. You will have to figure out the rest on your own."

She was about to ask him what there was to figure out when the waiter brought them their bill. Tyler then glanced at his watch. "Come on. I need to get you home. I have to fly to Philadelphia early tomorrow."

"Will you be gone long?"

He started to tell her that when he usually went to Philadelphia once a month to rotate his services at the zoo there, he was usually gone for a couple of days. But this was one time he intended to go and come back in the same day. "No, I won't be gone long. I plan to come back tomorrow night."

She nodded, missing him already. "I hope you have a safe trip."

He smiled. "Thanks."

The ride back to the ranch was done mostly in silence. She was hoping he would take her to Lover's Peak again and strip her naked, and was somewhat disappointed when she saw that he was taking her back home. But he did walk her to the door and the kiss he gave her was so incredibly gentle it almost brought tears to her eyes. When she tried to deepen it, he reluctantly pulled away.

"Don't tempt me, Megan," he growled quietly near her ear. He took a step back. "I'll call you when I return. Go on inside before I do something I might later regret."

She did as he requested and then stood at the window and watched as he drove off. She sighed deeply. She knew she was falling in love with Tyler all over again and had known it for weeks. If she was completely honest with herself, she would admit she had known ever since she had seen him that day tending Moonshine. Now she had less than two weeks before she returned to California and she wondered what, if anything, she was going to do about it.

Chapter 9

Megan sat on the wooden fence and watched a ranch hand attempt to break in one of the horses. Although she was seeing everything being played out before her, her mind was elsewhere as she remembered the reason Tyler had given as to why they hadn't made love.

"You're not ready for that part of a relationship with me."

A week had passed since Tyler had made that comment and she still didn't understand why he would think that way. They had seen each other practically every day, going on picnics together, she had accompanied him around to visit a couple of his sick animals and they had gone to the movies with Bryan and Tonya. They'd also had Sunday dinner at his grandmother's house, which Megan had thoroughly enjoyed. The only place they hadn't gone back to was Lover's Peak. And every day another vase of flowers was delivered to her.

Her heart fluttered at the sound of a vehicle pulling up. She turned, hoping it was Tyler dropping by unexpectedly. It wasn't Tyler but it was Tonya, and she was glad to see her. She and Tyler's cousin had become good friends over the past weeks and she enjoyed the woman's company and friendship. While growing up she hadn't had a lot of friends, especially other women whom she could talk to.

She jumped down off the fence and walked to the car to meet Tonya. "Hey, what brings you out this way?" she asked, giving her a huge hug.

"I had to make a delivery to Mrs. Collins and decided to stop by," Tonya replied, smiling. "How are things going?"

Megan shrugged. "They're going fine. Come on inside and let me pour you some ice tea to cool off."

Tonya chuckled. "That's sounds great."

Moments later, as soon as Tonya and Megan entered the house, Tonya stopped and glanced around. She then whispered to Megan, "Who died?"

Megan chuckled, understanding why Tonya had asked such a question. "No one. These are flowers Tyler sent me."

Tonya raised a brow. "Tyler sent all of these?" she asked, clearly astonished.

Megan grinned. "Yes, and aren't they beautiful? A different bouquet arrives each day."

Tonya shook her head, laughing and giggling. "I don't believe this. I've never known Tyler to woo any woman."

Megan smiled as she led Tonya through the living room and into the kitchen. "Tyler isn't trying to woo me. We're just good friends."

Tonya began laughing again as she sat down at the

table. "If you really believe friendship has anything to do with those flowers then you really don't know Tyler."

Megan lifted a brow after pulling the pitcher of tea from the refrigerator. "What does that mean?"

Tonya met her gaze steadily. "It means you need to wake up and really smell some of those roses in there. If Tyler sent you those flowers, then he is trying to tell you something. Maybe it's time you listened."

And hour or so later after Tonya left, Megan was still pondering her words. Coming back inside after riding one of the horses around the ranch, she glanced over at all the flowers adorning the living room. Was Tyler actually trying to tell her something, not only with the flowers but also with this courtship thing he was determined that they do?

She walked over and pulled off the card of the flowers that had arrived that day. It said the same thing the others did. *You're special.* Was he trying to show her the depth of just how special he thought she was? Was that the message he'd been trying to get her to see all this time?

She sat on the sofa and recalled what they had shared for the past two weeks and, no matter what, he'd always been the perfect gentleman and had brought her straight home from their dates. But she'd known he had wanted her, and on many nights he had fought for control when she'd gotten the best of him and had tried taking his chaste good-night kiss in another direction.

Sighing she suddenly realized something that she had forgotten, something very elemental about Tyler

Savoy. He was a man who'd been raised to do the proper thing. He never would, and she doubted if he could, take anything between them lightly. Ridding her of her virginity meant more to him than being a one time episode. His need to do things right by her outweighed any physical needs he had because he loved her.

He loved her. Just like she loved him.

Tears misted Megan's eyes when she finally realized why he thought she wasn't ready for that part of a relationship with him. He wanted to be sure that she understood the depth of what making love meant, and until she did he would continue to deny himself . . . and deny her.

Sighing she walked over to the phone, picked it up and punched in Tonya's number. A few moments later after hearing Tonya's voice she said. "I've smelled the roses and got Tyler's message. Now I need your help."

The huge vase of flowers was the first thing Tyler noticed when he walked into his house late that evening. He had met with the bankers in Baltimore that day, and after waiting for Keith, whose plane had been delayed, they had finalized all the paperwork that made him the rightful owner of the Palmer's ranch.

He frowned as he walked over to the flowers that sat in the middle of his table, and wondered who sent them and how they had gotten inside his house. For emergency reasons some members of his family had access to his home but so far none had ever done so. He pulled off the card that was addressed to him and read it. *You're special.*

A twinge of uneasiness hit Tyler between the ribs and he slowly turned around and surveyed his surroundings. And then he saw a trail of clothes that led from his living room toward his bedroom. After taking a few steps Tyler reached down and picked up a black bra. Not far away he retrieved a black half slip and in the hall area, directly in front of his bedroom door, was a pair of sexy black panties.

He lifted his brow as he stood in the doorway of his bedroom. Someone was definitely in his bed and from the looks of things she was still there and unquestionably naked.

"What's going on here, Megan?" he asked, barely able to get the words out. Although she was covered completely by the bedspread, she looked so good in his bed, as if she didn't belong anywhere else. And her scent was all over the place, mingling with the scent of the vanilla candles she'd lit. Evidently she'd heard him enter the house and was propped in bed waiting. Refusing to meet her gaze, he glanced around the room. In addition to the candles, soft music was playing. It was so soft he could barely hear it, which probably was the reason he hadn't heard it when he'd walked in the house. Her sundress was thrown over his recliner and a box of condoms, a huge box at that, was sitting next to the bed on the nightstand.

Seeing that his eyes were glued to the box, he heard her say, "The use of those is optional. You can take my virginity and give me a baby at the same time if you want."

His gaze snapped to her and he leaned against the

doorjamb trying to get his bearings. "I can?" he asked, his voice low and husky.

He head her soft chuckle. "Oh, from the looks of things, I definitely say, yes, you can."

He saw that her eyes had traveled the full length of him and had come to rest on the zipper of his jeans. It was evident for anyone to see that he was fully aroused.

Tyler shook his head. This was not how he intended for things to go. She was breaking the rules. "What are you doing here, Megan?"

When she stretched in bed, making the bedcovers dip low enough to see the top of her breasts, a hot erotic sensation seared through him. "Do you want me to tell you the truth," she asked softly, from lips that were wet and full of promise. He felt his body get harder the same moment his guts clenched.

"Yes," he said, nearly hypnotized as heat spiked through them. "I want you to tell me the truth."

Almost in a daze he watched as she pushed the covers back and a very naked Megan got out of bed and strolled, in the most erotic walk he'd ever seen, toward him. He tried not to notice how large and firm her breasts were or how her small waist curved into a pair of voluptuous hips—childbearing hips. But he couldn't keep his eyes off the area below her navel. He thought she was beautiful beyond words all over, but there . . . in that particular spot . . . it was his opinion she was undeniably so.

Every instinct he possessed told him to run, get the hell out of there, but he stood seemingly glued to the floor with his gaze latched on to her. He swallowed when she came to a stop in front of him.

"Okay, if you want honesty then here it is," she said softly. "The reason I'm here, Tyler, is to seduce you."

He blinked, astounded that she would admit such a thing. "Megan," he said hoarsely, trying to catch his breath and trying more than anything to do the right thing although she was definitely making it hard. "I want you to put on your clothes and I'll take you home." He wondered how she had gotten there in the first place since there wasn't a car outside. "You're not ready for this yet."

He suddenly felt a tug and she reached out and eased down his zipper. "Umm, I beg to differ. I've been ready for this."

When she reached inside his pants and cupped him he knew all control was lost, and although he knew he had to try to stop her, at the moment he felt too weak to resist. "I didn't want things to happen this way."

She met his gaze. "Why?" she asked while stroking him, and sending his mind on an erotic spin. "Don't you think I know the difference between the emotional and the physical side of things?"

"Do you?" he asked, barely able to get the words out. If he didn't get her hand off him he was going to embarrass them both, but her stroking felt so good.

"Yes, Tyler, I know the difference but I want to show you that when it comes to us there isn't a difference. They are one and the same. I know you love me and I know that I love you and—"

He reached out and stilled her hand. "What did you say?"

She met his gaze. "I said I know you love me."

"And?"

She smiled. "And that I love you."

He momentarily closed his eyes then reopened them. "Do you?"

She nodded. "Yes, I love you with all my heart, and now I understand what you were trying to tell me with the flowers and the courting. I know that you wanted me to know when we got into bed together that there was more between us than sexual satisfaction. I know that, Tyler."

His heart lunged in his chest and he pulled her into his arms, capturing her mouth with his, claiming her completely and kissing her with an intensity he'd held back the last two weeks. His tongue thrust deep, mating with a hunger that displayed just how much he needed her taste. Kissing her this way felt good but it wasn't enough, and when she wrapped her arms around him and sank her naked body deeper into his arms, he became aware that a certain part of him was exposed and, as if it had a will of its own, the hard length of him settled against her stomach.

Tyler groaned softly as he fought for control. He had to do something or else he would take her right there, now, standing up. He slowly pulled back from the kiss and, after shoving a certain body part back inside his pants, he whispered, "If you're sure about everything maybe we ought to get in the bed, what do you think?"

The eyes that were looking at him were filled with so much desire it made him inhale sharply. And it didn't help matters when she burrowed her hands underneath his shirt and caressed his bare skin with the tips of her fingernails, sending all kinds of sensations rocketing through him. "I'm sure about everything and yes, I think we ought to get into bed," she said, slowly walking backward and taking him with her. And when she got to the bed she lay back and pulled him down on top of her.

Megan then became the aggressor as she kissed him the way a woman in love was supposed to kiss a man. He had on too many clothes, but for now she was satisfied with just making love to his mouth, enjoying the level they were able to take their kiss. Gone were the gentle kisses they had shared. Now their kisses were hot, spicy, tongue-licking good.

"Megan," Tyler whispered, breaking off the kiss and trying to get his breath. He knew that if he didn't take care of the issue of protection he could be a father in nine months. Pulling back and leaning up, he knew that first he needed to touch her and taste her.

Reaching out he flattened his hand against her stomach, a stomach that would one day carry his child. He then slid his hand upward to her breasts, taking each in the palm of his hand, teasing the nipples between his fingers while thinking about how his children would one day take them into their mouths. He was suddenly hit with a need to be inside of her, to be joined as one with her.

Reluctantly pulling away, he stood to remove his clothes, watching her all the while he was doing so and seeing her watch him. The need and wanting he saw in her eyes had his body throbbing. And when he stood before her completely naked, the look of feminine appreciation in her gaze nearly took his breath away.

"You're beautiful, Tyler," Megan said, not knowing another word to describe him. Her body tingled all over and her nerves were stretched in anticipation. That area between her legs clenched and was becoming unbearably hot. She felt heavy, limp and filled with so much desire she couldn't believe he was actually standing there and wasn't a figment of her imagination.

"Make love to me, Tyler." She heard the words pour softly from her lips and when he took a step, coming closer to the bed and back to her, she reached out and caressed him, unable to keep her hands from wandering all over him, touching his chest, stomach and particularly that part of him she wanted.

"I need to put a condom on, Megan," he said, huskily, before going about doing the task. "We'll do things right and start making babies after we're married."

She nodded, not sure she could open her mouth to emit any sound other than a purr.

When he joined her back in bed, he gathered her into his arms and kissed her again, and when he pulled away he began kissing her neck and shoulders while telling her over and over that he loved her. The whisper of his heated breath on her skin as well as his tongue tracing a slow path downward, made a rush of sensations zing through her. This is what she had waited twenty-nine years to experience, and only with this man.

Tyler heard his name escape as a moan from Megan's lips. The tiny whimpers that followed sounded like music playing in his head. He knew just where he wanted to go next and slowly continued his trek downward. He felt her body tense up when he kissed the area around her naval, and knew the type of lovemaking he was about to do was something new for her, a first that he wanted her to experience with him.

When he saw she was pulling her legs together and trying to push him away he raised his head, met her gaze and whispered, "It's okay for me to taste you here. Please let me."

And she did.

Sensations Megan had never experienced before in her life ripped through her with this special brand of intimacy Tyler was giving her. It seemed that hard forces of sensations were hitting her at once, from every angle, in magnitudes of degrees, sharpening every erotic zone on her body with excruciating intensity. And she had to let go, or die from so much pleasure. She felt her body shatter into a thousand pieces yet he didn't let up as he continued to carry her to unbelievable heights as every cell in her body became electrified.

It was then, and only then that he eased up her body, moved in place over her. She could feel the heat from his skin and saw how his pulse throbbed through the arteries in his neck. Then she knew what the past couple of weeks had cost him. How much control he had endured.

Knowing what he had sacrificed to make sure she understood the depth of his love touched her. She reached up and traced the lines around his forehead, feeling how tense he was. Then she slowly traced the lines around his eyes and lips. She twined her legs with his, needing the contact. Their gazes locked and she whispered as she slid her hands down his back and buttocks, "Come inside me, Tyler. Make love to me. Now!"

She felt his muscles clench under her palms. She felt him ease downward slowly inside of her and this time unlike before she intended for them to complete what they started here. Boldly arching her body and lifting her hips, she met him as he pushed forward and when he met with resistance she saw the lines of his forehead deepen and sweat dampen his brow.

"It's okay, Tyler. The pain will be worth it. Do it. Please make me yours."

And he did.

She gasped at the feel of the sharp pain but it eased with the feel of him bedded deep inside of her. She smiled. They were a perfect fit. Then he began to move in and out, deep, steady, thrusting over and over.

She felt a renewing of sensations and when he stiffened and threw his head back while the corded muscles in his neck tensed into tight bands, she screamed when a turbulent wave of pleasure shot through her with a force stronger than before. And the only thing she could focus on was how Tyler was making her feel while the world was spinning out of control.

"Tyler!"

Tyler continued to mate with her, and when he felt the last of her shudder subside he drove himself inside of her for one deep final thrust and exploded in a way he had never done before, while expelling the breath he'd been holding. He knew that Megan James was his and that's how things had always intended to be. He continued to hold on to her as they collapsed together in the most luscious and sensuous oblivion any two persons could ever experience.

It had been the perfect seduction.

"You're something else, Tyler Savoy."

Even in the dimly lit room Megan could see the lines of his smile that appeared as a result of her compliment.

"There's nothing like the woman who has a man's heart saying words to stir his blood."

She leaned up over him. "And do I have your heart?"

He chuckled. "Baby, you have my heart so tight it hurts, and I know of only one way of easing the pain."

He pulled her closer into his arms and kissed her forehead. "Marry me. Will you marry me, Megan?"

Megan's throat tightened and then tears came into her eyes. "Oh, Tyler, I would love to marry you."

He smiled as he wiped away a tear that was slowly making its way down her cheek. "Is that a yes?"

She chuckled as elation soared through her body. "Yes, that's a yes."

"Good. I didn't want to think about running the ranch all by myself."

She lifted a brow. "What ranch?"

The smile he had deepened. "The ranch I officially purchased today, the old Palmer Place."

She pulled back far enough to be able to look at him, to make sure she had heard correctly. "The Palmer Place? You bought the Palmer Place?" she asked amazed. The Palmer's ranch was one of the largest in the area, almost as large as her stepfather's spread. "Why do you need such a huge place?"

He laughed as he pulled her back to him. "For my wife, our babies, my office and the animal hospital and clinic I plan to open. What do you think?"

She smiled down at him while thinking about all those things. "I think it's a wonderful idea and I'd love to be a part of your dream."

A grin tugged at the corners of his mouth. "You're more than my dream, Megan, you are my reality."

And then he proceeded to show her just how much.

Epilogue

Two months later—

"By the power vested in me I now pronounce you husband and wife. You may kiss your bride."

Megan smiled at Tyler and the love that swelled in her heart matched the love she saw in his eyes. And when he lifted her veil and captured her mouth she knew she would love him for the rest of her life.

Moments later he broke the kiss and sweeping her into his arms he carried her out of the church amid the clapping and cheering. A huge wedding reception was being held at their ranch. Tyler had moved in last month while she had been busy finalizing her move from California. She had decided to wait a semester before seeking a teaching job at one of the universities close by.

She laughed when Tyler deposited her in the back-seat of the limo and quickly got inside to join her. He immediately pulled her into his arms, framed her face and brushed a tender kiss across her lips. "I love you, Mrs. Savoy."

The emotions his words inflicted made her heart catch. "And I love you, too." They would be leaving in the morning for two weeks in Hawaii, and from there they would meet up with Bryan and Tonya, and the four of them would fly to Canada to pay a visit to Blake and his wife Justice.

"I have an idea about later tonight," he whispered as he pulled her into his lap.

She smiled down at him. "And what idea is that?"

"After everyone leaves and we have the ranch all to ourselves, how about we go parking at Lover's Peak. We own it now so we can go there and make out whenever we want."

She chuckled. "Good. You owe me a rain check anyway."

He leaned over and brushed another kiss on her lips. "Umm, is there anything else I owe you?"

She snuggled in his arms thinking this was the happiest day of her life. "Yes, but I have the rest of our lives to collect. And I *will* collect, Tyler."

"I don't have any complaints, because I like being in your debt."

Then he kissed her, deeply, thoroughly, and nothing existed for them at that moment but the overpowering love they shared and would be sharing for the rest of their lives.

Through the Fire

Monica Jackson

Heat

Two years ago somebody would have risked a sore jaw if he told Shepard Fraser he'd be painting pictures to decorate some backwater beauty salon chain in Kansas City. But in two years, things can change.

Shepard's eyebrows rose as he watched pink smocked magicians work their alchemy over women stretched out in pink leather chairs. R & B music thumped a loud bass beat, while the shades of raspberry and pink covered every surface, and caustic scents mixed with incense and perfume assaulted all his senses.

Cherice Givens had to be kidding. What was he supposed to do with a place like this? And where the hell was she?

A man in a bright pink smock approached him. "I assume you're Shepard Fraser?" he asked. Shep nodded. "Ms. Givens is waiting for you. Follow me."

The man led him into a small darkened room lit with pink scented candles. A woman was sitting on a chair in a white bathrobe, her head wrapped in a thick white towel. Another man was at her feet polishing her toenails.

"Shepard Fraser is here."

"Later," she told the man polishing her toenails. Then she stood and looked up at Shepard. For a second, he forgot to breathe. She was the most beautiful woman he'd ever seen in his life.

She had golden cat's eyes that set off light honey skin and full heart-shaped cherry lips. There was a beauty mark at the corner of her mouth that furthered the exotic, sexy effect. The robe was closed with only a belt, tantalizingly revealing her lush body with a wonderland of curves. Shep checked out the hills and valleys that begged for exploration, their endless softness, in surreptitious male fashion.

This lady was one hundred percent luscious, heavy-duty woman. The assignment was starting to look a touch more interesting.

"Shepard Fraser, it's wonderful to finally meet you," she said, holding out a small-boned plump hand with exquisitely manicured nails. He set aside his cane and she grasped his hand in a surprisingly strong grip.

"The pleasure is mine," he said.

"You're quite in demand. I appreciate you flying out here," she said.

Since she was paying quite well for the privilege, Shep simply nodded. He'd never guess that this kitten-ish bombshell with her dark velvet voice was a shrewd and successful business woman who'd grown a basement beauty salon into a multimillion-dollar profitable operation.

"I think you're the right artist to give our salons a new flavor," she said.

Shep decided to get right to the point. "You're going to have to lose the pink," he said. "Is that workable for you?" He needed to know—because if it wasn't, he might as well bounce now. There was no way his style would fit with the harem-boudoir-whorehouse look, if that's what she was going to insist on having.

"It's time for a new look. I want you to consult with a local designer I've contracted. She's quite good. I set up an appointment for tomorrow morning."

Shep exhaled in relief and then stiffened as he noticed her golden gaze running up and down the length of his body. He was intimately familiar with that look of assessment, but he wasn't used to it being used so directly on him by a woman. It both disconcerted and aroused him.

"I figured you were tired tonight, so why don't you rest at the hotel," she said in her husky voice. "We'll meet for dinner later. I'll pick you up in my car. Eight?"

She smiled at him briefly, then turned and exited, taking his assent for granted. The two men followed in her wake like lapdogs. Cherice Givens was a take-charge sort of woman. Shepard was unused to the type, but if that was her thing, he'd go along for a while. She'd come around to his way of thinking eventually.

Cherice studied the outfits in her closet. What should she wear for dinner with an artistic type? Was black too cliché? She wanted to impress Shepard Fraser. She took out a red suit and hung it back up. Too much. Slacks? No. Not sexy enough.

She'd been dying to meet Shepard Fraser for ages and lord a' mercy, the man looked every inch of his hype. He was off the hook fine. Tall, with long, lean muscles and high cheekbones, sexy, kissable lips and deep chocolate eyes fringed with lashes that belonged on a woman. His marked limp and cane gave him an air of vulnerability, making him more appealing. He was the type of man you wanted to take home and keep, preferably in bed.

He'd recently exploded on the art scene with passionate, impressionistic-looking artwork featuring black culture. Instead of gritty urban settings, his art reflected his people in beautiful, natural settings. His landscapes were as varied and expressive as the people in them. His art was incredible, as was his presence: sensitive, earthy and sexy.

There was nothing better than a fine man. Money had its attraction and power was intoxicating, but Cherice had always been drawn to fine, pretty types oozing sexual magnetism. Shepard Fraser was like candy and she was a greedy, greedy girl. She had to have him.

Her doorbell rang and Cherice sprinted to answer it, hoping to find one of her girlfriends. She pulled open the door and grinned at Rosaline and Brandy.

"What happened with Shepard Fraser?" Rosaline asked immediately.

"Do you have anything to eat?" interrupted Brandy. "I'm about ready to starve."

"Come on in and help me choose something to wear for my night out on the town. Brandy, you can pick up the phone and order food. Shep and I are going out to eat."

"So he was as good as you thought he'd be," Rosaline said.

"Honey, he's better than I hoped. The man is melt-in-your-mouth luscious."

"How about I order barbecue?" Brandy asked.

"That sounds fine," Rosaline said.

"I asked Shep out to dinner," Cherice said. "I think I'll take him to Jazz in Blue, but what to wear?"

Rosaline's brow creased. "Cherice, maybe you should take it easy with this guy. You know you tend to . . . take the upper hand."

"That's because they let her. Wimps. Admit it, Cherice, you're a dominatrix at heart," Brandy said, stretching out on the sofa.

Cherice's perfectly plucked brow shot up. "Please. What I get from my men, weaklings can't offer."

"That is correct, Brandy," Rosaline said, nodding.

"Just because a man can rock it, doesn't mean he isn't a wuss. I've seen you snap your fingers and your men flinch."

Cherice's eyes were wide and innocent. "Isn't that the way it's supposed to be?"

Brandy and Rosaline both laughed. "You need to quit," Brandy said.

"Cherice, you might as well admit it. You have issues with men," Rosaline said.

"I must agree," said Brandy. "You've got a giant heart, but for some reason, with men you always have to be in control. I've been your girl since childhood and I've never seen you trip over any man. No crush, no longings, no angst. You just decide who you want to get, go get him and that's it. It's not natural, girl."

"What's wrong with it? Think about it. Y'all are complaining because I don't need a man, and I use them as I see fit. I like fine men, and I like variety and I've never lacked for either. If I were a man, you'd be slapping me on the back and congratulating me."

"The point is that you're not a man."

Cherice turned back to her closet. "That fact has never ever been a matter of dispute."

"One day you're going to come up across a man who isn't going to give it up and give in to you. You are going to slam up into a jones so big and hard you won't know what to do with it," Rosaline said.

Cherice picked out a simple chocolate silk wrap dress that set off her skin and startling dyed blond hair. "Surely you jest. There's not been a man invented that is bigger and harder than what I can handle."

Rosaline smiled at her. "When you finally fall in love, girl, it's going to be like an earthquake. You're not going to know what hit you."

"Baby, I don't have time or space for earthquakes. I have way too much to do." Cherice considered an ivory lace dress. "Anyway, I know you're tied up at the hospital, Rosaline, but Brandy, how about you and Jackson coming with me for a relaxing weekend in California? There's a party at the record company and then we can swing on up and see Topaz, Jon and the baby. Arrival Records is going to let me fly with the company plane. Shelly owes me a favor for hooking her weave up real good. She headed on to New York on a 747."

"It sounds good, but I have to check with Jackson about his schedule."

"Shep doesn't know it yet, but he's flying back with us too," Cherice murmured.

"What if he wants to go home?" Brandy asked.

Cherice shrugged. "New Mexico's on the way. We can drop him off."

"Maybe we can get an invite to his place. I hear it's fabulous. He raises sheep, doesn't he? Or is it goats?"

"Sheep!" Cherice said. "I can do without the livestock. What's in New Mexico anyway?"

"Desert, some interesting plants, reported aliens, and caves," Rosaline answered.

"Some Native Americans, I believe," Brandy added.

"You are not talking me into asking Shep about a detour. Sheep, aliens, plants, and a few of the native peoples the white folk didn't slaughter—sounds exciting, but it doesn't quite measure up to the shindig that Arrival Records is going to be throwing in LA."

The driver pulled in front of Shep's hotel. Cherice bit her lip and took a deep breath. She returned the bottle of Perrier to the limo refrigerator and refreshed her lipstick. It wouldn't do to be nervous. There he was. She slid over on the leather seat.

Shep got in the car smoothly for a man with a cane. He smelled good, not like cologne or aftershave, but like clean soap. Fresh. He reminded her of crisp white sheets.

"Jazz in Blue," Cherice told the driver.

Shep smiled at her, a crooked grin that made her feel off-center. "You seem like a woman who knows exactly what she wants." His gaze dropped to her expanse of honeyed thigh. His eyelids were half-closed as he surveyed her body from the corner of his eyes. Cherice was practiced in reading a man's desire. *Warm it up.* She crossed her legs and swayed toward him.

"I am." Cherice decided that it was too early to add that he was high on that list of desires. Anyway, he'd find out soon enough. Shepard would make a nice dessert after a satisfying dinner.

The driver pulled up to the restaurant too soon. Inside, the atmosphere was right—close, intimate and sexy. A singer crooned jazzy love ballads.

When the waiter came to take their order, Cherice told him, "We'll have the lamb. It's very good here," she said to Shep.

"I'll have filet mignon, rare," he said.

Shep looked at Cherice. "I'm a man who knows what he wants, too," he said.

She sipped her wine. "Touché," she said, watching the couples filling the dance floor.

"I'm sorry, but I don't dance," he said, gesturing toward his cane.

"Did you dance?" Then she felt her face heat, realizing that asking that question to a man lamed in an accident was gauche.

"Not really. But there are a lot of other things I

miss quite a bit. I used to hike, to rock climb. I was quite active and I loved the outdoors."

Shep gazed at the dancers. "My lifestyle has changed considerably."

"Has it?" Cherice murmured, feeling awkward. This was not a sensation she was accustomed to, so she covered with words. "I hear your ranch is amazing."

"I wouldn't call it a ranch. I have a few animals. Some land. But I like it, it's home. The land is beautiful out there, you should see it. The colors . . ."

"Colors? Of what? The grass, the sky?"

"No, the land. New Mexico is unique. It's like God used a different set of paintbrushes."

"What made you decide to go into art?" Cherice asked, bored with the talk of the colors of dirt.

"You can say that I fell into it. I had time on my hands for the first time in my life. A buddy of mine had a wife with an art gallery. I've always played around with painting. She wanted to put on a showing of my work and the rest is history."

"That's it? Usually artists have a lot of passion behind their stories and suffering for their craft. They say that it's what they wanted to do their whole life."

"I don't think I'm the usual artist."

"No, you're not that, you came from nowhere."

"That's not true. Everybody came from somewhere."

Cherice laid her glass on the table and leaned toward him. "Tell me where you came from."

"I was born in Oakland. Yourself?"

"Kansas City." She studied Shep from under her lashes. He knew very well she hadn't been asking about the city of his birth. She was trying to get to the good stuff, what did Shep Fraser want, and what were his hopes and his dreams.

But he gazed out at the dancers with a pleasant, bland expression. Obviously, he was going to give her nothing.

They ate, and agreed the food was good. The conversation was light and soon the waiter came and removed their plates. "Would you like to order dessert?" he asked.

"No, coffee will do," answered Shep.

Cherice agreed, although she wouldn't have minded a bit of chocolate.

A short time later, Cherice was alone in the limo. She didn't get any dessert in more ways than one. After the meal, when the limo pulled up in front of Shep's hotel, he'd thanked her for a delightful dinner and gone to his hotel room without a backward glance. He didn't offer a touch of the hand, much less a kiss.

Cherice's ego deflated like a tire leaking air. He must not be attracted to her. A woman can't control a man's desires, but for a confident, attractive woman such as herself, it was rare that, once she fixed her attention on a man, he didn't respond.

It hardly ever mattered that she was big. She learned long ago that what mattered was the value a woman put on herself. When the clothes came off, if she knew without a doubt that her body was fine, he'd know it for sure too. She'd had plenty of men who once they tried her—the higher grade cut, the one with plenty of fat— they weren't about to go back to gnawing on soup bone and gristle. No, her weight never cost her any man worth having. It had to be more than that. What a disappointment. She swallowed hard.

Then she raised her chin. It wasn't like her to be defeated before the game had started good. She needed to pull up and regroup. There was something there between them. She could feel it. She'd sit tight. After all, tomorrow was another day. Cherice smiled to herself, her usual humor restored. She could hardly believe she was wasting time worrying over a man. She must have lost her mind.

Shep stopped outside Cherice's office door, filled with nervousness that he hoped didn't show. He'd never met anyone like her. She attracted him, aroused him, but something about her brought out his primitive male instincts. There was a place deep inside that wanted to knock her upside the head, duct tape her mouth, and drag her off to his lair. For a man who'd never come remotely close to oppressing a woman in his entire life, that need to dominate was scary.

A man in a hot pink smock walked by him and stared appreciatively at Shep's buttocks. Shep suppressed the urge to shake his head. That man should be ashamed to allow his boss to dress him in something like that. It would take a gun to his temple before he put on one of those pink things.

Shep knocked on the pink door. "C'mon in," she called.

He walked in and suppressed the urge to flinch. Cherice's office was decorated in hot pink and black, redolent of Oriental incense and outfitted with chaise lounges instead of chairs. It resembled the parlor of a

French whorehouse. A thin, intense looking white woman with short black hair and horn-rimmed glasses was perched uncomfortably on one of the lounges.

"Meet Fontaine, our interior designer," Cherice said.

"I love your work," Fontaine murmured as he shook her hand.

"Thank you. What do you have?" Shep asked, ready to get down to business. She handed him a portfolio.

Shep stretched out on the other chaise, leaving his shoes on the floor. If Cherice had the nerve to provide only the near equivalent of beds to sit on, he might as well be comfortable. He opened the portfolio and perused Fontaine's ideas for the salons, along with the color swatches. Cherice was right, she was good.

"Great stuff. I can work with this," he said, handing the portfolio back.

"The colors are fine with you?" Cherice asked, her voice almost sounding like a purr.

Fontaine's vision of the salon palette was a mixture of hip, urban smoky greens and grays, only accented by Cherice's trademark hot pink.

"It looks great. My art will fit in fine."

Cherice walked from behind her desk. "We have a deal then. I'll have the blueprints sent over to your hotel room and you can indicate the size and placement of the pictures along with the delivery dates."

He nodded. Cherice was paying him handsomely. He got some flak from his fellow artists about churning out originals for commercial purposes, but he needed the cash. He never understood the point of artistic sensibilities if you didn't have the sense enough to use your talent to pay the bills.

"Thanks for coming, Fontaine," Cherice said as the decorator gathered up her materials.

As soon as they were alone, Cherice came from behind the desk and sat on the edge of his chaise. Shep felt his pulse and blood pressure increase. Her perfume was so soft he could barely smell it. Feminine and sexy. Her breasts were full enough that each would overflow his big hand. He wondered what her nipples looked like. His mind snapped back to reality when she put her small hand on his thigh. He felt himself deflate and anxiety replaced his former inappropriate thoughts.

"Our business is almost wrapped up," Cherice said. "I'd like to treat you to the works, the complete salon experience on the house."

Her hand was burning through his trousers like a small brand. He intensely wished she would move it. "No thanks," he said. "I've never been the beauty salon experience type."

"Don't worry, we're not going to curl your hair or put mascara on your eyes. We have a spa special for men only. I want you to try it. To create art for us, you need to have at least some concept of what we're about."

He really couldn't argue with that, nor could he think straight with her hand on his body. *So why didn't he move his leg?* Because her hand felt so damn good.

"You're not going to try and make me wear one of those pink things, are you?" he said. "Because I'm not doing it."

Cherice squeezed his thigh and chuckled. "C'mon," she said.

* * *

Shep's hair was washed, scissor-cut and blow-dried. His face was shaved with way too much stinky cream rubbed into his skin. His toenails cut, feet scrubbed, prodded and massaged until the poor dogs wanted to beg for mercy. Now, he was buck naked, flat on his stomach on a hard table being enthusiastically rubbed by some queen who was showing far too much interest in his posterior area.

Shep would rather be in enemy territory under fire. Hell, people actually *paid* for this? "You need to head north," he growled.

" 'Scuuuuse me," the masseur said, lifting his hands momentarily and wriggling his fingers. "I was only trying to be thorough." He patted Shep's buttock.

Fortunately, just before Shep coldcocked the SOB, Cherice walked in. She took in the situation at a glance. "Antoine, I'll take over," she said.

Shep suppressed a groan. Just when he thought things couldn't get worse . . .

She laid small, soft, strong hands on him with smooth, even strokes, totally different from the pounding Antoine let him have.

And best of all, she didn't talk.

As the minutes passed he felt himself relax. Then he felt the press of her breasts against his back. Shep decided that he wouldn't complain a whit if her hands tended to drift southward. Surrounded by her scent and touch and blessed silence, his eyes closed as he dwelled on that pleasant possibility.

"Why did you dis my pink smocks," Cherice asked, jolting him out of his reverie.

"Hot pink smocks don't exactly project the image

of urban sophistication that you're going to try to cultivate," he answered.

A beat passed and the strokes of Cherice's fingers never wavered. "Then how do you suggest I approach outfitting my hair designers?"

"Traditional black smocks over blue jeans. It would be hip and it would have to be cheaper than those pink monstrosities you're having custom made."

He flinched as she gave him a sharp slap on the ass, the sound reverberating through the small room. But he didn't dare turn over because he had an obvious woody. How was he going to get up with her in the room and him buck naked except for this tiny towel?

"I have a favor I need to ask of you," Cherice said, her voice buttery.

He wouldn't mind if the favor was of a carnal nature. He turned his head to check to see if there was a lock on the door.

"I want you to fly to LA with me. There's a party at Arrival Records and I desperately need an escort."

Shep couldn't imagine Cherice being desperate about hardly anything, especially a man. She was as cool as they come.

He hesitated, and thought about how to answer her. He wasn't a hasty man.

"Chicken?" she challenged him.

However she must be a hasty woman. He could barely believe his ears. He turned over, forgetting his state, then quickly gathered the towel around his middle.

Cherice's gaze went unerringly toward his midsection, her mouth curved in a small smile.

"What did you say?"

"I asked if you were chicken."

"I'm never chicken."

"You should never say never. I say you're chicken."

"Why?"

"It seems as if you're afraid to play with me."

He caught his breath at the boldness of her challenge.

She leaned toward him, her perfect cupid-bow lips looking perfectly kissable, her hand on his thigh. She made him nervous as hell, but his woody had a mind of its own and it apparently wasn't a little bit afraid of her.

Shep, however, who had faced down assassins and flying bullets, who'd made it through minefields and entire enemy battalions, hesitated some more.

She withdrew. "That's all right. Most men aren't man enough for me."

Her words were a glove thrown in his face. Shep's eyes narrowed. She stared back at him, so cool, as if whatever he said or did, she really didn't give a damn.

Did she know who she was messing with? Once he got through with her, she'd be the one begging for mercy. Pleading for satisfaction. His woody apparently liked that thought.

Because, "Bring it on," is what came out of his mouth.

"I will do that, Mr. Fraser," she said as she slipped out the door, leaving him and woody all alone.

Spark

A few days later, and thousands of feet in the air, Cherice poured herself a glass of Cristal and replaced the bottle in the bucket. She didn't bother to offer Shep any. She was a one time learner, and he'd indicated that he wanted to help himself. So if he wanted some, he could do that.

The plane cabin was close, the air heated and stale. She unbuttoned one button of her shirt and dabbed a damp napkin at her neck. She noted how his gaze went straight down her cleavage like bees to honey. *Go ahead and help yourself, baby.*

They were alone with the pilot. Brandy and Jackson hadn't been able to make it. Not entirely a bad thing, because between her and Shep, the game played on, neither giving the other an inch . . . or anything else. Damn, because it was time she renewed her membership in the mile-high club. It had been almost a year since she'd made love amid the clouds. She glanced at Shep's lap. Sure enough, he was ready. The man had the quick responses of an adolescent. If he mixed that with the control and experience of an adult, it seemed mighty promising.

So when was he going to surrender to her? Cherice moistened her lips. She hoped soon. She was about to explode with the anticipation of him inside her.

"You should keep your seat belt fastened when there's this much turbulence," Shep said.

He sure liked to give orders. Cherice ignored his directives because she didn't much like following them. She glanced out the window at the mountains looming beside the plane. She needed to distract herself because the increasing turbulence was making her nervous. She glanced at Shep, wishing again that he'd get around to distracting her.

Then the plane lurched and she was thrown to her knees. Shep cursed and ran to the cockpit. A few moments later, Shep returned and helped her to her feet. He started wrapping some contraption around her. Cherice was in shock, following his command to lift one leg then the other. "I think the pilot had a heart attack," Shep said.

Her eyes fastened on his face. She was beyond words. Good thing, because what he said next was worse. "The pilot's dead. We're stalled and we're going down soon. We're going to have to jump."

"No," she whispered.

"Yes. I wish it wasn't so and I bet the pilot wished it more," Shep said as he struggled into his parachute.

She sagged down to the floor. "Oh, lord."

"Praying isn't such a bad idea about now."

"So we're going to die."

"I'm hoping we're not going to die at all. We're

extraordinarily lucky. The plane is well outfitted with equipment and we have a few minutes before the jump."

"Minutes?" Cherice's adrenaline kicked into gear. Her heart pounded so hard she felt it thumping in her ears.

Shep rummaged around the cabin.

"What the *hell* are you doing?" Cherice demanded.

"I'm gathering survival gear. My duffel bag doubles as a backpack."

"First you say we're going to jump out of the plane, and then you say we're going to survive?" Cherice asked, her voice rising to a shriek.

"Yes, that's the idea."

"Oh, lord, I'm going to die."

"Not if you follow my instructions exactly."

"I'm going to die."

"Will you shut up?"

He went to the cockpit, and when she heard him give the distress call on the radio, Cherice grabbed the whole bottle of Cristal that had fallen on the floor along with her and didn't bother with the glass. If she was going to die, it might as well be with good champagne. She looked around for something sweet to eat.

"Let's go. Listen carefully."

Cherice had a candy bar in one hand and the bottle of Cristal in another.

"Put the food down. You may puke it up when you drop," Shep said. She started to argue that she preferred to die eating, but reconsidered and laid down the bottle and candy with some resentment.

"The wind will be ferocious. You won't be able to talk. Keep your mouth shut and stay calm. Count to a hundred and pull here. There are backups. The chute will open automatically if all else fails, do you understand? Arch your back. Once the chute opens, try to steer clear of the trees, and definitely steer clear of power lines if there are any. Stay put. I'll come for you." He tied a knife onto one of her straps and strapped some more stuff on her back.

"Hold on to something," he said, as he pulled open the emergency exit. A windstorm swept through the plane and the plane tilted over. All Cherice could think was that they were going down.

"We have to go now," Shep yelled.

Cherice took a huge gulp from the bottle. "Ciao," she screamed over the wind. "Because if you think I'm jumping out of this damn plaannne—"

Nope, she wasn't prepared when he picked her up and threw her out of the exit door. Cherice figured she spent the first ten seconds trying to scream, but the wind screamed back in her ears and made her choke whenever she opened her mouth. So she started counting at ninety and pulled her knees up. It took her another ten seconds to realize that it was impossible to pray, count and cuss at the same time.

When she pulled the cord, she was yanked vertically and it got still, so still for a moment she wondered if she had died.

Unfortunately, that was when she made the mistake of looking down. She always had this phobia about heights, and here she was suspended in midair just under the clouds and over a whole bunch of trees with only straps and cord and nylon between her and oblivion. And to think some fools actually paid to do this, Cherice thought as she tried not to pee her pants.

She saw Shep's rectangular chute out of the corner of her eye to her left. Then she heard a whomp and saw a fireball rise to the west. The plane was gone.

Cherice supposed that hanging suspended among autumn leaves and drying wood in the tree branches was as safe a place to be as any, but the problem was that as the sun fell, the colder it became and the more she had to pee. If she let loose, wet pants were exponentially colder than dry ones.

Time passed. Time enough to muse on the experience of surviving her very first airplane crash. Time enough to savor the joy of living, alternating with the terror of being hung in a tree many feet up with only flimsy branches between oneself and terra firma. She never did like heights.

She wondered if Shep made it. She hoped so. She wanted both to kick his ass for throwing her out of the plane and smother him with kisses for saving her life.

He'd strapped a knife on her. She assumed it was to cut herself free if needed. But if she did, she might fall. And if she fell, well, she might fall. That was a bad thing. She never, never wanted to fall again. As far as she was concerned, skydivers and bungee jumpers needed committing at best, psychiatric drugs at least.

She'd stay put and somebody would rescue her.

So she hung in the trees and worried about the poor pilot's family and how they wouldn't even have the small comfort of burying his body.

She thought about the plane blowing up again, and wondered how it would have felt to be in it. She'd never spent much time thinking about it before, but she wondered what it would feel like to be dead. It was as if she'd been given a second chance at life. How was a person supposed to handle that? She wondered if there was something she was supposed to do, some purpose to accomplish.

It was about that time that the matter of waiting to pee became moot. It wasn't if she was going to pee, but how she was going to pee. Cherice decided to wriggle out of her pants, do the deed, and pull them back up. She had just got her rear exposed when she heard something making its way through the bushes down below. A bear? Bears climbed trees, didn't they?

Fear combined with nerves caused the trickle-down effect and it was pure happiness when she heard a curse uttered in Shep's dear voice. "Woman, are you peeing on my head?" he demanded.

"Up here, I'm up here!" Sheer relief caused Cherice to ignore his crass query, as true as it was.

"I see," Shep's dry voice echoed up. "Well, now I'm here. Come on down and we'll make camp for the night. Be sure and bring the parachute."

He had to be kidding. Did he think she was perched up here in this tree for her health and beauty?

"I can't get down."

"Sure you can. Use the knife I gave you. Climb

carefully. Common sense should tell you to use hefty branches." Then the SOB had the nerve to snicker. If he was up here she would have socked him.

"I can't climb down," Cherice said, slowly and patiently, as if speaking to a very young child.

"No such thing as can't. The problem is that if I come up there, I can't carry you down, the best I can do is lead you down. With my leg, you're able to climb as well or better than me. The tree is well and sturdily branched. If you slipped, you wouldn't go all the way down. I advise you to get started while there is still enough light. I'm going to start a fire. Gets a little nippy this time of year." He whistled as he started bustling around.

Cherice panicked. He really wasn't going to help her down. Apparently he'd just given all the advice he was going to give. He must think she liked being perched up in this tree like an enormous bird. Maybe he thought that she went looking for trees to hang out in during her spare time in Kansas City. Cherice fumed. She sputtered. She started to cuss him out but soon realized that he wasn't paying her an iota of attention.

Shep got a roaring fire going, close enough for her to smell the smoke, but way too far to feel any warmth. Then a short while later, she smelled a delicious aroma. Barbecue. The man had the nerve to barbecue. She was starving.

Her eyes filled. It wasn't fair. He helped her this far. He helped her jump (okay, be tossed) out of a plane. Did he help her to let her freeze and starve to death perched up in a tree?

243

Then she got madder. When she got down out of this tree, she'd kill him. She'd skin him like he did that poor, delicious, scrumptious animal that smelled so good. Except she wanted to do it while he was alive.

She struggled to untie the knife and cut away the parachute cord.

He must have heard. "Don't forget to try to get the chute free. We need it," he called.

She growled. She wanted to aim the knife for his head. But she knew there was no hope to hit that target so she'd save that pleasure for closer proximity.

The chute was huge. She pulled, tugged and hacked until she finally got it free.

Cherice had on a black silk pantsuit with a lace camisole and black lace insets that set off her honey skin, blonde hair and golden eyes. Worse, she had on no underwear. She wished she was wearing heavy wool coveralls, with white cotton drawers and a T-shirt under them.

But she was going to prove to Shepard Fraser that she could get down out of this damn tree, and then she was going to kick his ass all the way back to civilization, right after she had a drink and some of that barbecue.

Getting down was easier than she thought as long as she didn't look down and stayed mad.

She dropped out of the tree while he was lounging in front of the fire, cleaning a bone with his white teeth.

"You're bleeding," he said. "You should have been more careful."

The sight of her blood surprised her so much that

she didn't carry through her initial impulse to slap him upside the head as soon as her feet hit the earth. Her hands were scratched, her clothes were ripped and torn and there was a gash on her knee that Shep was examining.

"Good, it's superficial." He doused it with cool water from a small bottle he filled from a plastic bag of water he had hanging from a tree. "Hold on, this will sting." She didn't flinch as he cleansed it with what smelled unmistakably like aftershave. "Now, wash your hands."

Cherice obeyed him, her initial aggression completely eclipsed by a wave of hunger and fatigue. He made a seat of soft leaves for her and served her meat and vegetables on a plate of leaves. It tasted heavenly. Gourmet dining. Smoked to perfection.

"What is this?" she asked as she chewed.

"I came across a couple rabbits on the way here. Picked some wild onions and mushrooms. I even found a nice juicy root or two."

After a while, completely sated, Cherice leaned back against a rock. The sun drained out of the sky to the west. The fire warmed her like the last bits of the sun. "Thanks for saving my life," she said. She meant it. If he hadn't kept his head and known exactly what to do, they would have been ashes floating down the side of the mountain with the wreckage of the plane.

"My pleasure, ma'am." Shep answered with a warm, crooked grin.

"And I'm really sorry if I peed on you. I thought you were a bear."

"Interesting way of bear battle. But you missed." He looked up at the sky. "It's a clear night tonight. We can sleep in the open on the leaves."

Together they heaped up a great pile of leaves, the crisp, wonderful-smelling sort that Cherice loved to jump in as a kid. They nestled in, wrapped with the parachutes. The air was clean and crisp, and the stars shone clear and bright. She'd never seen them quite like this before, glistening like glitter tossed by the handful on a black velvet throw.

Shep fell asleep immediately. He didn't snore. She watched his breath, deep, quiet and regular. He hadn't jumped with his cane. She wondered how far he'd hiked to come and get her. He had a load to carry. He also somehow caught or trapped the rabbits and gathered the vegetables. Talk about cooking from scratch. Cooking was something she didn't do, from scratch or otherwise.

Cherice didn't feel like a person who survived a plane crash and harrowing drop thousands of feet into mountain wilderness. Because of Shepard Fraser, she felt contented and safe. Blessed. This wasn't how she usually felt.

She didn't like to admit it, but she usually felt something was missing. She tried not to let it bother her, but there was a hole there, a void she never could figure out how to fill. And now she was satisfied for some reason, the empty place no longer aching. What a strange state to be in while lost in the wilderness. Her eyes drifted closed as she settled into dreamless sleep.

*   *   *

Cherice woke wrapped around warm, hard man, in more ways then one. She looked into coffee-brown eyes with impossibly long lashes. Beautiful man. He started a long, hard grind. Answering heat flared within her and she felt herself moisten with readiness. She arched toward him. His head lowered. She covered his mouth, just for the moment it would take to dart to the bathroom and brush her teeth.

Then she remembered. This wasn't a pleasant erotic dream; she was a plane crash survivor presently stuck in the woods. And she was about to surrender everything to this man.

She realized that a look of horror must have crossed her face, because Shep was staring down at her in a bemused way, quite different from his former passion-filled gaze. "Reality bites, huh?" he murmured.

"Do you know where we are? What are our chances of being rescued? Can we walk somewhere?" Cherice peppered him with questions. She was diverting him from the issue at hand, the matter of her impending loss of control. It terrified her.

"Vaguely, slim to middling, no."

"What do you mean?"

"In short, none of the above covers it pretty well."

"What are we going to do?" Cherice was staring at her hands. Four nails had completely broken off.

"We need to get to better shelter and closer to water. Winter's setting in. We have to prepare for the snows. Lay in food."

"Prepare? What! You seriously don't think we're going to be rescued soon?"

"I hope we are, but I believe in being prepared for the worst."

"What do you mean, prepare for the freaking snows?"

"It does that when it gets real cold, you know. White stuff from the sky."

"There's no need for sarcasm. Anyway, camping out in the woods in the snow is out of the question. My idea of enjoying the great outdoors during snow season is at a four-star ski resort in front of a roaring fire while somebody else's silly rear is outside in the white cold wet stuff sliding down hills on wood slats with poles."

"Not the nature-girl type, huh?"

"Do I look like the nature-girl type?"

Shep shook his head, probably wisely deciding to stay silent.

"Look at my nails," Cherice said, her voice starting to quaver. "My hair! I've had twice a week salon appointments since I was fifteen. What's going to happen to me?"

Shep's eyebrows shot up. "Twice a week? You've never seen your roots?"

"Never. And you see how silky my highly processed hair is? I'm a walking advertisement for my salons."

"Look at the upside. You should lose some weight."

Cherice's neck started to swivel. Anybody who knew her well would have started backing away at that point. "Why would I want to lose weight when I'm faced with looking like hell? So I can be scrawny and look like hell? Unlike you brainwashed folk, I don't think the be-all and end-all to a woman is how bony her body is."

Shep shrugged. "Frankly, I never preferred skinny women either, but all the women I've known have been concerned about their weight more than anything else. Even when I told them it didn't matter, that I liked them the way they were. I assumed you were the same."

"Spend less time assuming and more time finding out."

"Fine." Shep rolled out of their makeshift bed and stalked into the bushes.

Cherice frowned after him. He assumed that a woman was more concerned about what she weighed than anything else? Pleeeze! That man had been hanging around too many thin women.

She shivered. It was too cold to worry about Shep, to worry about anything really. Cherice burrowed back into the leaves. Fact was she wouldn't last long out here without Shep. The other fact was that he was fine, all man, and they were alone. The inevitable was inevitable.

Once she knew without a doubt that she could handle what any man had to offer. But as cold as it was, Shep was way too hot for her to fool with. Her stomach didn't feel right when she was around him. Her skin was heated and flushed, then cold and clammy. Sometimes she didn't know what to say. Worse, he made her feel uncertain, about herself, about everything. This was nothing like her and it was totally unacceptable. If she wasn't stuck with the man, she'd have tried to get away . . . or get closer. See, what he did to her? The man was driving her crazy.

But she needed him now, so she needed to stay clear of emotional entanglement. She had to keep her head. Because otherwise she was certain to cuss him out or try to knock him out and neither would do at all. She had to hold off sleeping with him somehow, because her woman's heart simply knew that it would just make everything so much worse.

She heard him approach. "If you lose weight," he announced, "you'll be able to work harder. We are going to have to work hard as hell to survive the winter. But don't worry. It'll be fun."

Somehow she had to avoid killing him, too. Cherice glared at him. He grinned back.

Right before she took off her shoe and aimed it at his head, he turned away and started gathering their supplies. "We need to head out. I'm going to go up and get the other chute." He threw clothes at her that he'd pulled from his duffel bag. "Put these on, you'll need them. A knife is over there."

It didn't take long for her to figure out why he told her where the knife was. There was no way she was going to get Shep's pants over her hips. She ended up taking two pairs, cutting open the inner seams and wearing them over each other like a layered long skirt. She looped the parachute cord through the belt loops to hold them up since there was no chance of zipping them closed. She put on a couple of his sweaters over that. They stretched tight, but at least she could get them on. And she was much warmer.

He strapped a makeshift backpack on her back that

gave her flashbacks of the jump from the plane. Cherice shuddered.

"You okay?" he asked.

She couldn't answer, because she wasn't. This survival stuff was so far outside of her ken of experience it wasn't even funny.

"I want to get closer to the water. If we can find a cave a little higher up, it would be ideal," Shep said.

Cherice avoided the park. She was a high maintenance town girl. The country was something you drove through at high speed on a strip of asphalt to get to another town. She knew there were worthy purposes to grass, bugs and dirt, so didn't begrudge their existence. She simply was grateful that she didn't have to deal directly with any of them.

"We're going to be okay," he said. "I'm trained for this. This is nothing."

"Why would you train for something like this? Masochism?"

"You might say so. I trained extensively in survival techniques, in far harsher environments than this. We have a good, fresh water source, plenty of game . . ."

"Did you get injured in the military?"

"Yes. I was a Navy SEAL." His voice was clipped and short.

Cherice's eyebrows shot up as she reviewed what she'd seen in movies about Navy SEALs. Weren't they supposed to be the ultimate badasses?

"So can you kill me with your bare hands?" she asked.

"Without a doubt. But since it's not freezing yet, I'd have to bury you and it would be hardly worth the trouble."

"Very funny. So what happened? Why did you stop beating up on bad guys for our great nation?"

Shep gestured to his leg. "Physical disability removes you from the team."

He tried to disguise it, but she heard the undertone of bitterness. "Do you miss it?" she asked.

"You don't go through something like what it takes to become a SEAL without wanting to do what you're doing. Yeah, you could say I miss it."

He was at his prime, oozing masculinity and, despite his disability, fitness and strength. From what she knew of him, she guessed that to be relieved of duty must have almost killed him.

From Navy SEAL to celebrated artist was quite a leap. She was aching to ask him about it, and she wanted badly to know how he received his injury, but sensed that he had enough conversation on the topic. Shep Fraser was a man of action disguised as an artist. His artistic talent was amazing, but it wasn't his passion. He'd been denied that. He had layers to unpeel and a story to tell. Cherice sighed. An interesting man was an even more attractive one.

They trudged on. Cherice observed him with a sideways gaze. Shep's limp was less pronounced. He made a tall staff from a branch, and his step was definitely surer. He smiled more than when she first met him and seemed in a damn fine mood. Like this was a picnic in a park or a resort vacation.

"I bet you could stay out here for a while," Cherice said.

"Years, probably forever. It's pristine, damn near

paradise. One of the few true livable wilderness areas we have left."

"Years . . ." Cherice breathed out the word.

"Maybe you and I could make like Adam and Eve. Raise some kids wholesome-like."

She looked at him as if his brain had squeezed out of his ear holes, which made about as much sense as the craziness he was talking.

"I can't believe you don't appreciate this fresh mountain air, the open spaces, the scenery, the naturalness of it all," Shep said, interpreting her look.

"The cold, the dirt, the lack of . . . shoot where to start? Let's just say lack of *everything*."

"Too bad. And here you can be where nature intends a woman to be happiest . . ."

Cherice's eyes narrowed. "Happiest?"

"You know, in a woman's natural place."

"Pray tell me what that is?"

He had a wicked glint in his eyes. "Under a man."

Flame

Just when she was starting to feel sorry for him, he showed his true colors. She had no idea that Neanderthals like him still existed. Chauvinist . . . The pig was too fine a creature to be sullied by being likened to him. He'd ordered her to gather wood and carelessly tossed her a small hatchet. She hefted it, gave him a dangerous look and he had the nerve to *laugh*. She didn't want to kill him, because she was well aware that she needed him. Her fantasy was to tie him down and spank him. Whip his ass until he begged for mercy. *Under a man, indeed.*

"Take that, take that," she muttered as she swung the hatchet with great energy and satisfaction. She had no idea where he found the small ax in the plane, but she was very pleased that he had it. Chopping wood was excellent at releasing fury.

When she delivered Shep's shirt full of wood to the stack, she noted that it was now almost as tall as she. When she asked him how much wood she was supposed to gather, he said more than she could possibly imagine. She'd made a start.

He said to gather roots. That was a hoot. She had no idea what edible roots looked like growing up out of the ground versus packaged prettily in the supermarket. It all looked like grass, weeds and dirt to her. Cherice did a double take as she approached a small, bushy tree. She did know what nuts looked like, even in their ugly husks. Bingo. She filled Shep's shirt full of readily available fat and protein. Yep, she was survivor wonder woman. If this place had central heat and a lot less dirt, she might be all right out here.

If it wasn't so damn cold, the place they settled down in wouldn't be half-bad. It was a sandy cave, secluded by a stand of trees. There was a bubbling mountain spring close by, lots of green piney trees, and dirt galore.

Cherice surveyed the cave. It wasn't really a proper cave like she'd seen in the movies, more like a rock ledge. She couldn't stand up in it. There was enough room for a small fire at the opening and for them to lie down. Maybe a little storage. That was it. It didn't have much in the way of décor possibilities. She thought the soft carpet of pine needles where she'd been gathering wood might be a nice start on flooring.

The sun sank low in the sky and the cave floor was covered with about an inch of pine before she realized how much time had passed.

What if the Neanderthal was injured? He said he was going to go and hunt a deer, but what if he ran into a mountain lion doing the exact same thing?

What if he was lying somewhere cut to bloody tatters of bloody flesh?

She started to bite her nails, pulled short, looked at them and groaned.

But her nails were the least of her worries right now. If Shep was gone, she'd be alone in the wilderness. How long would she last? Not years. Why couldn't he just keep his rear home and gather roots? She didn't need a deer. She didn't even know if she liked deer meat, since she'd never tried it. When she asked Shep, he just grunted and said, "When in doubt, always assume that it'll taste like chicken."

He had to go and spend all day trying to kill a poor deer. How like a man. Always going overboard.

The sun settled lower and the air grew chill. Cherice longed for a fire, but she didn't know how to light one. She couldn't light logs without lighter fluid and she had no idea how Shep did it.

As she shivered, she heard a rustle and reached for the hatchet. "Go away, bear," she yelled. Shep had told her that it never did well to surprise a bear.

Her hand tightened on the hatchet as she debated what to do about the possible bear. Playing dead seemed the best alternative, with hatchet in the brain, hopefully before it decided to take a chunk out of her, as a backup plan.

The sound drew nearer, and then much to her relief, the rustling coalesced into Shep-sounding footsteps.

"Thank heavens you're not a bear," she said.

"You should try to get over that unnatural fear of bears," Shep said, as he dragged a smallish deer on a pallet into the clearing in front of the cave. "What, no fire?"

"My bear phobia never much bothered me in Kansas City for some reason," Cherice said. "By the way, I don't know how to start a fire."

"You better learn. It's an indispensable skill in subfreezing weather. We need to start smoking this deer tonight. Hope you like venison jerky."

Cherice had always been more of a champagne and caviar sort of woman, but venison jerky was better than starving. "I hope you like nuts," she said. She darted into the cave and returned with a handful to pour into Shep's lap.

"Filberts," he said. "They look good." He eyed the pile of wood and the soft carpet of pine needles lining the cave. "You've been busy."

"I have. It was interesting that you said that when I lost weight that I'd be able to do more work. You didn't make a lick of sense. Fat is nothing but stored energy. I'm quite fit, with energy to spare and lots of insulation to boot. Isn't it logical that a hefty sista would be able to work harder while stranded in some cold-ass mountains than some underfed, bony heifer?"

Shep cocked his head and stared at her. "Apparently so," he murmured and busied himself arranging the campfire. "Come and watch what I'm doing."

A while later, Cherice warmed her face and hands in front of the fire, pleased with her handiwork. He'd made her light the tinder that eventually ignited the logs. Strips of venison were roasting, flavored with hazelnut and onion.

Shep stretched with pleasure. "This is the good life," he said.

Cherice shook her head. "Not stinking is a large portion in my idea of the good life—not to mention . . ." But why get started? Bottom line, she was grateful to be alive.

"We'll heat some water in bark and wash up tomorrow. I have some soap."

Visions of Shep naked, with soap suds dripping down his brown skin, caused her pulse to do strange things.

"We'll freeze," she said.

"It'll have to be a washup, one body part exposed, washed and dried well until we can get walls constructed so we can heat this place."

"Walls?"

"Sure. There's nice clay by the stream. We can make some pots too."

The temperature fell as fast as the sun, and as hard as Cherice had worked, exhaustion soon followed.

She started to carry in leaves for a bed, but Shep stopped her. "Why not?" she asked.

"Leaves rot. You're complaining about stink. Rot really stinks."

She couldn't argue with that. She curled up on the pine needles, wishing she'd brought in more. Shep piled on all the fabric they had, and then pulled her to him spoon fashion. Once her heart settled down, she welcomed the warmth of his body and was grateful that she was too tired to fully appreciate its masculine length.

"Tomorrow, I'll prepare the deer hide. It'll be warm. I'll get more, too," he whispered in her ear.

"Mmmmm," she whispered. Him, big hunter, was her last thought before sleep claimed her.

Cherice watched the sun rise, like a swash of gaudy watercolors splashed across the sky. They rose and set with the sun also. She supposed this is what being close to nature meant. She stretched and yawned. She'd also never slept this much or as soundly in her life. So this was what lots of exercise and no caffeine does to you—it makes you sleep your life away. But *no,* nobody warns you about that adverse side effect of the outdoor life.

Shep was leaving when she woke, gone down to the stream to get water. She'd felt bereft when he unwrapped himself from her, but she understood. He had to go to the bathroom and frankly, she had to also. She was grateful that their bladders gave them an excuse to flee the cave.

His nearness hurt. She awoke wet and aroused, ready for him. She'd never wanted a man so much for so long and didn't reach out and take him. She'd partied hardy before and it never stopped her from burning up the sheets, so it wasn't merely fatigue and exhaustion. She knew he was ready for her also. When they were together, the temperature rose ten degrees. Something was holding Shep back too. He'd rushed away this morning, talking about going to the stream.

Cherice clasped her arms around her knees. It was nice to worry only about physical labor instead of going in to work. No employees or customers, thus no griping and complaining to deal with besides her own, no wheeling and dealing, nothing extraneous. Everything she did mattered out here, and she didn't do anything if it wasn't worth doing. Such a contrast to her day-to-day life in Kansas City.

Were facials, nails and hair superficial? Something within rebelled at such fundamental questioning of dearly held values, and Cherice studied her ashy legs under her makeshift denim skirt. When she got back, she'd need the works. She'd soak for two hours in a hot Jacuzzi to get the dirt out of her pores. Then a massage, complete body wax, facial, and pedicure. She'd need a set of new nails. Her hair would need rebuilding from the ground up. It would take two days.

That could be a marketing concept. She could name it the Extreme Beauty Package. Get thrown from a plane into the mountain wilderness for three days topped off by an overnight at one of her spas. She could charge a fortune.

She heard Shep approach before she saw him and she stood and stretched, ready for what the day was going to bring.

He was carrying the duffel bag filled with clay from the stream. "I'm going to start the wall with this. Why don't you start scraping the deer hide. You saw me start it. Take care with the skin. I want to get as big a piece as pos—"

"I'm not touching that deer."

Shep cocked his head and looked at her as if he hadn't heard correctly. "Excuse me?" he asked.

She repeated herself real slow to make sure he got it. "I'm not touching a dead animal except to eat it."

He stared down at her in full glower. Cherice supposed a lesser woman would have been intimidated, but there was nothing lesser about her.

"You are going to do what I tell you to do. Furthermore, you're going to do it without bitching, moaning or complaint. I don't want to hear any back talk from you except yessir. Do you understand?"

"Oh, I understand. You're allowed to run on at the mouth all you want. But I'm still not touching that damn deer." Cherice put her hands on her hips.

"If we're going to make it out here, I demand one hundred percent cooperation."

"This doesn't sound like cooperation to me; it sounds more like tyranny."

Shep gritted his teeth and went and picked up the deer hide and extended it to her.

"What letter of the word no don't you understand, the n or the o?" Cherice asked.

"That's it," he said, dropping the bloody hide. "I'm going to do what I've wanted to do for a long time." He dropped the duffel bag from his shoulders and took off his belt. Then he headed toward her with determination in his eyes.

"I know you don't think you're going to lay a hand on me, Mr. Navy SEAL, because you best not ever go to sleep at night if you do. Have you heard what happened to Bobbitt—eeeeee!"

Shep tackled her like a running back going for Super Bowl pigskin. He had her flat on her stomach and ass up within ten seconds. She struggled, she really did, but it was like trying to fight with warm steel. Son of a bitch!

"Do you not agree you deserve this spanking?" he asked in a calm, matter-of-fact tone.

"If you hit me, I'll never forgive you, never!"

"I realize that this is coming a little late, since your home training seems to have been sorely neglected, but how else are you going to learn to follow directives?"

"I'm not cutting into a dead deer. You can forget about it," she yelled.

She felt his arm rise, and panic filled her. She started to struggle in earnest. "I hate blood," she screamed and started to cry.

His arm lowered. "Well, hell. Why didn't you just say so?" he said.

She was beyond responding, her body shaking with sobs. Memories she never allowed to surface flooded her. Memories of masculine arms raised and lowered, hitting her. Beating her body over and over, not stopping, never stopping. She screamed and begged and it didn't matter. He didn't stop. Not stopping, not stopping, the pain, the pain.

But the arms holding her now were different from her memories, tender, contrite, cradling and rocking her. She tried to pull away, but Shep wouldn't let her go. "I'm sorry, sorry, sorry," he said.

It seemed hours later when she was able to raise her head. Her gaze met his anguished eyes, full of guilt. "I wasn't really serious about spanking you," he said. "I was only going to give you a few taps . . . I'm sorry."

"Some things you can't play around with and some places you don't go. If you had hit me I would have hated you forever." When she uttered the words, she knew she meant them.

"I'll never hit you," he said. Cherice looked into his eyes and knew he meant what he said. "I was way out of line," he said.

She settled back in his arms and it was her way of saying she forgave him. His arms tightened around her.

"What happened?" he asked a few moments later.

She shifted, not wanting to talk about it, but knowing she should. "My father died when I was ten. He drank a lot. He beat my mother and occasionally he beat me. A sad story, but a common one, I guess."

"How did he die?"

"A car accident." She paused and took a deep breath. "I wished he would die."

"Do you feel guilty about that?"

Cherice's chin lifted. "No. I only feel bad that it took me so long to make the wish."

"You don't like men too much, do you?" Shep asked after a pause.

"I like men. Some people say I like them too well."

"Maybe I should rephrase that. What I was wondering was if you trusted men."

Trusted men? The question took her aback. Had she ever trusted a man not to hurt her? Had she ever trusted one with her secrets? Her heart?

"No, I don't trust men," she answered, her voice low.

Shep sighed. "I can't blame you. With a brutal father—Jesus, I'm sorry I raised my hand to you. I was so stupid. I wish I could rewind time."

"Have you ever hit a woman before? Be honest."

"I knocked the hell out of Sheniqua Gates, but we were both eight and I recall when she got up, I paid dearly." Shep stared at his hands. "No, I've never hit a woman as an adult, even in jest. I don't know what I was thinking when I threatened to spank you. I believe only a weakling and a coward would hit a person who he knows is weaker. I'm a lot of things and not all of it is good, but I hope I'm more than that."

He let her go, stood and walked over to the deer hide, standing over it. "You seem so confident. You throw me off balance. I don't know any woman who's affected me that way. My reflex was to want to . . . spank you."

"Frankly, Shep, my fantasies run along the lines of whipping your ass, too."

A look of shock crossed his face. Then he grinned.

Burn

Maybe Shep was right, Cherice decided as she went to the stream to get water. Maybe this place was a little bit of paradise. It was the sort of day that was the reason the good Lord made autumn. The sky burned blue and the air was fresh enough to cut. She took a deep breath and smelled fall receding and winter coming in.

The thought didn't strike fear into her as it once did. She knew Shep would take care of her. A couple of weeks ago, if she had known that she'd be stranded in the wilderness without a lick of makeup for nigh on a week with only a man for company, slaving at menial tasks like chopping wood, catching fish and gathering nuts, she would have said that it would be the most miserable time of her life. But she'd never been so content. She could barely believe it herself.

Most of all, if someone had said that she'd be cooped up all alone with a highly attractive man that she was highly attracted to without some serious clothing ripping and boot knocking, she'd say they'd lost their minds.

Not that she wasn't about to lose hers. She was one huge sexual ache. She was like to die. But as far as ways to bite the dust went, she could think of worse.

Her waking moments were consumed with thoughts of parts of Shep's slammin' body in relation to hers. It hurt so damn good because she knew he wanted her, too. She saw the evidence in his body, and she saw it in his eyes. It was only a matter of time.

They didn't have much of an opportunity yet because they spent most of their waking hours working. They'd settled in. The walls were made and their little cave was now cozy and warm. Now they could sleep apart. Far apart. Shep didn't enter the cave until after she was asleep and left before she awoke.

She was getting extra water because today Shep wanted to show her how to make soap from the wood ashes so they could wash clothes. The stream was stiller than usual, probably from the freeze settling in higher up in the mountains. She bent over it and looked at her reflection in the clear water. She froze in place, shocked. Her features were washed out and bland. Cherice's once vibrant honey skin, gold eyes and gold hair all blended to dull yellowish beige. Her hair resembled old straw. Worst of all, although it was barely perceptible yet, she spied roots. Frizzled sandy brown roots, probably no more than a millimeter, next to her scalp. Cherice sank to the ground, horrified to the cellar of her soul.

She stared at her hands, callused and ashy, every single blessed nail broken off and with only specks of polish. She was a mess, a woman who built her fortune on appearance, a complete, sloppy, trifling mess. It wasn't acceptable. She clasped her shaking hands together. She had to get back home.

Cherice filled her bag with water and made her way back to the cave, heading straight for Shep. "Don't you think we should be doing more to be rescued? Maybe we should make some sort of SOS?" she asked, trying to keep the anxiety out of her voice.

"It would be hard for anything to be seen through the tree cover," Shep said.

There were a lot of trees, but still . . . "So what are we going to do? We can't stay here forever."

"We probably won't have to, but it's wise to be prepared for all contingencies. Check it out up there." Shep pointed upward to where he'd lashed branches together to form a platform. "That makes a dandy food storage area this winter."

To her dismay, her eyes filled with tears. "I don't want to stay in this place through the winter." The tears spilled and Cherice fled to the cave.

A moment later she heard Shep come in. "Go away," she said. "I hate to cry."

He sat down beside her. "I know. You don't seem like the crybaby type."

She wiped her face with her hands and sat up. "I'm not. I've never cried in front of any man but you—except my father."

She turned her head away from him. "You probably think I'm awful."

He reached out to touch her, then pulled his hand away as if she might burn him. "Baby, I don't think you're awful. I think you're kind of fabulous. I'd cut off my good leg before I'd hurt you."

Damn, she was going to start crying again. Why did he have to be so sweet like that?

"I want to tell you something and it's hard to do it," he said.

Cherice turned toward him, fear rising. What was he going to tell her?

"It's about me. I have a daughter."

Of all the things she was thinking he was going to say, that was not it.

"She's five now. I never married her mother. I never knew she was pregnant until I was served with the paternity papers. I'm not a part of my girl's life and if it's up to her mother, I may never be." He studied his hands with an expression of pain on his face.

"I'm sorry," Cherice said.

"One thing I never wanted to do was to scatter children around like my brother did," Shep continued. "But I met this woman. She was fascinating and attractive, but I wasn't ready to marry and besides, I was a SEAL, always putting my life at risk, always on the go at a moment's notice. I wanted to be a family man someday, but not then. If you're going to have a family, I've always believed, you should be with them, be a husband and a father. She laid down an ultimatum that I produce a ring, and when I didn't meet it, she broke up with me before an assignment. I wasn't too upset."

Shep sighed. "Two years later she pops out of nowhere with a baby and says I'm the father. She expects me to marry her and us to ride off into the sunset. I was beyond pissed that she didn't tell me she was pregnant. She deprived me of a year of my child's life. I took her to court for sole custody. I lost. I got joint custody, but I got injured right afterwards. She then went for sole custody and got it. She told me she'd do everything in her power to keep me away from my daughter. She's bitter about her fantasized happily-ever-after ending not turning out."

He touched Cherice's cheek. "So as you see, I'm wary of making any stray and unplanned babies. I don't think my brother is a true man, because he doesn't care for his own. I need my children to be cared for, loved and fathered, to be mine."

His light touch on her cheek was like fire, melting her inside. "Understand?" he whispered.

His lips were perfect. So close to hers. Closer. Cherice moistened her lips, her need turning into a familiar ache, but steeling close to her heart. She didn't want to understand. She really didn't. She just wanted them to make love and to hell with the consequences. But that wasn't her style either. She knew about responsibility and how could she have anything but respect for his?

"I understand," she said.

His gaze dropped. "Thank you," he said. He started to make his way outside of the cave, then stopped. "Cherice, I'm sorry."

"That's the way it is. It's nobody's fault," she said.

He shook his head and walked outside the cave.

Apparently he changed his mind about the soap because he gathered up supplies. "I'll be back well before twilight," he said.

She didn't want him to go. "We have more than enough meat. Why hunt today?" But she was speaking to his retreating back. He was already gone.

The sky darkened and grayed. Cherice made a small fire at the mouth of the cave to warm it and retreated there. She usually didn't rest during the day, but she felt wrung out.

If only the world was big enough to walk from one end to the other in an hour and she and Shep were the only two in it. Shep was a man who could tolerate weakness in others far better than in himself. If he gave in, Shep would hate himself and lay claim to her. So, here they were. Two grown people without a living human soul in heaven knew how many square miles and they couldn't do the natural thing that happens between a man and a woman.

Maybe they should talk about it. But talking about it meant facing it. Facing it meant dealing with it. Dealing with it meant ripping each other's clothes off and . . . Cherice sighed.

There was a distant rumble of thunder. She strained to hear Shep's footstep through the patter of icy sleet that started to drizzle down. Her enchanted day ended in a dreary freeze. She put on several layers of clothes to haul in more wood to get them through the spell of icy rain. When Cherice was done, she was frozen on the outside and heated and sweating from the exertion.

Her fingers were too numb to get the fire started again, so she snuggled in a niche behind their supplies to get warmed by her body heat in the small space and to catch her breath.

After a few minutes she heard Shep's comforting footfalls. "What, no fire?" he asked, his tone kind and worried and joking all at once.

"The sleet put it out. How did the hunting go?"

"The weather's bad. Thanks for getting the wood." He busied himself with the fire. "It looks as if the storm is headed in from the west and here to stay through the night, maybe through tomorrow. The temperature's dropping."

Cherice didn't like ice storms when she had the benefits of central heat. She could hardly imagine enduring one stuck outdoors. The past week the weather had been relatively mild with the night temperatures rarely dipping to below freezing. This was the real deal. Cherice's teeth chattered in anticipation.

They had two small deerskins in addition to rabbit and squirrel skins that Cherice had been stitching together with a crude bark needle. Even with the sputtering fire at the mouth of the cave, they would need to huddle together for warmth.

Eating smoked fish while playing a makeshift game of checkers, they talked about the weather and how to vent smoke from the cave better. Cherice didn't register their superficial words. The more important conversation was nonverbal.

His eyes on her breasts. Fingers accidentally brushing with the voltage of lightning bolts. Tongue wetting lips. Breath coming faster, heart beating wildly. The scent of arousal. It was as if a freight train was bearing down on them.

They'd given up on the words and allowed laden silence to overtake them. Cherice shivered uncontrollably, fear, longing and anticipation filling her, as the temperature dropped.

Shep groaned. "It's as if I told you the reason why we can't just in time to make myself out a liar," he said.

She reached out for him. It was as if her hand had a life of its own. She touched his lips. "Don't say that. We can stop."

He looked into her eyes. His eyes were storm black with longing. "We'll never stop." He kissed her fingertips. Cherice's eyes closed. His lips were firm, sensual, masculine. They moved over the pulse point of her wrist. She never imagined that a touch on her hand could move her as much as a passionate kiss.

She raised her head. That was before he kissed her. His mouth lowered, infinitely tender, gentle. She felt his restraint, tempered steel held back by velvet, and if she could have one wish, it would be to have all of him unleashed. "Please," she whispered.

It was as if a dam broke and a hot, wild river rushed in and drowned. His mouth became passionate, bold, and his body covered hers. The sun had come down to earth and settled within her core, he heated her that much. She entwined her arms around his strong shoulders; her legs spread and straddled his slim hips.

The freight train kept coming hard and pounding . . .

Blaze

Swept up in thick honeyed passion, her breath came in gasps as she felt his lips trail down her neck. He opened her blouse reverently and cupped her breasts in both hands, thumbs slowly rotating around her nipples. "I've wanted to touch you for so long."

And she wanted him inside her ever since she first laid eyes on him. *Please, now.*

His mouth lowered to her breasts. He played with them, a delicious tease. His tongue swirled around one nipple, then another, sucking, heating her to a burning frenzy.

Cool hands slid across her burning belly and she reached to him. "I want to make love to you. I've dreamed of this." He pinned her arms up, over her head. "I've dreamed of making you surrender to me."

She arched up blindly seeking him, arms encircling him, inhaling his masculine scent, drawing him close, drawing him in.

The gentle massage across her belly seared hot into her flesh. His hand edged lower and there was nothing but need. He touched her, explored her, tasted her until she gasped . . .

Into her skin, a part of her. Yes, forever. *Now, don't wait.* She groped for his waistband and they came together with the intensity of the too long denied. He sprang free, beautiful, big and proud, and she opened for him and took him in. No thoughts, only sensation, her one desire satisfaction.

"Do you want me?" he breathed. Their clothes had melted away and his tip, so hard, rigid and big was at her entrance. She widened, aching for him.

"So much."

"How much?" He eased into her a fraction of an inch, teasing, tantalizing, his hard smooth rod parting wet gates.

She bucked, at the brink, if he would just give . . .

"How much?" he asked, holding back, wanting something from her, what, what, oh lord, she had to have it . . .

"Please," she begged. "Please give it to me, I need you."

And with those words he broke and plunged home, filling her so good and hard, hurting so damn good she felt the tears leaking from her eyes as they beat that old-time rhythm. They took a wild ride, bucking and pumping, plunging back and forth, the delicious friction of his thickness pulling at her velvet walls, pushing her over, over, so tight, to the edge . . . and she fell, down and down to the point where pleasure and pain crossed and she never wanted to reach the bottom.

* * *

It was the first time in her life that Cherice felt as though she regained consciousness, but that's the best way she could describe how she felt after Shep's love-making. The charcoal outlines of the cave lit by orange embers were fuzzy and out of focus. There was residual stickiness between her thighs, and she turned to him to glean his reaction to doing something he'd said he was determined not to do.

He was lying on his back, arm covering his eyes. She watched him, afraid that a word from her would change everything even more.

So she waited for a word from him. A gesture. She waited to feel his arms around her, the comfort of his warm body. She waited to hear that everything was going to be all right.

Shep burrowed under the coverings, and turned his back to her, curled up into a ball, inward toward himself.

Waiting in vain. A too familiar feeling attached to wanting. It was a bad thing to want from a man.

It was a long time before she got to sleep.

Shep was gone before she woke. Thankfully, the ice and sleet had stopped falling from the sky, leaving the landscape bleak and frozen. She restarted the fire, heated water and washed up. When she walked outside, she smelled far-off wood smoke. Where was Shep? Certainly not hunting in this weather, they had plenty of meat. He simply was gone. Gone from her. She felt empty. Everything changes.

For the first time she wished she had a television or a laptop for games or any passive modern pastime.

She simply wanted to sit without thinking and be entertained while time passed. The key to modern life was not thinking overmuch. It kept one sane. Out here there was nothing else to do but think and reflect. There was no hiding from yourself, no escaping reality, no easy way out of dealing with a situation.

Maybe that's why what she looked like was so important to her back home, because she presented the construct as who she was, instead of taking the time and anxiety of finding out.

Here and now, in the past hour, she'd come to realize something about herself that didn't fit well and she didn't quite know how to wear. She, Cherice Givens, loved a man for the first time in her life. Poetic justice, wasn't it? A sort of wicked irony that here she sat, after the first time they made love, waiting for him to come back and drop the other shoe on her heart.

And she could control none of it. She braced herself for the emotional ass-kicking that she'd tried to avoid for nigh on thirty years.

What else could you expect from a man, after all?

Cherice didn't look at him as he approached. She couldn't, she really couldn't. He touched her cheek. Just before she turned to him, he said, "I have something to say. You're not going to like it."

Her heart started to pound like it was outside of her chest. Here it comes. She studied her feet and tried not to curl her hands into fists.

"I've not been completely honest with you."

So was he married? Gay? She prayed he had no communicable disease.

"I wanted to get to know you, spend time with you. I knew I'd never be able to do it in Kansas City. Your shell is so thick. Once this happened—the crash was terrible—but, this place seems like paradise to me. I feel completely safe here. Once I saw you weren't hurt . . ."

What the hell was he talking about? She hated folks who didn't get to the point.

"I thought it wouldn't hurt to stay for a little while. But when I saw you cry, it tore me up inside. Jesus, baby, I'm sorry." He looked like he was going to cry himself. "It seems like I'm always apologizing to you. It's not a good omen for any sort of relationship." He swallowed hard.

"What are you talking about?" Cherice demanded, what was left of her patience wearing to a thread and snapping.

"I thought I could handle everything, that I had myself completely under control." His head dropped. "That obviously isn't the case."

"Will you pleeeeze get to the point?" Cherice begged.

"We could have been out of here days ago, but I didn't want to go."

Cherice stared at him. "You're joking, right?"

"Uh, no."

"So you're telling me this is your idea of a vacation?"

He nodded, looking miserable. "I'm sorry. I truly apologize for lying to you. I honestly thought it would do you good. If there is anyway I can make it up—"

"You're out of your freaking mind." Cherice got to

her feet and headed toward the woods. She stomped through the trees, feeling incredulous, furious and somewhat relieved that it wasn't worse. But as it was, it was too much emotional fallout for even a big woman to handle.

She must have tromped on in a dazed flurry of emotion for about an hour when she stopped in her tracks. There was a huge bear in front of her sharpening its claws on a tree. It turned and stared at her. She stared back. They stared at each other for what seemed like hours, but must have been only seconds. Then her survival instinct kicked in. Cherice had already gone over what she would do if she came across a bear, and in her terror, it was very natural to execute. She fell over. It hurt when she hit the ground, but she hoped that being already dead was nonthreatening and unappetizing to Mr. Bear.

She squeezed her eyes tight and tried not to think about what being torn apart by a bear would feel like. She tried to perfect playing dead by barely breathing, but it didn't work well. Right before her choices narrowed to frost-bitten versus bear-chewed ass, she opened her eyes and looked around without moving a muscle and sniffed. She smelled no bear. She heard no bear. She cautiously lifted her head. She saw no bear.

Now she only had one problem. She had no idea where she was. Cherice tried to retrace her steps. "I will not panic. I will not panic," she repeated, both as a handy herald of her approach to warn any nearby bears and a positive mantra of affirmation.

She almost cried in relief as she heard Shep calling her name. "Over here," she answered.

He pulled her to him in an embrace as soon as he reached her, and everything faded away but this man's arms around her. She raised her head and looked into his brown eyes. She was drowning, drowning, but right now his arms held her up. Nothing was resolved. But she saw the caring and passion in his eyes and for some reason, for right now, that was enough. She could breathe. They walked back to camp in silence.

Inferno

The stars blazed and ice crunched underfoot when they returned to camp. Shep made a fire and they ate. The day had been exhausting physically and emotionally. After they ate, Cherice followed him into the cave and he gathered her in his arms. There was no room for words.

She curled up in the warmth and comfort of his arms and felt as if she were home. Tomorrow they would talk and she would make sense of what he'd said to her. Tomorrow they'd start again.

That night she dreamed of doves, thousands upon thousand of doves beating their wings and whipping up a mighty wind. Cherice woke shivering and alone. There was a commotion outside. She struggled to her knees and made her way out of the cave.

Her heart flipped over to see a helicopter in the clearing and Shep talking to the pilot. He spied her and approached. She couldn't read his face. "Is there anything you want to take?" he yelled over the whir of the blades.

She shook her head, in shock. It was over, just like that. She was going home.

He helped her in the helicopter and they lifted off. She looked down at their camp and melancholy filled her. It was over.

They set down at the Kansas City airport. Her girlfriends barely waited until she was off the helicopter until they rushed her, their faces drawn with concern; Topaz, Rosaline, and Brandy, her family more than her real family. They fluttered around her. She cast one last look at Shep. He was standing alone, gazing in her direction.

Rosaline helped her into a wheelchair and pushed her toward a waiting limo on the tarmac. They all moved to help her in, like she was an invalid. She shook them off and looked toward where Shep was standing. He was gone.

An hour later, she was in her home, in her bubbling hot tub, a glass of champagne in hand, her girlfriends ministering to her. Rosaline rinsed her hair.

"When we thought you were gone," Topaz paused. "It was as if we each lost a part of ourselves. Funny how you think nothing ever will change until it does."

Cherice took a sip of her champagne. "Everything changes."

"Even you?" Brandy asked. "You seem different. What happened out there?"

They all grew still as they waited for the answer to the question that they had been reluctant to ask.

"Less then you'd probably guess. I worked. Fished, gathered nuts, roots, anything edible. Hewed wood, carried water and such. It was a very back to the earth experience."

"Back to the earth experience? I didn't think you'd ever experienced earth, as in ground cover, to begin with," Rosaline said, eyebrow lifted.

"Yeah, and you aren't even acting overly traumatized. Hewing wood? Roots?" Brandy shuddered.

Topaz poured herself a glass of champagne and settled back in one of Cherice's chaise lounges. "What does your back to earth experience have to do with what had to be your more earthy experiences with the very handsome Shep Fraser?" she asked.

Cherice stared into her champagne. She wasn't ready to talk about Shep yet.

"Yes, tell us," Brandy urged.

"He made no effort to get us rescued," Cherice said slowly. "He wanted to hang out in the wilderness for a while. He liked it out there."

They all stared at her, speechless.

Finally Rosaline pulled herself together. "Are you saying that he tricked you?"

Cherice hesitated, then nodded.

"Goodness," Topaz murmured. "And your roots are showing."

Cherice touched her hair. Topaz knew how to get directly to the heart of the matter. The roots were the point of offense, the evidence of the heinousness of the crime. He'd deprived her of civilization against her will, allowed her roots to show for the first time in her adult life.

She heaved a sigh. "You know what? All of a sudden I don't give a damn about my roots."

There was a shocked intake of breath, one sound from three women. Topaz drained her champagne glass and poured another. "Tell us about this Shepard Fraser. He must be a hell of a man."

Cherice held out her glass for a refill. "I have to admit he is that."

Despite her declaration of nonchalance, Cherice went ahead and got her roots touched up, her body waxed, her nails done and her skin properly pampered.

She went through the motions of running her business, but it no longer thrilled. Her life seemed empty, her home nothing but a gilded cage. Thirty is old for self-realization and it was layered with surprise that she understood that the time with Shep was the most meaningful in her life. The happiest. She took long walks in the park, and spent time in the silence, simply sitting around doing nothing but staring into her fireplace.

She was waiting. Waiting for the phone to ring, waiting for the door to open. Waiting for Shep to show up. How could he not come to her after all they went through? But days passed, then another, then another.

Finally a letter came with a New Mexico return address. She ripped it open with trembling hands. Two sentences. *You'll let me know, won't you? I trust you.*

She closed her eyes, yet tears leaked out from under the lids as the pain of the realization racked her. He wasn't coming for her. The fantasy that she was holding dear crumbled to ashes. All Shepard cared about was whether or not she was carrying his child. Her hand drifted down to her lower belly.

Cherice turned the ignition in the rental car and perused the map. She drove along the asphalt, taking in the land. New Mexico was rugged, beautiful. Colors not usually used in the palette spread across the landscape. She could see why an artist would love living here.

She sped toward Shep. His truck was there, but he didn't answer the door. She walked toward the barn. The side door was open and she entered. She drew in a breath as she surveyed canvas after canvas of the wilderness, their cave—and her. Images of her laughing, sleeping, and . . . making love.

She closed the door behind her as she left. He was in a field, sitting on a rock, sketch pad in hand. When he saw her, he didn't react, as if she were a dream or a ghost.

Then when she approached, his eyes widened. "Cherice," then they dropped below her waist.

She raised her hand. "Let me first put your mind at ease, I'm not pregnant. I came up here to tell you something else."

On the plane trip here, she expected to see relief when she made her announcement. There was no relief. He dropped his gaze. "It's good to see you again," he said.

Cherice felt disconcerted, confused. "I wouldn't have guessed you felt that way," Cherice said.

He frowned. "I've always been clear about how I felt about you."

"You didn't call, you didn't come. I waited for you, Shep."

"I thought you hated me. I betrayed your trust. I lied to you."

Cherice started to pace, the enormity of what he said shaking her. "You mean for these past few weeks, I've been torturing myself, thinking you rejected me for nothing?"

Shep grimaced, nodded.

Cherice's voice trembled. "I've been driving myself insane worrying that all you cared about was whether I was pregnant or not." She faced him and put her hands on her hips. "So you wussed out on me because you thought I was mad at you. If I hadn't dragged my ass all the way out here to confront you, I would have gone on suffering indefinitely? Ain't this some bulls—?" She wheeled and stomped away.

Shep was right behind her. He grabbed her shoulder and swung her around. "I was coming!" he yelled.

"And when were you going to get around to it?" she yelled right back. "After we were both committed to the funny farm?" They glared at each other.

Shep shook his head and laughed. He reached out and pulled her into his arms. "I'm so glad you came," he whispered into her ear. "We're lucky at least one of us has good sense."

"I'm just impulsive. I also have a terrible temper. I planned to cuss you out."

"Refreshingly tempestuous."

"Geez. Big words," she said.

He smiled at her, and then his smile faded.

His head bent to hers and their lips met, tender, full of trust, love and the promise of passion that would soon be theirs.

"I love you, lady," he whispered, nuzzling her neck. "Wherever you want to be, that's where I'll be, too."

Cherice looked into his eyes, stunned at what he said he'd give for her. She gazed out over the sweep of the magnificent land, the wild beauty of it. This was where she belonged, by Shep's side, on the land they would both love.

She surrendered fully to his strong embrace, her refuge, her haven . . . her love. "It feels as if I've found my way home," she said.

"Our home," Shep said, his words a promise sealed with love.

His
Everything
Woman

Francis Ray

Acknowledgement

Special thanks to my daughter, Carolyn Michelle Ray, who asked me one night why the heroines I wrote about weren't full-figured. A good question deserves a good answer.

. *Chapter 1*

Neal Dunbar's well-ordered life had taken a dramatic turn and not for the better.

With wide-palmed hands braced on his lean, jean-clad hips, Neal stared at the packing boxes scattered on the gleaming hardwood floor of his living room. Boxes were in practically every room of his 1928 brick adobe cottage home that sat on a heavily wooded two-acre lot. What had seemed like a great idea six months ago no longer felt that way.

He'd lived in an apartment or condo since he'd graduated from college and had planned on continuing the trend. But a few weeks after he'd relocated from Miami to Austin, Texas, he had seen a HOUSE FOR SALE sign tacked to a rickety wooden gate. His natural curiosity had kicked in. He'd immediately wondered what lay hidden behind the dense crop of mature oak and sycamore trees.

Two days later Neal had his answer when he'd seen the two-story home surrounded by a yard that had gone wild with gladiolas and waist-high johnsongrass.

Dandelions muscled their way through the cracked pavement of the walkway. Pieces of asphalt shingles were scattered everywhere.

As a renovation designer, Neal had seen worse. Walking through the comfortably sized rooms with fading wallpaper, orange carpeting, and a kitchen too small even for a noncook like himself, he'd seen the possibilities instead of the glaring flaws and the costly repairs needed before the house was habitable again; flaws that had probably helped keep the house on the market for the past two years.

Ideas had whirled though Neal's head as he looked out through the dirty window panes and visualized wide, arched windows and the enormous undisciplined crepe myrtle in the front yard shaped and ringed with hosta and dragon-winged begonia.

The tiny sewing room next to the kitchen could be renovated to allow for a pantry and a little breakfast nook for those rare mornings he wasn't rushing out the door and had time for a leisurely cup of coffee. He could take the house with its electric mix of English Country and Tudor details and turn it into an inviting and comfortable living space.

He'd checked wiring, plumbing, insulation and a number of other areas to assure himself that there were no major problems, then he'd put in a bid on the house. By the time he'd reached his apartment, the realtor was calling him back with a counter offer. Although Neal was excited about the house, he didn't budge. He could bluff with the best of them. Fifteen days later he'd closed on the house.

Then the tedious work of bringing to fruition what he'd envisioned began. Luckily his older brother, Michael, was a landscape designer and owned Evergreen Landscaping in Dallas. Brody, his younger brother, was a building contractor and lived in Albuquerque. The three of them had spent long hours on-site and on the phone, first planning, then working on the renovations. He'd used aged English bricks for the paving of the walk, steps and area around the newly constructed swimming pool.

Now, five months later, he could proudly say he'd accomplished most of what he had set out to do with the help of his family, but he had yet to enjoy the fruits of his labor.

Worse, he wasn't about to relax until he unpacked some of the 50-plus boxes from his condo. He hadn't so much as stuck his toe in the rectangular pool tucked between the piazza and the kitchen. It had gotten so bad, he dreaded pulling into the garage because he knew all the work that waited inside.

In his profession as well as his home, he liked order. Chaos unsettled him. He enjoyed his work, but it was often stressful and demanding, so when he came home he wanted an oasis of calm, a sanctuary that soothed his nerves and fed his soul.

He wasn't even close to having either.

Neal blew out a breath as he glanced around the living room with its eggshell walls and khaki-colored trim and saw the hand-carved dining table that was hidden beneath several months of professional magazines he subscribed to. When he had the time, he'd go through them and keep the articles that interested him. In the meantime, they were the least of his problems.

In the weeks he'd lived there, only his clothes were unpacked. And that was due to necessity, because he had to get dressed for work.

After his father's death, when Neal was eight, money had often been tight. His mother worked hard to keep her three growing sons clothed and fed with a roof over their heads. She had done without to see that they wouldn't. He and his brothers quickly learned to take care of their possessions so they'd last, and then perhaps their mother would buy herself a new dress.

A smile curved Neal's mouth as he entered his office with cherry paneling and built-in lighted bookshelves. Their mother might not have bought many new clothes then, but she was making up for it now. She lived to shop. In fact, her shopping was what had brought his brother Michael and his wife, Stephanie, together.

Michael had been searching for their mother when he'd gone into a boutique where Stephanie worked as the assistant manager. He'd found their mother and had been instantly taken with Stephanie. Luckily she had felt the same way.

Placing the box on the polished cherry desk, one of the few clear surfaces in the house, Neal began pulling out books. If anyone had told him that his older brother would fall in love and marry within three months of meeting a woman, Neal would have laughed his head off.

Michael might have fallen, but not Neal. There wasn't a woman alive who could get him to the altar. He enjoyed women too much to settle for one.

Neal picked up another book. He liked to read and collected first editions as well as historical textbooks on architecture and design. With six remaining boxes, he'd be at this for a while.

His mother had offered to fly down from Dallas to help him, but he'd told her he could handle things. He wasn't about to take her away from helping Stephanie get ready for the opening of her own clothing boutique, The Wright Solution.

He realized how crucial timelines and openings were. He was dealing with both. Fincher and Fincher, the architectural firm he worked for, had beaten out firms from across the country to renovate the seventy-five-year-old Alistair Hotel located in the heart of downtown Austin. Once finished, the Alistair would hopefully reclaim the five-star status it lost over thirty years ago after going through a series of owners and a steady decline in bookings.

The present owners had hotels across the country and not one had a rating below four-star. It had been a coup for Neal's firm to be selected. But it also meant his workdays would get longer. At the rate he was going he would be unpacked about the same time he finished the hotel.

Irritated at the situation, he shoved another book onto the shelf. He couldn't last that long living out of boxes.

He supposed he could hire someone, but he didn't like the idea of just anyone going through his things.

Besides, they'd probably put them in the wrong place and he'd just have to do it all over again.

If you had a wife like Michael has, she could get the house in order for you.

Neal shuddered as he recalled his mother's words when they'd spoken last night. He headed back for another load. Stephanie was a great woman and he was pleased for his oldest brother, but marriage wasn't in his immediate plans.

Settling down with one woman was like asking a starving man to choose one item from an eleven-course meal. Impossible. That was another reason he had to get his place in order. With moving, the renovations on the house and gardens, he hadn't been on a date in seven months, which was a record for him. He didn't even have time to look at a woman, which in his humble opinion was a crying shame.

Back in his office he placed another box on the desk. On the wide-screen television across from his desk, a local talk show had taken the place of the nightly news. Pert and cheerful, Pamela Camp, the pretty hostess in her early thirties, went through the lineup of guests, people with unusual jobs.

Neal could not have cared less. He didn't watch much TV. He'd turned on the set to catch the news. Besides, on a beautiful spring Friday night he should be on a date with a woman, not watching one on television and unpacking boxes.

"Our first guest is Cara Scott, often referred to as the Domestic Diva."

Neal reached for the remote. He didn't want to hear about some woman cooking. His thumb was over the

POWER button when the camera zeroed in on a woman in a high-backed chair sitting next to the hostess. Neal froze. She was simply gorgeous, with dark, laughing eyes and a sultry mouth that begged to be kissed.

"Welcome, Cara," the hostess said.

"Thank you, Pamela. It's a pleasure being here. By the way, I'm also known as a hired wife," Cara said, with a husky just-shy-of-wicked laugh that went straight to Neal's gut.

"Where do I go to sign up?" Neal quipped to himself with a grin. Now, that was what he called a woman. Poised and voluptuous, she was stylishly dressed in a black pantsuit and white blouse with the collar upturned and the cuffs peeking over her wrists. Easing a hip onto the corner of the desk, he kept his eyes glued to the television screen.

"I'm also a personal shopper, cook, housekeeper, gardener, designer," Cara went on to say. "Anything my client needs to make their life easier, more enjoyable and fulfilling, either I or one of my three employees will do it. No task is too small or too large."

"I'll start making a list." Neal's grin was pure sin.

"How do you ensure that a design project suits the client's taste and not yours?" Pamela asked.

"By meeting with them, getting to know them over a casual dinner, observing how they work and relax, finding out what's important to them," Cara said. "Some of my clients want a room designed around an antique piece handed down from one generation to the next. Others want sleek contemporary with stainless steel and strong colors, while others prefer a soft romantic feel with crystal and flowers or even a combination. There is no right or wrong way to decorate a room. It's what makes you feel good."

"Exactly," Neal said, nodding his head in agreement. Too many decorators he'd worked with felt their way was the only way.

"Cara, let's get back to the hired wife," Pamela said. "Have any of your clients ever tried to take that literally?"

Cara's dark eyes momentarily narrowed. Unconsciously, Neal's hand tightened around the control. "If they do, they become ex-clients. Hired wife is a moniker one of my first clients gave me and it stuck. She referred me to several of her friends who also became clients. I handle things for busy working mothers or women executives who simply don't have the time. If a male client thinks I'm there for any other reason he's dropped immediately."

"Come on, Cara," the announcer cajoled, glancing briefly at the camera in a conspiring way. "Hasn't there been at least one drop-dead gorgeous man in the five years since you began developing Cara's Innovations who has tempted you?"

Cara's smile slipped for a fraction of a second, then firmed. "I've worked with some gorgeous men who were charming and attentive, men who made me happy to be a woman, but so far none has been the one for me." Cara paused, her expression serious. "However, being gorgeous isn't enough. He would have to have other qualities, like integrity and dependability."

"Have you found such a man and, if so, does he have a brother?" Pamela asked with a laugh.

Neal straightened. "Please say no."

Cara laughed as well. "No, much to the annoyance of my mother and grandmother."

"Yes! Neal pumped his fist.

"I can make any home a pleasure to return to where the meal is prepared, the table set with fresh flowers, the house immaculate, the scent of their favorite candle in the air," Cara went on to say.

"*Any* home?" Pamela asked.

"Any home," Cara said with confidence. "I'm building a reputation, and the satisfaction of the client is paramount to my success. If I can't do the job, I won't waste my time or the potential client's time."

A gleam entered the hostess's dark eyes. "What if we put you to the test?"

"How so?" Cara asked, a slight frown knitting her brow.

Pamela leaned forward. "Let's say we select a new client from those you take on after tonight's show and film the before and after of their home. You and the client then come back on the show."

"Some clients are very private," Cara said. "I'm sure you can understand that. Or they just don't want people to see their home in a light that might reflect badly on them."

Pamela nodded. "Understandable. I'll leave it up to you to select a client who would be suitable for our purposes."

Cara didn't hesitate. "As long as my client is comfortable with the situation, I have no problem with it."

The announcer laughed. "You forgot to mention price."

Cara's sensual mouth curved into a smile. Neal imagined seeing that look just before his lips touched hers.

"After being raised by parents whose grandparents lived through the Great Depression, if necessary, I can pinch pennies with the best of them. However, I won't bat an eyelash at suggesting a hard-carved table that could cost twenty-thousand dollars if I think it would complement the setting I've created."

Pamela's eyes widened in disbelief. Neal smiled. He'd seen the same shocked expression on a few of his clients' faces when he suggested using authentic pieces or having an item made for an authentic look.

"Whew," Pamela finally said, then looked at the camera. "Well, you heard her, audience. If you want the Domestic Diva to straighten out your life as your hired wife or just to help you decorate your home on a budget or the sky's the limit, her phone number is at the bottom of the screen. And if it's decorating a room or the entire house, please be agreeable to us coming out to film." Pamela glanced over at Cara. "If you're single and handsome or just the kind of man to make a woman swoon, so much the better."

"But don't feel bad if I'm more interested in selecting the right accessory for a room than in you," Cara quipped.

"All right, fellows, she has issued a challenge," Pamela said. "There's got to be a man in Austin who can at least tempt her to date a client. So pick up that phone and call Cara's Innovations and make an appointment. I look forward to meeting the winner, and no offense ladies, but I hope it's a single guy."

Neal rounded the desk and wrote down the number. Pamela was right, the challenge was too blatant to let pass, especially since it was given by such a stunning woman.

He was taking his mother's advice and getting a wife . . . a hired wife.

Chapter 2

Saturday morning Cara woke with a smile on her face. Why shouldn't she? Life was great! Her company, Cara's Innovations, was thriving and after the interview last night on one of Austin's top-rated talk shows, business should pick up considerably. Pamela's suggestion that Cara select a client for a before and after shoot would certainly help. She had been truthful when she said some people were private, but many would jump at the chance to be on Pamela's show.

Cara wasn't worried about Pamela's challenge. Earl Peters had taught Cara to never mix business with pleasure. Just thinking about the low-down rat made her want to hang her head in embarrassment, then hang Earl up by his toes. He had dated her until she had decorated his apartment with ten thousand dollars worth of furniture and accessories before breaking up with her. He'd refused to pay the bill, saying they were gifts. She'd been gullible and stupid enough to put the purchases on her credit card.

Luckily the threat of taking him to court had pried

the money out of him. The investment company he worked for would have taken a very dim view of their accountant being taken to court, especially when she had a contract and his signature signing off on every purchase. But the experience with Earl had taught her a lesson. Dating clients could lead to problems. Thus far, keeping her resolve had been easy.

Thrusting Earl from her mind, Cara stared up at the ceiling covered with fat, drifting blue clouds in a clear sky. In those lean and scary early days of her first year in business it had been difficult to keep doubts at bay. Earl's duplicity hadn't helped. During the most trying times she had decided she'd wake up to a glorious day no matter what her mood or what the weather might be outside. The ceiling she'd painted ensured she kept that promise.

After that first bumpy year she'd steadily built a client base by meeting the varied needs of people who simply didn't have the time or the talent to do things for themselves. The nesting instinct was strong and people wanted their surroundings pleasing and restful after a stressful day.

From an early age Cara's mother had taught her that philosophy in caring for her family. Home was a haven. Problems stopped at the door and if they dared intrude, the surroundings, preferably a garden setting with running water and a sympathetic, loving family, would soothe.

Despite Cara following a different career path that her parents had initially wanted, they still loved her. And she loved them. She just couldn't be what they wanted or expected.

Cara was supposed to go into dentistry like her older brother and sisters. Although she admired her siblings for their dedication and hard work and had the grade point average and SAT scores to follow in their footsteps, she'd majored in Interior Architecture. Her interest lay in colors and design, turning the ordinary into the extraordinary.

Today, Mother Nature was certainly cooperating. Even at seven in the morning, sunlight poured through the single window directly behind her white iron bed. Diaphanous white curtains hung from a circular rod over the three-foot graceful spiral of the headboard, then draped to the white-carpeted floor.

Reaching over, Cara turned off the alarm she no longer needed. Next to the radio on the nightstand were some of her favorite possessions: a milk white pitcher filled with the graceful branches of apple blossoms from her parents' backyard; her first black porcelain doll; and the china cup and saucer her grandmother had given her when she'd mastered the fine art of serving tea at six years old.

Cara couldn't imagine anything better than being surrounded by things that held cherished memories of those you loved. Her father had always said, "You couldn't have a future without a past." And despite her parents' and grandparents' worry, hers certainly looked bright.

Still smiling, Cara threw back the hand-stitched bedspread handed down from her great-grandmother and headed for the shower. Life was outside waiting.

* * *

An hour later, Cara pulled into the upscale shopping center where Cara's Innovations was located. The rent was steep, but the location was ideal. With the varied mix of stores, it was also tough to get a parking space. Even the space for tenants in back of the stores was often filled.

Seeing a spot a hundred feet from her store, Cara pulled in and got out of her bright yellow SUV, quickly heading for her store.

When she saw a man with his hands cupped to the sides of his face peering through her plate glass window, a frown darted across her face. Women stopped and stared all the time at the different drapery treatments or the queen-sized four-poster bed luxuriously covered in imported silks and fluffy pillows. She couldn't recall a man doing so, especially one wearing creased jeans that fit his long muscular legs and cupped his tight behind as if they'd been molded to him. He was certainly built well.

She did not ogle men, but she did admire beautiful things and he was certainly that. With her most professional smile she walked up to the man and said, "Good morning, may I help you?"

He turned. Midnight black eyes narrowed, then he slowly smiled and it was like coming upon a perfect rose in a hedge of thorns. Breathtaking.

For a moment she felt light-headed. He was simply gorgeous, with a strong chin and a full, neatly trimmed beard. She'd always been attracted to men with beards ever since, as a teenager, she'd seen an old movie about swashbuckling pirates.

"I certainly hope so," he finally said. His slow, deep voice was as wicked as the half smile on his handsome face.

Disregarding the warm tingle that went through her, she said, "I'm Cara Scott."

"I'd know you anywhere." He extended his wide-palmed hand. "Neal Dunbar. I saw you last night on television."

Cara tried not to be affected by a face handsome enough to tempt any woman and a muscular body shown to perfection in a white shirt and sinfully tight jeans. But it was difficult. She felt a slight jolt as he took her hand in his. Last night's boast of her ability to resist men came back to her. She hoped he wasn't a potential client.

Trying to appear casual, she withdrew her hand. "What can I do for you?"

"I'd like to hire your services," he said.

Regret swept through her, but she didn't let it show. Business always came first. "I'm not open for another hour. I can give you my card or you can call back later to discuss how Cara's Innovations might help."

"Can't you spare a minute or two? You're looking at a desperate man."

He didn't look desperate. He looked like a man who took what he wanted. A little chill ran down her spine.

"I got your address from the phone book and took a chance since you're self-employed that you might come in early." He smiled again. "I wanted to put my request in before anyone else. As I said, I'm kind of desperate here."

Disregarding all the warnings her family had ever told her about being in the shop alone with a man, Cara stepped around Neal and opened her door. "Please come in, Mr. Dunbar."

"Please call me, Neal, and thanks." Following her inside, he closed the thick wooden door behind him.

"Have a seat, I'll be right back."

"Take your time," he said, still standing by the door.

For a brief moment Cara thought she might have made a mistake. He was a large, powerfully built man and although she was a full-figured size twenty-two, she would be no match for him.

"Your first instinct that you could trust me was correct," he said.

Not knowing how she felt about a man who seemed to read her so easily, she went to the back to turn off the alarm. When she reentered the front of the shop he had wandered to the display of seashells and candles on a sofa table. He faced her almost immediately.

"You have a great place here."

"Thank you." Since he had not taken a seat, she didn't either. "You mentioned you were desperate."

He nodded. "Three weeks ago I moved into my first home, a home that needed major renovations, as well as the property around it. Since moving I've only gotten around to unpacking my clothes and my computer equipment." He blew out a breath. "I can't continue to live out of boxes or in chaos. Please help."

"Mr. Dun—"

"Neal," he corrected.

"Neal. You can hire any number of services to unpack your clothes. You don't need me." Why did just saying the words fill her with another twinge of regret?

"But would they know how to establish a focal point and tailor the interior colors, select accessories and furnishings to complement the rooms, know where to hang my art, be able to tackle window treatments, stock the pantry and refrigerator, then visualize how to finish off the flower garden and pool area?"

As he'd listed the areas he needed help in, her interest piqued. She enjoyed decorating a room, but she had always wanted the challenge of tackling an entire house. But she had to be honest. "I've never had a project that was this extensive."

His dark brow lifted. "Do you think you can handle it?"

"Yes," she answered immediately. "The house and the grounds should have a natural flow and be totally integrated."

"I agree," he said. "Now that I have a house I'd like to enjoy it after all the hard work my brothers and I put into getting it and the grounds in shape."

"You have family here?" she asked, finding it easy to talk to him.

"Mother in Houston, brothers in Dallas and Albuquerque," he told her, then glanced at his stainless steel watch. "Sorry, but I have an appointment in ten minutes. If you have no other plans, how about dinner tonight to continue this discussion?"

It wasn't an unusual request and she often used it as a means of getting to know clients. If Neal had watched the entire program last night he was aware of this. However, she didn't usually see clients after five on Saturdays.

"Please," he said persuasively.

With the beckoning smile on his handsome, bearded face there probably weren't many women who could say no to him. "I'd rather see your house."

"Why don't we do both. Would six be convenient? There would still be enough light to see the grounds."

Cara stared at him a long moment. He hadn't missed a beat with that suggestion of combining the two. It was reasonable. So why did she feel like Little Red Riding Hood with the Big Bad Wolf?

"The house is situated on a wooded two-acre lot. It's isolated," he said. "Feel free to bring an associate or a friend."

He was reading her mind again and she definitely didn't like it. "What do you do for a living?"

If he thought the question odd, he didn't look like it. "I'm a renovation designer for Fincher and Fincher."

Her eyes widened. The company was one of the most prestigious architectural firms in the state. "Are you working on the Alistair Hotel?"

"Yes. Thus my hectic schedule." He glanced at his watch again. "I'll call later. I have to go. Good-bye and thanks for seeing me."

"Please call with the address." Deciding she'd been overreacting, she handed him her business card. She'd met male clients by herself on many occasions. There was nothing to fear from this man.

He placed the card in the pocket of his white shirt.

"By the way, you're even more beautiful in person. Bye."

Cara was left staring after him. As if compelled, she moved to the glass window to watch his long, ground-eating strides carry him quickly to a big black pickup truck. He was six feet plus of coordinated muscles and drop-dead gorgeous. He wore jeans that looked as if they'd been poured on, but the worst thing was the sexy smile on his handsome face that she had no doubt could tempt a saint.

She wasn't a saint. What she was was in trouble.

Chapter 3

For the first time in weeks Neal rushed home with a smile. The meeting with Cara had gone better than expected.

She was as warm and as open as she came across on television. She was also more beautiful in person and wore the most intoxicating fragrance he'd ever smelled. He'd wanted to sniff and investigate all the places she might have put the scent. She wouldn't have liked that . . . at least not this soon.

Smiling, he pulled into his driveway, retrieved the mail from the mounted mailbox, then activated the iron gate to slide open. His Cara was the cautious type. He shook his head at his phrasing. In his mind he'd already claimed her. He just had to make it a fact. It wouldn't be easy, but then he'd never liked anything that was.

He'd seen the wariness a couple of times in her beautiful, dark brown eyes. He didn't blame her for being cautious, but he planned to show her that she had nothing to fear from him.

Continuing the half-mile drive to the house he pulled into the double garage in the back. Grabbing the bags of food from the passenger seat and his attaché case, he got out of the truck and went inside.

The kitchen, with its warm oak cabinets and rough-beam ceiling, was a chef's delight with the latest appliances in black and stainless steel. His mother had fun picking them out, saying even if he didn't cook the kitchen would still be pretty. The accoutrements were in cobalt blue.

Placing everything on the smoky-colored granite countertop, he opened the glass-front cabinet and took down a bag of paper plates. The dishes were someplace, but since he didn't like loading and unloading the dishwasher, paper suited him just fine. Then, too, he wanted Cara to see how much he needed her.

Finished with setting the table he picked up his attaché case and started to his office. In the living room he happened to look out of the large plate glass window and stopped dead in his tracks.

Cara stood in the midst of the garden Michael had so painstakingly designed. His brother had insisted on flowers, vines, trees and shrubs that offered blooms with year round color. The results were spectacular. The yard was alive with pink, red, and yellow blooms that were everywhere and which invited the eyes.

Neal had appreciated Michael's ability to create such beauty, but his appreciation went up a notch as he moved closer to the window. He couldn't imagine a more beautiful sight than the one he was viewing now. A slow smile curved his mouth. He placed the attaché on the nearest box and opened the door.

Cara glanced up. Neal's hand on the doorknob tightened. Beautiful couldn't define the exotic looking woman staring back at him with wide, wary eyes. She was absolutely stunning.

She moistened her lips, and Neal groaned, fantasizing of closing the distance between them and satisfying his curiosity about the sweetness of her mouth. Soon, he promised himself as he continued toward her, hoping the hunger in his body didn't show in his face and scare her away. "Hello, Cara."

"Hello. I hope you don't mind that I'm early. I wanted to be sure I found your place," she said. "You're right, it is isolated. You certainly have your privacy."

"Initially that wasn't my intention, but I'm enjoying the peace and quiet. I can turn my jazz up as loud as I like and only disturb the wild animals," he said with a smile.

She glanced around. "It's absolutely breathtaking."

"I was thinking the same thing about you," he said softly.

Cara's head snapped back around. Something she saw in his eyes must have alarmed her because she took a step back. "I think we need to get something clear. I don't date clients."

"I believe what you said on television was that none of your male clients had been the one for you," he reminded her. "Would you like to look over the grounds or go inside and eat? I have stuffed chicken breast with green salad. I hope you're hungry."

"Did you hear what I just said?" she asked.

"Every word." He gently took her arm and drew

her closer just to tease himself with the tantalizing floral fragrance she wore. "You smell delicious."

Freeing her arm she stared up at him. "What do you think you're doing?"

"Paying you a compliment," he said easily. "Surely you have no objection to that?"

It sounded reasonable, but something about the determined look in his eyes wouldn't let her relax. "I do when they're personal."

"That's the only kind worth saying."

Cara had a feeling she could argue, but she'd lose. Her chin lifted and she gave him her most professional-no-nonsense look. "I'd rather see the grounds first."

"This way." He took her arm again.

There was both strength and tenderness in his touch as he led her to a curving stone pathway. Cara had to remind herself he was a potential client and not let herself lean closer and enjoy being held with such care.

"As you can see, the ground was uneven in front, but instead of grading, I decided to use the natural sloping to give it a terraced look and let my brother do his thing with plants and flowers."

"He didn't suggest any pots of flowers for the front or edging the terrace with a small tree. Perhaps a Japanese maple? She asked as they followed the path.

"He did, but I wanted to wait until I could find pots I liked and until I'd decided on the color to paint the adobe brick," he explained.

Stopping, she stared at the side of the house. "The existing red brick does nothing for the house."

He turned with her. "I agree. And the custom color I ordered didn't either. The shutters are in the garage, waiting to go up once I decide. We did the structural changes and left it at that. I decided I could paint after I got a feel for the place."

Cara gazed up at Neal with new respect. "Some people rush headlong into things to get it done, and then regret it later."

His gaze drifted to her mouth. "I'm a man who takes his time and savors things."

Her breath fluttered out over her lips. She was positive he wasn't talking about the house. Deciding that discretion was the better part of valor, she turned and continued on the path just wide enough for two. "The garden looks as if it's been here for years."

"Thanks to Michael." Rounding the corner of the house, they passed beneath an arbor with yellow roses in full bloom, then followed the winding path down a slight incline.

"It becomes more beautiful and breathtaking with every step," she said, moving away from Neal to look at the abundance of flowers, the dark waters of the rectangular, reflecting pool and the shooting fountain at the end of the well-tended yard. "You must love it out here."

Neal sighed. "I probably would if I had time to come out here, and if I had someplace to sit when I did."

"Since the area is open, I'd suggest a cast aluminum table set. You could come out here to relax or enjoy your meals."

"Speaking of food, let's go inside." Taking her arm

again, he led her up the curved steps to the back door and into the spacious kitchen. "Excuse the mess."

"If it were neat, you wouldn't need me." She looked around the kitchen with the built-in refrigerator, graceful swirl of granite on the counter and island, the unique glass-front cabinets over the counter that allowed a person working in the kitchen to still be a part of what was going on in the living room. "If the rest of the house is as well laid out as this area and the grounds, I'd say you did a fantastic renovation job."

"Thanks." Neal pulled out a chair in the breakfast nook, which looked out into the side yard. An arbor of yellow roses arched over the window. "Let's eat and then I can show you around."

After taking her seat, Cara picked up her napkin, then smiled, finding a paper plate in front of her. Reminds me of when I eat at my brother's house."

Neal poured iced tea, served her the chicken and then served himself. "Does he live in Austin?"

"Yes, along with my two older sisters. I'm the youngest." Cara picked up the container of mixed vegetables and roasted potatoes and, following his lead, served him before serving herself.

"Parents?" he asked, pulling a loaf of French bread from the bag on the table.

"The same." She placed the carton on the round oak table. "They're all in practice together."

"Decorating?"

"Dentistry." She waited for his reaction on why she didn't join the practice.

"Dentistry's loss is my gain," he said easily, then bowed his head and said grace. "Don't let all the

314

boxes scare you," he said when he raised his head again. "You can take as long as you like." He paused, noticing she wasn't eating. "The food not to your liking?"

"You're the first person I've ever told about my parents who hasn't asked me why I didn't follow in their footsteps," she told him in amazement.

He sliced a chunk of bread for them. "It's obvious you enjoy decorating more."

Smiling, she leaned back in her chair. "I do, but it was difficult at first to get my family to understand. Now they're my biggest supporters." She chuckled. "They have my business cards and brochures all over the office."

"My mother doesn't hand out cards, but her friends probably get tired of hearing about us."

Cara nodded, then took a bite of her meat. "Delicious. I haven't eaten since breakfast."

"Do you have many days like that?" he asked, enjoying being with her and seeing her drop her guard and relaxing.

"Fortunately, yes," she told him. "I remember the lean years too well to complain when I'm on the run all day. As expected, the show last night generated a lot of interest and I'll be even busier." She picked up her glass of tea and sipped. "I have appointments scheduled for the next three weeks."

Neal frowned. "You'll have time for me, won't you?"

"I haven't decided to take on this project." She glanced around the room. "It would take me a week just to unpack . . . and that's just the boxes I've seen."

Neal pushed his empty plate aside. "Then hire someone to do that while you coordinate the finishing touches on the house, like the color of the house, the gardens and pool area. I told you I need you."

Her heart did a little leap as he stared intently at her. Cara realized the reason she was reluctant to work with Neal was because he disturbed her in the most elemental way. He wasn't a man a woman could easily resist or forget. He was too tempting. "What if I wanted to paint the house pink?"

"Which shade?" he asked without batting an eyelash.

Her mouth dropped open, then she snapped it shut. "Do you ever react the way people think you should?"

"Probably not." He placed his napkin beside his plate. "If you're finished, I can show you the rest of the house."

She owed him that much, but she would be asking for trouble if she agreed to work for him. Earl had taught her a valuable lesson about the hazard of dating clients she couldn't afford to forget. "All right."

Standing, he reached for her chair and pulled it out. "My office is on this floor, along with the master bedroom, kitchen and living area. Upstairs are the two guest bedrooms, connecting bath and theater room. This way."

To Cara, each room held more possibilities than the last one. The white walls in the guest bedrooms begged for a splash of color, the windows in the master bedroom longed for wooden blinds, the addition of a sofa table in the living room would be wonderful, and so much more. The house was beautiful, but it could be spectacular.

They ended the tour in the living room amid the packing boxes. Against the walls were several African-American paintings.

Neal caught the direction of her stare. "I started to hang them, but then I thought I'd wait until the furniture was in place."

"I'd like to see all of them before we decide on their placement." Next, she explained her rates and how she worked.

Eyes wide, Neal stepped in front of her. "You're taking me on."

Cara refused to listen to the little voice of caution in her head or to react to the arousing closeness of Neal. Being her size it wasn't often that a man towered over her, and never had one made so many emotions flow through her. Taking on Neal as a client would test her self-control every time she was with him. Yet, the house called to her. Or was it the man? "If you're agreeable to my terms."

Laughing, he grabbed her arms and stared down into her eyes. "When can you start?"

His rich laughter vibrated through her. "How about Monday morning at eight? I could be here by the time you're ready to leave for work, if that's all right. I could bring the contract with me."

"Great. This calls for a celebration with a glass of wine." Releasing her, he went into the kitchen and took a bottle of chardonnay from the refrigerator, opened it, then filled two paper cups and handed her one.

Her lips twitched as she took the paper cup. "I'm definitely unpacking your dinner and glassware first."

Neal held out his cup. "To a long association as a hired wife and all its benefits."

Cara's smile faltered for a second. Neal had that hungry look again. Had Little Red Riding Hood willingly entered the Wolf's den?

"Cara?"

She touched her cup to his. She could handle Neal or any other attractive man.

"How about I pick you up tomorrow afternoon and we can go look at furniture for the pool and garden area?"

Cara blinked. Most men would rather have their toenails pulled without anesthesia than go shopping for furniture. "The decorator showroom where I can get a discount is closed on Sundays."

"The Internet is open 24–7 and I have a few contacts of my own," he said. "We can do it all here."

Reasonable. But then she was quickly learning that Neal was always reasonable. That's what made him so dangerous. "I have plans."

Midnight eyes narrowed. "Oh."

"Church and then Sunday dinner with my family," she told him. Immediately she wondered why she was explaining herself to him.

Neal nodded his dark head. "If my mother lived here, that's where I'd be." His expression forlorn, he glanced around the room. "Not by myself eating take-out again."

"Would you like to come to dinner?" she said before thinking.

"Yes," he answered almost before the invitation was out of her mouth. "You just saved me from another lonely Sunday. Thank you."

"Y-you're welcome," Cara said, still a bit stunned. She hadn't invited a man to Sunday dinner since she'd broken up with Earl.

"What time should I pick you up?"

Time to put a halt to this. "I'll drive myself. I don't want anyone getting the wrong impression. You're a client."

He grinned. "And you're my hired wife."

Chapter 4

Neal could tell that Cara was leery of him, but he planned to change that. He was a patient man when it came to obtaining what he wanted. He wanted Cara.

Turning into the tree-lined street where Cara's parents lived, he smiled, realizing that he hadn't been invited to Sunday dinner by a woman since high school. That he'd finagled the invitation was beside the point. Neal was convinced that Cara would realize that she'd finally met a client who tempted her, just as much as she tempted him.

Moments later he pulled to a stop behind a snazzy red BMW sports car. Parked in front was a Mercedes. In the driveway sat a Hummer and Cara's yellow SUV. Without asking, he knew business considerations, not finances, had factored into her choice of a vehicle.

He walked up to the door and rang the doorbell. Before the chimes stopped ringing, the door opened.

"Hello, Neal," Cara greeted him.

Warmth and a nip of lust zipped though him. The lemon yellow suit she wore complemented her caramel complexion. The straight skirt she wore showed off her figure and nice legs. "Hello, Cara."

Her welcoming smile slipped, when she saw the potted basket of pink tulips in his hand. "I told you this isn't a date."

"I know. This is for your mother." He held up the other hand with a bottle of sparkling cider. "This is for dinner."

"Oh," she said.

He leaned in close to her. "Don't worry. I have something else for you."

Her eyes widened. She took a quick step back, and Neal entered the house. He wasn't surprised to see a group of attractive people in the great room watching him. Only the older woman he assumed was Cara's mother was smiling.

It was easy to see the rest were reserving judgment. He planned to do his best to put their minds at ease. He moved forward and stopped in front of the one friendly face in the group.

"Hello, I'm Neal Dunbar. Thank you for allowing me to intrude on your family dinner."

"Hello, Neal, and you're not intruding," said the attractive, middle-aged woman wearing black slacks and a white blouse. "I'm Susan, Cara's mother."

"You're as beautiful as she is, Susan." He handed her the basket of flowers. "And just as gracious. Your daughter is saving my sanity."

"She'll have your place looking like a page out of *Southern Living,*" an older gentleman in navy slacks and a light blue shirt said, extending his hand and introducing himself. "Anthony Scott, Cara's father."

Neal shook the older man's hand warmly. "I brought sparkling cider. I also have a bottle of chardonnay in the car if you'd prefer wine."

"I love a good bottle of wine. We'll get it later. I'm Brandi, next to the oldest."

Neal tipped his head. "I can see where Cara gets her straight-forwardness. Do you by chance drive the Hummer?"

Chuckles came from everyone. "Guilty." Brandi put her hands on her ample hips. "I confess to being a road hog."

"I'm Sandra. Offspring number three."

Neal smiled at the pretty woman with braids in a snug white top and slacks. Then he turned to a tall, muscular man in tailored gray slacks and white shirt. "From the family resemblance you must be the oldest, Victor. It must have been tough keeping the guys away."

"Nothing I couldn't handle then or now," Victor said.

Brandi and Sandra rolled their eyes. Mrs. Scott frowned. Mr. Scott looked pleased.

Neal was unfazed. "Only now, you have a dentist drill in your hand."

Victor's mouth twitched. "Something like that."

Neal turned to Cara, who stood quietly behind them. "You can take care of yourself."

Cara wasn't sure if it was a question or a statement. "Yes, I can."

"Dinner is ready," Cara's mother said. "I hope you like ham, yams and mustard greens."

Neal groaned with pleasure. "Mrs. Scott, I'm in your debt forever."

Beaming, she said, "Let's go sit down." The little group turned toward the dining room.

Neal touched Cara's arm. "Victor doesn't have to worry about you."

"He never did," she informed him. "As I said, I can take care of myself."

"Life has a way of throwing little surprises at you," he whispered just before they joined the others at the table.

He had charmed them all. Arms folded, Cara watched Neal from the living room window. He had his head stuck beneath the gigantic hood of Brandi's Hummer along with that of her father's and brother's. Neal had gained the mens' approval by being a graduate of Georgia Tech and rooting for their basketball team as they beat Oklahoma to advance to the Final Four. Just by showing up, he'd made points with her mother. Being handsome, courteous and thoughtful had given him a slam dunk.

"If you don't want him, I'll gladly take him off your hands."

Cara didn't look around at Sandra. Another conquest. "He's a client."

Taking her younger sister's arms, Sandra turned Cara around to face her. "If you pass up a fabulous guy like that just because you had one bad experience with that no-good Earl, you're crazy."

"If I forget what he did, I may be just as crazy."

Cara turned back to look out of the window once again. A few of their neighbors, one of them, Lisa, a slim, attractive dietician who lived across the street, had joined them. "What does a woman do with a man that gorgeous and charismatic?"

"She holds on and enjoys the ride," Sandra quipped. Then, noticing Cara was still troubled, she put her arm around her baby sister's shoulders. "I've dated more than you, but there is no easy answer. You take it for what it is."

"I suppose," Cara said, but she was still disturbed. Neal turned and looked directly at her. Her heart thumped hard in her chest.

Cara sighed. She had been fooling herself. She couldn't handle Neal or all the new emotions he brought out in her. It was too new and scary.

Looking back on the fiasco with Earl, she knew she had been more in love with love than with him. He'd angered and embarrassed her more times than he'd hurt her with his callousness. "I may have bragged to Pamela too soon. I just hadn't met the *right* man."

"Don't be too hard on yourself," Sandra said. "That's what makes meeting that special someone so scary and wonderful and so very special."

"Whoa." Cara held up both hands. "Back up. He hasn't even asked me out."

Sandra chuckled. "He will. And if he doesn't, we'll pull straws to see who has the honor of doing an extraction without an anesthetic."

"Don't you dare touch a perfect tooth in his mouth," Mrs. Scott said as she joined them at the window. "I was just telling Mother about Neal. She can't wait to meet him."

True panic gripped Cara. She should have known her mother and grandmother would make more out of her inviting Neal than they should. "Mother, he's just a client. I felt sorry for him since he has no family here. I invited him for Sunday dinner so he wouldn't be alone."

Mrs. Scott patted her daughter's arm, then looked outside and frowned. "Why don't you go outside and join them?"

Cara followed her mother's gaze. Lisa Sims clung to Neal's arm as though they were old friends or potential lovers. Pretty and single, Lisa had tried to snag Victor at one point, but he'd quickly found out she was only interested in how much money he made.

Annoyance swept through Cara. She took one step toward the front door and stopped.

"Well, go on and show Lisa she should keep her distance," Sandra urged.

Cara shook her head. "See, this is exactly my point," she continued at the puzzled look on her mother's and sister's faces, "I have a full schedule next week. I should be thinking about my clients instead of wasting my time on Neal and Lisa. My company *has* to come first."

"But, Cara, you can't just stand there and do nothing," her mother told her.

"Yeah, you have the rep of the Scott women to uphold," Sandra urged.

Laughing, Cara hugged Sandra and kissed her

mother. "I'll leave that up to you and Brandi. In the meantime, I have work to do. Bye." With a wave, she grabbed her keys from the table in the entryway and was out the door.

She didn't stop until she was on the sidewalk with the small group of people. "I'm going. I'll talk with you all later this week. Good-bye."

Frowning, Neal untangled his arm from Lisa. "I thought we could go for a drive and discuss decorating plans for the house."

Cara fingered her keys. So now he had time for her. "I can't. I have work to do."

"Neal, perhaps I could help," Lisa chimed in. "I have excellent taste. I live across the street if you'd like to see for yourself."

"Perhaps you'd also like to take my place for the drive." Cara stared at the brazen woman. A two-year-old had more decorative skill. Cara happened to know Lisa had professional help with her house.

"What a wonderful idea." Lisa smiled up into Neal's frowning face, then glanced around. "Which car is yours?"

Cara's eyes widened at the greed in Lisa's voice.

Neal inclined his head toward the cars parked at the curb. "The black Jag."

Lisa practically drooled. "I *love* sports cars."

Her patience quickly growing thin, Cara got into her SUV and pulled out. She promised herself she wasn't going to look back. Reminding herself of Earl's duplicity, she was able to keep that promise.

By the time Cara pulled into the driveway of her cottage, she had progressed beyond annoyed to being really ticked. Lisa was shameless, but Neal didn't to let himself fall victim to her. Not that Cara cared what he did or whom he did it with. It was just the principle of the thing. After all, he'd been her guest.

Getting out of the vehicle, she slammed the door and started for the house. If it weren't a matter of ethics, she'd withdraw from working for Neal. It would serve him right if Lisa ruined his house.

"You're a speed demon on or off the highway."

Recognizing Neal's deep sexy voice, Cara froze for a split second before spinning around. Seeing the smile on his handsome face somehow set her teeth on edge. "What are you doing here?"

"You left before I had a chance to thank you for the invitation," he said, strolling toward her as if he didn't have a care in the world. "My mother would disown me." He glanced around her tiny yard. "Nice."

It didn't compare to his. She'd gone for bold and beautiful with simple plants with striking colored leaves that were easily maintained. She loved flowers, but with her hectic schedule she didn't have time to care for them. "Thank you, and you're welcome for dinner. Now, if you'll excuse me."

He caught her arm as she turned to go. "If you're upset about Lisa, you're the one that tossed her at me."

Cara's chin lifted. "It seemed to me, from the way she was clinging to you, that you'd already caught her."

"Looks can be deceiving," he said. "Do you have nosy neighbors?"

The oddity of the question made her blink. "What?"

"I don't want them gossiping about you being kissed on your walkway," he explained. "Maybe we should go inside."

For a moment she couldn't speak. "You are the most exasperating man I have ever met."

"I guess kissing is out, so how about we go inside where you can relax and I can pour you a glass of wine." He held up the bottle of wine. "Or a foot massage? Maybe help you with whatever you're working on?"

Cara rubbed her temple. She had never met a man with such single-minded purpose. Then another thought struck. Quickly she stepped away. "Is this because of Pamela's challenge? Or are you trying to come on to me to win some bet with the boys?"

Neal's eyes went glacial. "Is that what you think? That I'd stoop to something that low and underhanded?"

Instantly she regretted the words. Although she hadn't known him for very long she trusted him. "No, I . . . I'm just tired."

His face softened. "You work too hard. Go inside and rest." He handed her the bottle of wine. "Perhaps one day you'll invite me over to share a glass. Bye."

Cara watched him walk away. Instead of feeling relieved, she felt . . . lonely and miserable. She took one step then another after him. Perhaps Sandra was right. "How . . . about now?"

He turned, but he wasn't wearing his usual smile. Slowly he retraced his steps. "I can take a rain check." The back of his knuckles tenderly grazed her cheek. "Someone should take care of you."

Warmth coursed through her. She couldn't remember anyone outside of her family and close friends being concerned about her. "I'm fine. Now, let's have that wine." Opening the door, she invited him inside. "Please have a seat and I'll be right back."

"Thanks." Neal stepped inside and was immediately taken with the warmth and simplicity of the house. Cara had limited the floral patterns to the matelasse accent pillows on the white denim slipcovers on the sofa and chair. The walls were buttery. A hand carved honey-colored mantle surrounded the small, white brick fireplace.

A low coffee table sat on a round Oriental rug. On top was a milk white bowl of pears, a wooden box, a couple of hardback books, and a bouquet of red and orange roses that looked like the roses he'd seen in her mother's front yard. Her home was restful, comfortable and romantic.

"Here you are."

Neal turned and took the crystal wine glass with a smile. "No paper cups for you."

Her smile warmed his heart. "Today. But if you promise not to tell anyone, I do use plastic and paper when I have friends and family over for a cookout in the back. It's easier to clean up."

"Your secret is safe with me." Glad that she felt comfortable enough with him to tease and share a secret, he lifted his glass. "To a long relationship."

Her smile faltered for a second, then she touched her glass to his and took a sip.

"Not to your taste?" he asked.

Cara shook her head. "Low tolerance. One glass and I'm sleepy. I have too much work to do."

Neal took her glass and his own and put them on top of the mantle. "I can give you the foot massage or get out of your way so you can finish and get to bed early."

"I really do need to get to work."

Did she look regretful or was it just what he wanted to see? "All right." He leaned over and gently brushed his lips against hers. The brief taste, intoxicating and sweet, made him want to deepen the kiss. With sheer force of will, he pulled back. Wide-eyed, she pressed her trembling fingertips against her lips.

"See you in the morning. Sleep well." Neal let himself out the door. Whistling, he strolled to his car.

Cara stared at the closed door, then plopped onto the arm of the sofa, her entire body trembling. Initially the kiss had startled her, then pleased, and finally thrilled and scared her.

It would have been so easy to let herself go, to succumb to the need that rushed through her. So very easy and so very dangerous.

She didn't have time for a relationship, especially with a man who was a client. She'd worked too hard to build her business. Her focus had to be on developing Cara's Innovations, not on a man who made her heart yearn, her body want.

So what was she going to do when she saw him in the morning?

Heaven help her. She wished she knew.

Chapter 5

When Cara's yellow SUV pulled up in front of Neal's house the next morning, he was waiting for her. After thinking about her after he'd left her house and all morning he was anxious to see her. She was an enticing mixture of sensuality and innocence that simply got to him. He could visualize making love to her all night or strolling hand and hand with her in his gardens. If he wasn't careful, he might not get to do either.

The kiss had obviously rattled her. It had done the same to him. He had intended it to be a tender gesture. The fierce need to keep holding her, to make her his, had totally caught him off guard. No kiss had ever taken him so far, so fast.

He also couldn't remember being so attuned to a woman or so protective. Yesterday, at her parents' house, he had seen the hurt and uncertainty in her face when she came outside to say good-bye and saw him with Lisa. His only thought had been to reassure

Cara. He had done that, but the kiss had scared her. He'd have to fix that.

Cara emerged from the vehicle and paused on seeing him. Then she continued. She didn't return his smile.

Neal sighed inwardly. They were back to square one. Winning Cara was going to be a lot harder than he originally thought, but he didn't have a doubt in his mind that he would or that it wouldn't be well worth the effort. His Cara was uniquely special. Today she wore cropped blue pants and a matching floral blouse with a multi-pocketed apron tied around her waist.

Opening the glass storm door, he stepped back, allowing her to enter. "Good morning, Cara."

"Good morning, Neal," she said, entering the house. "I'll begin in the kitchen, if you have no objection."

"Whatever you say. I left the numbers where you can reach me by the phone in my bedroom."

She moistened her lips and Neal wondered if he'd get slapped if he did that for her. "Thank you. If you'll excuse me, I'll get started." Without waiting, she went into the kitchen.

Neal's hot gaze followed. She had the sexiest walk and hips that made his hands itch. Slipping his hands into the pockets of his slacks, he followed. Seeing her lifting a box from the floor, he rushed to help. "Let me take that."

"Thank you, but I'm used to lifting boxes. With the number you have, I'll be doing that a lot today." Removing a box cutter from one of the apron's pockets, she quickly cut the tape and opened the box he had placed on the countertop.

"I didn't realize that." Neal rubbed the back of his neck. "You work too hard. Maybe you should hire someone to lift the boxes."

Cara glanced up from unwrapping the glass from bubble wrap. "Neal, I'm fine."

"You certainly are, and I want you to stay that way."

Her fingers tightened on the glass. There was no mistaking the husky inflection of his voice. "Shouldn't you be leaving for work?"

Folding his arms, he leaned against the counter. "I have a few minutes."

Determined to ignore him, Cara set the glass aside then picked up another wrapped package just as her cell phone rang. Pulling it from the waistband of her pants she glanced at the number before answering. "Hello, Pamela. How are you doing?"

There was a pause, then "No, I haven't found anyone willing to do the before and after. I'm sorry if your producer wants to do a promo piece today."

Shoving her fingers through her hair Cara gazed out the window. "You didn't specify any time limits."

She jumped when Neal tapped her on the shoulder. "What's the matter?" he asked.

Cara held up her hand for him to wait a moment. "Pamela, I'm with a client, can I call you back?" Her startled gaze flew up to Neal. "No, I don't think he'd go for it. Pam—" Cara held out the phone toward Neal. "She wants to speak with you."

Neal took the phone. "Good morning, Ms. Camp,

Neal Dunbar, please hold." He pressed the mouthpiece to his chest. "What's going on?"

"As you know they need a client for the makeover for Pamela's show. With the popularity of all the reality shows, Pamela's suggestion struck a responsive chord. The station has received a lot of positive feedback." Cara sighed. "The advertisement department has also received inquires from a couple of home improvement chains and furniture stores. The station manager wants to keep the buzz going and bring in revenue."

"So why are they hassling you?"

If nothing else Neal was astute. "If I'm such a Domestic Diva the station manager feels it should be a snap for me to find a client. So, he's pushing Pamela and she's pushing me."

Neal's mouth tightened briefly, then he lifted the phone. "Ms. Camp. I'll allow you to use my home if you put it in writing not to divulge the address or general location of the house. I won't be in the footage either. It's non-negotiable."

"No." Cara reached for the phone, but Neal stepped away. Helplessly she listened as he gave Pamela his address.

"I'll be at the gate waiting for the film crew in thirty minutes. Good-bye." Shutting off the phone, he handed it to her.

Taking her phone, she glared at him. "You didn't have to do that."

"It's done. Looks like you're working for me until my house is the way I want it."

Something about the way he looked at her caused a return of the uneasiness she had first experienced that morning when she saw him waiting for her. "You thought I might bail, didn't you?"

"Since you haven't mentioned the contract this morning, I thought you might have changed your mind because of the kiss yesterday," he told her.

Heat flushed her cheeks. "There will be no more of that."

"Didn't you enjoy it? I did."

Something flickered in her eyes. "I don't date clients."

Neal folded his arms and leaned against the counter. "So you enjoyed it as much as I did."

"I didn't say that," she flared.

He straightened. "No, you simply avoided the question, which told me all I wanted to know. What I can't figure out is why you're so set against us becoming better acquainted." He stepped closer. "I watched you closely that night on the show. Did something happen between you and a client?"

Her eyes widened, then she turned away to pick up another glass. "Give it up, Neal. I'm just not interested."

"It's a good thing for both of us that I don't believe that," he said, running a lean finger down her spine.

She whirled. "Stop it or I'm leaving."

"What about the shoot? Pamela is expecting you to be on the footage," he said calmly.

"What?" Cara's jaw dropped. "I can't be on camera dressed like this."

Neal gave her a slow once-over. "If you looked any more sensational I don't think my heart could stand it."

"Will you stop saying things like that!" she admonished.

"It's your own fault for being so incredible." Ignoring her glare and the stiffness of her body, Neal gently took her elbow. "Come on, we have work to do."

"Where are we going?"

"To my office to show you a few of the ideas I have for the house and garden," he said, never breaking his stride until he reached his destination. "We're in this together."

Cara watched Neal take a thick folder from his desk drawer. A tiny suspicion resurfaced. "Some people might think a renovation designer shouldn't need any help with decorating."

Neal looked her straight in the eye. "They would be right in some cases, wrong in others. It often takes a team consisting of architect, builder, craftsman, and designer to pull a project together. I learned early that I didn't know it all and was never too proud to admit I didn't and to ask for help. I'm too busy to finish this by myself. I need someone I can depend on."

Warmth she didn't want to feel coursed through her. "How do you know I'm that person?"

"I knew the moment I saw you," he told her. "I'm attracted to you, but I wouldn't let you loose in my house if I didn't think you had the necessary skills and if I didn't trust you." His hand lifted briefly to stroke her cheek and he felt her quiver beneath the light touch.

"Your sense of style is evident in the way you carry yourself, the flirtatious way you dress, your house, which is simple and romantic. You have solid ideas. I learned that Saturday from the comments you made when you toured the house."

Her crazy heart started pounding again. His words pleased her. Neal confused her more than any man she'd ever met. She could keep running from it or she could be honest. "I don't want to be attracted to you."

"I know. You kind of blindsided me as well. I need your help to finish this house. But to be honest, I can't wait to taste how sweet your lips are again," he said, his voice husky with suppressed longing. "Who says we can't have a great business *and* personal relationship?"

Her gaze went unerringly to his mouth. She couldn't deny her own need. "I just don't know, Neal."

"Just give me a chance to show you how wonderful it can be." He placed his hands on her waist to keep her in place and also for the sheer pleasure of it. "I'd like to take you out. After that, if you tell me you're not interested and to leave you alone, I won't like it, but I'll respect your right to say it."

"And you'll stop trying to entice me," she asked softly, regret already sweeping through her.

He chuckled. "Probably not."

She found herself laughing with him. "You're incorrigible."

"I go after what I want. What do you say we give each other a try?"

An honest man. "You attract women like a homing device."

337

Strong, determined hands pulled her closer. "The only woman I'm interested in is you."

Her body quivered with his nearness, the arousing scent of his spicy cologne, the heat of his muscular body. Could she take a chance? If she did, she had a feeling that Neal wasn't the staying kind. She'd be left again and this time the consequences would be disastrous. But was turning her back on what she felt any better?

Gently she pushed out of his arms. "I need time to think."

"Reasonable. I'll come by your place tonight around six with dinner. You need to eat and take better care of yourself."

Neal was pushy, but his concern was endearing. "You aren't going to let this go, are you?"

"Nope."

"Make it six thirty." She wanted to show him she had some semblance of control of the situation.

His expression showed that he realized her intent. "I'll be there." With a brush of his lips against hers, he was gone.

Her stomach quivering, Cara watched him leave. There was no turning back now.

Chapter 6

Cara was running late. She looked at the clock on the dashboard of her SUV just before pulling through the stop sign. It was six twenty.

The day had been nonstop since she'd left Neal's house around eleven that morning. With the help of two of her employees, they'd finished the kitchen and made good headway in the living room. They were on a tight schedule to finish in four weeks.

Cara blew out a breath. Perhaps she should have given herself more time. She really didn't know if she had set the time limit to finish quickly so there wouldn't be a conflict with dating Neal, or if she wanted to be away from the temptation of him as soon as possible.

Pamela, as expected, had flipped when she'd seen Neal. Filming the house had been incidental to her. She'd taken every opportunity to speak with him and let him know she was available. Cara had been surprised and ridiculously pleased when he'd made it clear that he was seeing someone. However, she hadn't known how to react to Pamela's comment to her that they had both lost out. Luckily, Neal had saved Cara by telling Pamela the film crew was ready to leave.

Neal had left soon afterward, but he'd made sure they had signed the contract. Before leaving he'd given her keys to the front gate and the house. That morning he had left it open for her. There was no backing out for either of them.

Cara turned onto her street and saw Neal's black truck. Her body tensed, but there was also anticipation. She really didn't know what to do about Neal. Calls from her mother, her maternal grandmother, and her sisters left no doubt that they wanted her to jump into the relationship with both feet. She had no intention of doing so until she was sure she'd land on solid ground and not fall into quicksand.

Nearing her house, she saw Neal talking with her next door neighbor, Mrs. Newton. She grinned and shook her head. Mrs. Newton, a retired school counselor, was a spry eighty-year-old widow who was as bad as Cara's mother and grandmother in plotting to get her married. She kept a close watch on Cara's house and the people who visited.

Stopping in her driveway, Cara got out with her briefcase and a book on patio and lawn furniture. "Good evening, Mrs. Newton. Neal."

"Hi, Cara. I've been keeping your young man company." Mrs. Newton glanced teasingly up at Neal. "Thought of keeping him for myself."

Neal chuckled. "There's still time."

"My hands are full, and I couldn't stop you," Cara said.

The older woman laughed, bracing herself on her cane. "You two have a nice dinner. It isn't often a man is that thoughtful."

"You're welcome to join us. There's plenty," Neal invited.

Cara couldn't imagine any man she'd previously dated inviting an elderly woman he'd just met to dinner. "Knowing Neal, there's plastic ware and paper plates so we don't have to worry about doing the dishes."

"You two go on. Time for my television program." Mrs. Newton turned toward the house, her steps slow.

"Cara, I'll see that Mrs. Newton is settled then I'll bring the food inside." With his hand at her elbow, he matched his steps to those of the older woman.

"What's for dessert?" Mrs. Newton asked as she made her way cautiously up the first step.

"Chocolate soufflés with pistachios. I'll bring you one." Neal opened the door.

"I'll hold you to that." Mrs. Newton went inside and Neal followed.

Cara caught herself staring after them. She was amused and touched by their light-hearted banter. Neal might attract women, but there was substance to him. He cared. Resisting a man like that would take a very strong or a very stupid woman.

"Dinner is finished, the kitchen is cleaned up, and I've taken Mrs. Newton her dessert." Neal flexed his fingers. "Time for your foot massage."

Laughing, Cara pulled her feet under her on the sofa. "Stop that. I want you to look at the patio furniture."

"If I must." Sitting beside her, he draped his arm around her shoulders.

The muscled warmth of his body seeped through her clothes. It became difficult to concentrate on patio furniture instead of on Neal. "I-I looked at your folder and I think you're right about going with teak instead of the solid-cast aluminum as I first thought. As the honey-colored wood ages and acquires a silver-gray patina, it will blend better."

Neal played with a lock of her hair. "What else did you decide?"

That you're the most tempting man I've ever met. "You need a round dining table out by the pool, a table and two chairs beneath the piazza, and perhaps a small cushioned bench by the kitchen window. The overhang of roses would make it a wonderful spot to just sit and enjoy the night."

"Only if you were there with me," he whispered, his warm breath against her ear.

She shivered and sighed at the same time. "Neal."

"You'd say my name just like that." He turned her in his arms, his mouth finding hers. He couldn't get enough of her sweetness and fire. He knew if he didn't pull back now he wouldn't be able to stop.

Lifting his head, he pulled her tightly to him, trying to control the wild need surging through him. "Cara."

Her breathing labored, she lay quietly in his arms. Concerned, he lifted her chin. Her eyes were closed. "Cara, what's the matter, honey?"

Opening her eyes she gazed at him a few moments

then tucked her head again. "I dated a client once. I thought we were in love. It turned out he was just using me to furnish his apartment."

Neal's arms tightened. "Is he still in Austin?"

Cara sat up and stared at Neal. The coldness in his face matched that in his voice. "No."

"Maybe I'll meet him one day."

"He doesn't matter anymore," she said.

Neal palmed her face. "He does if he's coming between us. For that I'd like to have a conversation with him."

Cara could well imagine the type of conversation Neal meant. With his muscular build he'd pound Earl into the dirt. Once upon a time the idea might have been appealing, but not anymore. It was time she moved on. "I can make an appointment to visit the showroom after hours tomorrow night. If you find pieces you like, they can be delivered in two days and we can test out my theory of sitting outside to enjoy the night."

"Make the appointment and in the meantime I want to test something else."

"What?"

"How long I can kiss you without going over the edge." His mouth took hers again.

Cara was smiling when she pulled up in front of Neal's house the next morning. She'd been doing that since last night. She enjoyed being with Neal, laughing, talking, letting him kiss her breathless. By the time she was out of the car, Neal was there, his mouth claiming hers once again.

"I can't get enough of you."

Her arms around his neck, she smiled up at him. "You're rather potent yourself."

"You look beautiful as usual. It will be difficult to leave for work." Sighing with regret, Neal put his arms around her waist and started for the house. "You made good progress yesterday."

"Thanks. I can only do a couple of hours today and then I have appointments."

He stopped and stared down at her. "Did you leave time for lunch?"

"Skipping a few meals won't hurt me," she told him.

"You skip too many and it might. I like your sexy body just the way it is."

He always said the right words. She was comfortable with her size, but it was heady knowing Neal thought she was sexy.

Neal opened the door and they went inside. "After we visit the showroom, do you want to watch a movie here or go out to eat?"

She glanced around the living room. She was anxious to get it finished and the artwork hung. "Let's stay in. I'll cook something easy and we can tackle this together."

"I was with you until the last part."

Smiling at the disgruntled expression on his face, she stood on tiptoe and brushed her mouth across his. "It won't be so bad."

His hands curved around her waist. "I'm still not convinced."

"Let me see what I can do about that." Circling his

neck, she pulled his head down and kissed him until they both were breathless.

Two weeks later, Neal could proudly say the house was taking shape and it was all because of Cara. Plucking two glasses from the cabinet, he added ice, then filled the tall glasses his mother had given him years ago with tea. He hadn't had to ramble in the cabinet or in the refrigerator for what he needed. Everything was neat and orderly, just the way he liked it.

He started from the kitchen, reversed his steps to pick up a couple of napkins, then hurried out again. Cara liked things done right and he liked pleasing her. She'd even made the tedious and boring task of unpacking enjoyable.

The main floor of the house was almost free of packing boxes and every day looking more and more like what he had envisioned. One guest bedroom was finished with antique white furniture and soft sheer curtains his mother and Stephanie would love. Neither Michael nor Brody would notice or care. The patio furniture had been delivered, and to his delight, he and Cara had spent several pleasurable evenings sitting in the pergola, necking like teenagers. They'd even managed to take a dip in the pool.

"Neal, come here, quick."

Hearing the urgency in Cara's voice, Neal broke into a run to his office where they had been working to shelve the last of his books. "What is it?"

"The promo for Pamela's show is about to be shown." Taking one of the glasses of tea, she waved her hand toward the television set. "I was hoping we'd finally get a chance to see it. It's really brought in a lot of business. Almost everyone in my family has seen it. Mother even made a tape and sent it to my grandparents."

Neal took a sip of his tea. "People at work have been talking about it too. Since none of them have been out here they don't know it's my place. Apparently Pamela was able to work in the footage I gave her of how the house looked before we began the renovations."

"Their eyes are going to pop when they see what you and your brothers have done."

"And you." Neal pressed a kiss to her temple.

"Shhhh. Here it is."

The television screen filled with the house as Neal had first seen it, neglected and surrounded by weeds and dense vegetation, then showed the interior before the renovations began. Pamela, smiling and vivacious, replaced the house on the screen. "This week you'll get a chance to see the changes the owner made to the outside of the house, but finishing touches are still needed inside and out. Remember all those packing boxes? The Domestic Diva, Cara Scott, has her work cut out for her. She has two weeks left. Can she make it? Stay tuned."

"I'm glad you rescued this house."

"So am I. It brought us together." He put his glass on the blotter and reached for her.

"No, you don't." Laughing, she set her glass beside his and moved away. "We have to finish shelving these books."

He went after her. "Kissing is more fun."

"True, but we're on a schedule here and I don't want to get behind." She put the desk between them. "Let's finish this and I'll come over in the morning and cook you your favorite breakfast."

He stopped. "What time is your first appointment?"

"Ten. My secretary is opening the shop. Now, what do you want?"

"You. Just you."

The teasing smile slid from her face. His words went straight to her heart and clogged her throat. He made her feel so many emotions. She was awfully afraid one of them was love.

"What's the matter, honey? You looked scared to death."

Unable to tell him the truth, she lay her head on his broad chest and listened to the steady beat of his heart. How could she have been so foolish?

"Don't worry. We'll finish on time. I finally thought of a color for the house."

"Hot pink?"

His chest rumbled with laughter. "Pale yellow with olive green shutters."

Glad they were on a safe subject, she lifted her head. "That color will go perfectly with the green striped cushions on the teak furniture. Instead of pots you could use limestone urns planted with formal boxwood at the corners of the pool, and filled with cascading flowers on the terrace."

"You think fast on your feet."

"Have to in my business."

"Let's see how you think off of them."

With no more warning than that she was lifted and held easily in his arms. Her eyes widened in amazement.

Placing her on the leather sofa on the far side of the room, he followed her down. "I figured since I've solved a big obstacle to finishing on time we don't have to rush as much, and we can get back to this."

He started at the corner of her mouth, nibbling and tasting and tempting. By the time he covered her mouth with his she was more than ready for the kiss. She forgot everything but the man driving her slowly wild with need. His hand closed over the rounded mound of her breast, causing her breath to stall.

Her hands were doing exploration of their own. Touching him, feeling the ripple of his warm muscled flesh beneath her fingertips always made her feel powerful.

He nipped her ear lobe. "You're going to get in trouble."

"So are you," she moaned.

"Let's see how much."

The buttons on her blouse slipped free. Neal stared down at the lacy bra. This time he was the one sucking in his breath. "You're beautiful all over."

She felt beautiful in his arms. Not wanting to think of a time when they wouldn't be together, she circled his neck and joined their lips. For now, for this time, they were together.

Chapter 7

Saturday morning Neal had just stepped out of the shower when he heard the doorbell ring. He glanced at the clock on his night stand. It was seven-thirty. Reaching for a towel he quickly dried off, then grabbed a pair of jeans and tugged them on. Cara was as anxious to see him as he was her. She wasn't thinking about pulling back as he had feared last night.

Something was bothering her, but his stubborn Cara wouldn't tell him until she was good and ready. Since she had clammed up last night he'd used his own method of taking her mind off whatever had her worried—with blazing passion. He sensed she wasn't ready for total intimacy and was content to wait until she was.

Although seeing how close they could come to the edge without going over was sheer pleasure not to mention madness, it made him that much more anxious to see her and hold her again. He definitely liked having her around. Oddly, the best times were when they were doing something for the house. He'd never had so many dates at home. Cara was not only changing his house but she was changing him too.

Opening the front door, his eyes widened in surprise. "Mama!"

Corine Dunbar lifted a brow at the stunned expression on the face of her middle child. "I'd hoped to surprise you and obviously I did. Who were you expecting dressed like that?"

Explanations raced through Neal's mind. The one paramount was that his mother not get the wrong impression of Cara.

Opening the storm door, he hugged his mother and explained. "I was in the shower when I heard the doorbell. You know I'm always happy to see you. Is Stephanie finished with getting ready for The Wright Solution?"

"Yes, and don't think you can change the subject."

Neal decided to put off telling his mother about Cara for the moment and picked up her overnight case and glanced around the porch. His mother loved shopping and clothes. She always took at least one suitcase and often an empty one for her purchases. "Where is the rest of your luggage?"

"I'm waiting for The Wright Solution to open next weekend. I went with Stephanie on a buying trip and have my eye on some lovely things." She smiled. "I never plan to pay retail again."

Chuckling, Neal opened the door. His mother loved shopping, but she also loved a bargain.

Just inside the living room his mother stopped abruptly, then continued further into the room. "I can't believe it. You're finished." Her searching gaze went to the fresh cut flowers on the coffee table, the colorful throw she'd never seen before draped casually across the side chair, the new sofa table with her wedding pictures, and photographs of Neal and his brothers as small children. "Neal, it's beautiful."

"Thanks." He set the luggage by the bottom of the stairs. "Wait until you see the kitchen."

She hurried into the adjoining rooms. It was just as spectacular. The bold floral print valance over the sink matched the new pads on the chairs in the breakfast nook and coordinated with the small yellow check napkins and placemats she'd purchased for all her sons years ago. To her knowledge, none had ever used them.

The window by the breakfast nook had been left open so the wonderful view of the yard was unimpeded. The crystal that she had despaired would ever be used was displayed in the glass front cabinets.

"Neal, it's wonderful." She looked around the kitchen again. "I can't believe you got so much done and that it's so absolutely perfect."

"I didn't." He leaned against the countertop. "I owe it all to Cara."

His mother immediately focused her attention on Neal. "You finally picked a girlfriend who wants to do more than have fun."

Straightening, Neal frowned. He opened his mouth to defend his choice of women, then snapped his mouth shut when he realized that was exactly the reason he had chosen them. He hadn't wanted anything heavy or long lasting. "What's wrong with having fun?"

His mother patted his cheek the way she had done when he was a small child. "Nothing at the time, but I'm glad you've moved on. Now, tell me about Cara."

Once again Neal opened his mouth, then closed it before saying anything. It didn't take a genius to see where his mother's mind was going. "She's the decorator."

"Is that all she is?" his mother asked.

Neal was fumbling for an answer when he heard the doorbell. His head jerked toward the sound, then he looked back toward his mother who had started for the front door.

In two hurried steps, he caught her arm. "I'll get it."

"Is it Cara at the door?"

Neal didn't know why he couldn't answer or why he felt nervous all of a sudden. His mother had met a couple of the women he had dated and he hadn't thought a thing about it at the time. "She's nice, Mama."

His mother rolled her eyes. "Of course she is. Now, please go open the door and let the young woman in so I can meet her."

He hesitated.

"One of us has got to answer the door," she said reasonably.

Left without a choice, Neal went to the door and opened it. As expected, Cara stood there. She had a covered dish in her hands. She looked positively mouthwatering in a lemon yellow camp shirt and cropped pants.

"Good morning, Neal." A frown raced across her brow when he simply stood there.

His shoulders slumped because he wouldn't be able

to do any nibbling this morning. "Good morning, Cara. My mother is here," he blurted.

Shocked surprise raced across her face. "I see. I'll just leave this with you. I hope you enjoy your visit."

Neal opened the storm door, but couldn't bring himself to reach for the dish. The smile on Cara's face was strained. He didn't want to hurt her or let her leave. As much as he hated the speculation her visit would raise and all the questions he'd have to endure once his mother had him alone again, he couldn't bring himself to let Cara leave.

"Not so fast. She'd like to meet the woman who turned my jumbled mess into something beautiful and comfortable." Opening the door, he pulled her inside and took the dish out of her unsteady hands. He wished he could put his arms around her to reassure her.

"Mother, I'd like you to meet Cara Scott, the owner of Cara's Innovations. Cara, my mother, Corine Dunbar," he introduced.

"Hello, Cara. I'm so pleased to meet you." His mother extended her hand. "I love what you've done with Neal's house."

"Thank you. The structure of the house and the things he already owned made working for him a pleasure." Cara responded to the warmth of Neal's mother. For a moment she had been afraid Neal didn't want them to meet.

Corine smiled. "It's nice seeing things I've given him over the years being used."

"I always planned on using them, Mama," Neal defended.

His mother threw him an indulgent smile. "But when?"

"He probably didn't have room for them before." Cara didn't know why she had jumped to Neal's defense, but she certainly didn't like the speculative expression on his mother's face. "I really must be going."

"You're leaving?" Neal and his mother questioned at the same time.

"I don't want to intrude on your visit," Cara explained.

"Nonsense," his mother said. "Have you had breakfast? I can fix something quick. The airline served only peanuts."

"It will be my pleasure to cook you an omelet," Cara said, taking Mrs. Dunbar's arm and leading her into the kitchen. "Why don't you sit down. It won't take very long since I know where everything is."

"You do?" his mother questioned.

Cara's gaze met Neal's. He answered first. "Cara is known as the Domestic Diva. I hired her to do everything."

"I see."

Cara didn't know if his mother understood or not, but the way Mrs. Dunbar kept looking from one to the other was making her nervous. "I baked strawberry cinnamon muffins. Would you like one now?"

"They smell delicious and probably crammed full of calories, but I'm too hungry to care." Taking a dessert plate from the cabinet, Mrs. Dunbar took the dish from Neal.

"They're low fat, low calories," Cara told her.

Mrs. Dunbar took a bite and sighed. "They taste as good as they smell. Neal, please put my suitcase in the guest bedroom. Call Michael about the yard. And you might consider putting on a shirt."

He flushed and shot a look at Cara. She was biting her lower lip. He couldn't tell if she was embarrassed or trying to keep from laughing. "Yes, ma'am. I'll be right back."

His mother waited until he left the room. "You'd think I was an ogre. I've never seen Neal so protective of a woman."

Cara didn't know what to say. She couldn't very well ignore Neal's mother, nor did she want to read too much into his mother's statement. "He just wants to make sure I stay and finish the house," she said, trying for humor.

"I don't think so." His mother wandered to the counter where Cara was working.

Cara busied herself making the omelets for Mrs. Dunbar and French toast for Neal. She planned on getting out of there as soon as she finished cooking. "Neal tells me you live in Houston."

"Yes, but I've been in Dallas a great deal lately helping Stephanie, my daughter-in-law, get ready for the grand opening of her clothing boutique next week." Mrs. Dunbar opened the bottom cabinet, found the skillets needed and placed them on the stove. "You take care of Neal's toast and I'll do mine. You better fix more or you'll be hungry."

Cara sprayed the skillet. "I'm not eating."

Mrs. Dunbar stopped and stared at Cara. "If I weren't here, would you be eating?"

"Yes," Cara admitted, then quickly added, "You don't need me intruding on your visit."

"A wanted guest is never intrusive. Neal wants you here and that's all that matters."

"Thank you." Seeing the omelet sizzling around the edges, Cara handed Mrs. Dunbar a spatula. She accepted with a nod.

"I haven't gotten a chance to see the rest of the house. Are you finished?"

"No, ma'am." Cara took out the golden brown French toast and added two more slices of battered bread.

"Were you planning on working today?" the older woman asked, expertly sliding the food onto a plate.

"Yes, ma'am. I'd only planned to work a little while after Neal left because I have an appointment at ten. But afterward I wanted to go antique shopping at a few estate sales to see if I can find an armoire to complement the bed in the guest bedroom. Neal enlarged the bathroom during his renovation, but not the tiny closet. He said you liked antiques."

"I do." Mrs. Dunbar took the three plates of food and set them on the table. "I haven't been estate sale hopping in years."

A thought struck Cara. "If you'd rather I buy new or from an antique dealer, I certainly understand."

"No. You can find some excellent buys that way."

"Would you like to come with me?" Cara asked impulsively. "After all, I'm decorating the room with you in mind."

"I was hoping you'd ask." Corine's eyes gleamed. "I'll be waiting."

Neal hurried back into the kitchen not knowing what to expect. The two women were talking and apparently getting along. The tension seeped right out of him and warmed his heart.

Cara knew she was asking for trouble, but that didn't stop her from swinging by her parents' house to see if her mother wanted to join them. Her parents' house didn't need anything, but her mother liked to browse just the same. Cara hoped the two women would hit it off and was pleased when they did. By the time they reached the first estate sale, they were chatting like old friends and Cara couldn't find a parking place fast enough.

"Your son is such a wonderful young man."

"Thank you. Cara's done a fabulous job on his house."

"Neal has invited the family over for dinner when it's finished."

"He actually had napkins when we ate. Cara is a good influence on him."

"They're good for each other."

"We're here." Cara quickly unbuckled her seat belt. "I see a few things I want to check out." She was gone in five seconds.

The two mothers looked at each other and shook their heads. Corine spoke first. "She's perfect for Neal."

"Same thing I thought the moment I saw them together." Susan scooted forward in the back seat. "Is Neal as blind as she is?"

"As a bat," Corine said with disgust. "He's protective of her, hovers over her, worries about her, and is so proud of her."

"Cara spends every free minute with him or working on that house. You can't tell me it's all business or it's because of that TV show."

Corine turned around in her seat. "What TV show?"

Susan quickly explained. "Cara's business has almost doubled since then. She's even hired another woman to help out. But what worries me is whether the two will realize their feelings by the time they're supposed to be finished with the house."

"If not, we'll just have to help them." Corine stuck out her hand and Susan gladly shook it.

"I think our mothers are up to something."

Neal looked up from cutting his grilled T-bone to see the two women in question sitting at the picnic table with Cara's father and a couple from next door. Cara's parents had invited Neal and his mother over for a cookout in the Scott's back yard. Cara's brother and sisters had dropped by earlier to visit, then left. All three had dates.

"Why do you say that?"

"I've caught them whispering and, every time I do, they stop and look all sweet and innocent," Cara explained, still watching the two.

"Honey, it's nothing. Knowing Mama, they're talking about shopping." Neal cut into his juicy steak and took a bite.

"We went shopping today. I made three stops and the only time they got out was when I found that armoire for the guest bedroom and wanted your mother's opinion," Cara told him.

The fork laden with potato salad stopped midway to Neal's mouth. "Mother loves shopping more than anything."

"She loves her sons more." Cara picked at her salad.

"Sure, but what's that got to do with anything?"

Cara started to tell him her suspicion that their mothers were matchmaking, then she decided not to. The M word scared men more than the L word. She wasn't going to jeopardize the time she and Neal had together. "You're right. I'm probably imagining things."

Chapter 8

On the way back from Cara's parents' house, Neal's mother couldn't stop talking about what a fantastic job Cara had done decorating his house and what a fabulous woman she was. Since Neal agreed, he didn't find the conversation out of the ordinary. In fact, it pleased him.

They hadn't been home five minutes before she informed him not to worry about her if he wanted to go out again. "I'm going to bed early. You don't have to stay with me."

Neal's concern was immediate. "It's barely nine. You never go to bed this early. You feel all right?"

"Never better." She continued up the stairs. "But wouldn't you rather be out than stuck here with me?"

The only person he wanted to be with was Cara. "I'm in for the night."

A frown darted across her brow. "Cara's mother told me how you two met. Susan says Cara's business has doubled."

"It has." Neal was the one frowning now. "She works too hard."

"She's a very conscientious young woman. I wonder how many clients have hired her as their hired wife?"

Neal's head jerked up. Somehow hearing Cara being the hired wife for another client disturbed him.

"She's excellent at what she does." Corine climbed another step. "Too bad after she's finished she won't need to come by so frequently."

Something like panic gripped him. "There's no reason for her to stop coming over. There'll still be things she can do, like grocery shop and such."

His mother tsked. "Anyone can do that. Susan told me Cara hires young college students for those types of things. Cara reserves her time and talent for the larger jobs. Yes, I'm afraid in two weeks you're going to lose her. What a pity. Good night."

"Good night," Neal mumbled.

Lose Cara? He couldn't. She'd still be around.

But as he walked through the room to the patio, he recalled the many hours they'd spent together getting the house in order, and realized his mother was right. Once Cara finished decorating the house and patio area, the time they spent with each other would decrease dramatically.

She'd move on to another client. She'd move on from him.

Cara sensed Neal was troubled the moment she opened her door Sunday afternoon. "Did your mother get off all right?"

"Yes." Closing the door behind him, he took her in his arms and his mouth found hers.

The kiss, deep and passionate, left Cara trembling. "Maybe we should skip seeing each other every day more often." His hands tightened on her waist. The teasing smile left her face. "Neal, what's the matter?"

He shook his head. "I just missed you, that's all."

Her heart sighed. "I missed you, too. Come on. Sit down. Would you like a drink?"

"No, thanks." He pulled her down beside him on the sofa. "I see you've been working."

Cara wrinkled her nose at the papers covering the surface of the round coffee table. Beside it were various sample books. "I need a desk."

"New client?"

"Two. Both want me to redecorate the entire house and grounds." She sighed. "I told them your brother had done the yard, but they still want me." She bit her lip. "You think your brother would mind me running my ideas past him."

"No." His hand flexed on her shoulder. "Seems you'll be pretty busy."

She smiled up at him and his heart turned over. "I told you I enjoy being busy. Keeps the wolf from the door."

It would also keep her away from him. "When do you start?"

"Next Monday. The painters start tomorrow on your house. I know just the place to pick up the limestone pots and plants I'll need for the pool and terrace. The carpenter is scheduled to hang the shutters Tuesday. The pots will be delivered Wednesday. By

Thursday morning everything will be in place. Just as soon as you can work it in your schedule, Pamela can come out and film.''

"Four days," he said softly.

"We did it. Ahead of schedule." She palmed his face. "You'll have the house exactly as you wanted."

He'd have the house, but not Cara.

"You have a spectacular home, Neal," Pamela said as she ended her tour of the house and grounds Friday morning. "Cara, your phone is going to ring nonstop after the show next Friday."

"It already is," Cara said, then glanced at Neal who had been silent most of the tour.

"Neal, since we honored your request that you not be in any of the promo shots, you're still available to come on the show live next Friday night, aren't you?"

"Yes."

"Thank you." Pamela leaned over and whispered to Cara. "I think Neal and his lady friend must have had a lover's spat."

Cara barely kept from looking at Neal again. "Why do you say that?"

"Can't be work. I happen to know the renovations of the Alistair are ahead of schedule, and word is the reason is Neal. He'll probably get a big fat bonus. He could sell this house for probably triple what he paid for it. The only other thing that could have taken his smile is a woman." Pamela leaned in closer. "Maybe there's a chance for me now. You had yours."

"We're loaded and ready to go, Pam," said the cameraman.

"I'll be right there," she said, winked at Cara and started toward Neal.

Cara stood there for all of two seconds then she went after Pamela and caught her arm. "Pamela, if Neal has a problem, I'll take care of it."

Pamela blinked. Her gaze went from one to the other. "But—"

"I finally found a man who tempts me," Cara admitted. "I'm making no excuses that I'm rather territorial about him."

As if she didn't believe Cara, Pamela turned to Neal. "Is that the truth?"

Neal's lazy gaze went to Cara. "Whatever I need, she has."

Pamela shot her a look of annoyance. "Well, you picked a fine time to take the plunge. See you Friday night." Pamela went to the van and they pulled off.

Cara went to Neal. "All right. What is it?"

"You."

She frowned. "What?"

Neal paced away then back. "It's you. You're as much a part of this house as I am, maybe more so. You're in every inch of it."

Something in her heart cracked. "And you resent that?"

His head came around sharply. "Resent you? How could I resent the person who gives me a reason to smile, who makes the day brighter."

"Oh, Neal." She launched herself into his arms. "I was so afraid you wouldn't love me the way I love you. I was so afraid to tell you. You love me, too. I can't believe it." Cara finally realized Neal was stiff.

Lifting her head she looked at his face, saw the shock and wanted to run away in shame. "You weren't talking about love, were you?"

"Cara, I'm sor—"

Shaking her head she stepped back. "No, please don't say anything. I'm the one who should apologize for embarrassing you."

"Cara, don't. I care about you."

"But you don't love me," she said, her voice trembling. His silence was his answer. "There doesn't seem to be anything else to say. Good-bye, Neal." Getting in her SUV she drove away. Once out of sight of the house, she stopped and let the tears fall.

Some obligations you couldn't get out of no matter what. Attending the opening of your sister-in-law's boutique was one of those. Neal had never felt less like being cordial. Seeing Cara's family who were invited by his mother without her made the ache in his chest worsen. As expected the sisters cornered him. "How is she?" he asked.

"How do you expect she is?" Brandi asked, a glint in her eyes.

"To think I told her to go after you," Sandra said. "You hurt her!"

"It wasn't my intention," he said. "I care about her."

"Your kind of caring causes too much pain," Brandi said. "Just stay away from her."

The women walked away, leaving him feeling helpless and cruel. He started to take a sip of wine, then recalled that Cara preferred tea. Setting the flute on the tray of a passing waiter, he went to find his brother or Stephanie to let them know he was flying back to Austin that night.

He didn't find them in the crush of women shoppers, but his mother found him. "I thought you were smarter."

He rubbed his throbbing temple. "Mother, please."

"All right, I can see you're hurting over this, but Cara is hurting, too."

"If I could change that I would." He shoved his hand over his head. "I can't give her what she wants, needs."

"You can," his mother said softly. "Just search your heart and you'll see, just as I do. You love her."

He took a step backward. "No, you're wrong. I just like being with her."

"And you're miserable without her," she said accurately. "What is love but finding the other half that makes you whole. Cara is your other half. Don't wait too long to come to your senses or she'll become someone else's wife and not just for hire."

"No, I don't love her. I just care about her," he said, but his mother had already walked away.

Neal could hardly stand to be in the house he had taken such enjoyment in. Everywhere he went there was a memory of Cara. He couldn't keep her out of his thoughts any more than he could walk into a room and not remember her being there in it.

He'd go to bed thinking that in the morning it would be better, but instead the aching loneliness would be worse. He'd driven by her store just to see if he could catch a glimpse of her. He hadn't had any luck there, nor when he had gone by her house. Mrs. Newton had been sitting on her porch.

The older woman had five curt words for him. "I thought you were smarter."

Neal thought he was smarter, too. He enjoyed women, but once it was over, it was over. The way they had broken up had thrown him. A woman telling a man she loved him would certainly do it. He just needed to see her, reassure himself that she was all right. Then he'd be able to move on. Once he saw her, his life would get back to normal.

Cara bought a snazzy black pantsuit with a hot pink blouse for Pamela's show. She'd forbidden herself to cry. There would be no red, puffy eyes. If she couldn't have Neal's love she didn't want his pity. Flipping through a magazine in the waiting area of the television studio, she tried to appear as if she didn't have a care in the world.

"Mr. Dunbar, you can wait in here until Pamela is ready for you."

"Thank you."

Cara's body tensed. Just the sound of his voice went through her like chain lightning.

"Hello, Cara."

Swallowing the lump in her throat, she glanced up. He looked as handsome as ever. He'd gone for casual with tobacco-colored slacks and a wheat-colored sports coat over a white shirt. "Hello, Neal. How are you?"

"I was about to ask you the same thing."

"Fine." She went back to her magazine.

"I'm glad to hear that."

"Pamela is ready for you," the stagehand said. "Ms. Scott, if I could afford you, I'd certainly hire you for my apartment."

Cara gave him a card. "Call me. Perhaps I can help you come up with some ideas. No charge."

The young man's eyes bugged. "Cool!"

"You're sure you should take on more clients?" Neal asked from beside her.

"What I do is no longer your concern," Cara said, then walked away.

Perhaps she'd listen to her mother, Neal thought. She needed to take more time for herself. His mouth tight, Neal followed.

Pamela's smile slipped as she looked from Cara's solemn expression to Neal's. "Whatever the problem, please fix it before the show airs in five minutes."

Cara blinked and looked away.

Neal reached for her before he thought. "Honey, don't."

"Please let me go," she said, her voice muffled against his coat.

His hold tightened. "I tried. I can't."

Her head lifted, hope shimmered in her eyes. "Neal?"

"Two minute warning. Two minutes."

"Please take a seat or I'll be looking for a job," Pamela told them.

"We're going to talk when this is over." Kissing her hand, he took his seat, feeling better than he had since Cara had walked out of his life.

* * *

The show was a resounding success. As soon as they were off the air, Neal grabbed Cara's hand and they were out the door. Neal saw Cara to her SUV, then followed her to his house.

He rehearsed what he planned to say, but nothing seemed right. By the time he pulled up behind her, he was no closer to finding the right words. Getting out of his car, he opened her door. "Let's go to the piazza."

"All right."

Once there, Neal seated her on the cushioned bench and took her hands. With the overhang of fragrant yellow roses and the reflection of the pool a few feet away, the alcove had a romantic air about it.

"You remember the first time we sat here together?"

"Yes." Her voice trembled.

"It's one of my favorite places because we shared it together. We made it ours."

"I felt the same way."

His hand touched her cheek. "I didn't understand at the time what that meant."

"Neal, what are you trying to say?"

He got down on one knee. "I want to share a lifetime of firsts with you. I know it took me a long time to realize it, but I love you. I don't want you as a hired wife, I want you to be my wife, my confidante, my friend, my lover, my everything. Will you marry me?"

Tears crested in her eyes and rolled down her cheeks.

"Please don't say no," he cried frantically. "I want to care for you, hold you, take care of you. Don't walk away from me again."

"Oh, Neal. Of course I'll marry you."

Relief swept through him. "Thank goodness! I'll spend the rest of my life making you happy."

Her arms circled his neck. "How about starting now?"

Grinning, he pulled her into his arms.

About the Authors

Donna Hill has more than twenty-three novels to her credit and dozens of short stories. Her work has appeared on several best sellers lists and she has received numerous awards for her writing as well as her community service. Three of her novels were adapted for and aired on television. She co-wrote the screenplay for the independent film, *Fire*. She has been featured in *Essence, Black Enterprise, USA Today, New York Daily News* and others. Donna operates Image-Nouveau Literary Services, her own publicity business for special projects, and works full time as a Public Relations Associate for the Queens Library. She has recently launched a nonprofit organization *Divas Inc. Society* which offers scholarship and grants to deserving women, among other ventures. Donna lives in Brooklyn with her family. For more information you can visit her Web site http://www.donnahill.com.

Brenda Jackson lives in the city where she was born, Jacksonville, Florida. She has a Bachelor of Science degree in Business Administration from Jacksonville University. She has been married for thirty-two years to her high school sweetheart, and they have two sons, ages twenty-six and twenty-four. She is also a member of the First Coast Chapter of Romance Writers of America, and is a founding member of the national chapter of Women Writers of Color. Brenda is the recipient of numerous awards, including the prestigious Vivian Stephens Career Achievement Award for Excellence in Romance Writing; the Emma Award for Author of the Year in Romance; the Shades of Romance Multi-cultural Award of the Year, and the Romance in Color Award of Excellence.

The Perfect Seduction is her twenty-fourth story.

You can visit her Web site at www.brendajackson. net.

In addition to being in love with words, **Monica Jackson** has worked in the field of nursing for over twenty years. She is now a registered nurse with experience in coronary intensive care, community health, psychiatric and nursing administration, and management.

Descended from the "Exodusters" who migrated to Kansas from the South, her roots are deep in the Kansas soil. But her adventurous spirit has led her to live in several different places—St. Louis, Houston, greater San Francisco, and Atlanta. She has also spent extended amounts of time in South America and the Far East.

Monica is now back in Kansas, where she's a single

parent happily nurturing her child and her muse and writing tales she hopes you will love.

Visit her Web site at www.monicajackson.com.

National bestselling author **Francis Ray** is a native Texan who lives in Dallas with her husband. A graduate of Texas Woman's University, she was twice nominated for the Distinguished Alumni Award. Ms. Ray has twenty-three books in print. Her awards include the Romantic Times Multicultural Career Achievement award, Emma award for single title and novella, Atlanta Choice Award, The Golden Pen, and finalist for the Holt Medallion. Award. You can visit her at www.francisray.com.

A WHOLE
LOTTA LOVE

Four bestselling authors deliver for larger-than-life
stories of bold, beautiful woman.

Featuring all-new tales of love from:

Donna Hill,
Brenda Jackson,
Monica Jackson,
and
Francis Ray

0-451-21090-5

Available wherever books are sold or at
www.penguin.com

S905

The National Bestseller

GOT TO BE REAL

Four Original Love Stories

E. Lynne Harris,
Eric Jerome Dickey,
Colin Channer,
and Marcus Major

0–451–20432–8

A sensational anthology of love stories
from "some of the biggest male names
on the African–American
literary scene."*

"This anthology features the qualities that
distinguish [the authors'] best
writing—enduring characters,
touching story lines and new insight
into the world of love."
—*Ebony*

"Groundbreaking...
Succeeds on a grand scale."
—*Publishers Weekly*

Available wherever books are sold or at
www.penguin.com

All your favorite romance writers are coming together.

SIGNET ECLIPSE

COMING FEBRUARY 2005:
Across a Wild Sea by Sasha Lord
The Love of a Lawman by Anna Jeffrey
The Duel by Barbara Metzger

COMING MARCH 2005:
Dare Me by Cherry Adair, Jill Shalvis, and Julie Elizabeth Leto
A Knight Like No Other by Jocelyn Kelley
The Perfect Family by Carla Cassidy